I0712916

Cruel Devices

George Wright Padgett

Text © 2014 by George Wright Padgett
Illustrations © 2014 by George Wright Padgett
Design by Grey Gecko Press

All rights reserved. Other than for review purposes, no part or portion of this book may be reproduced or transmitted in any form or by any means, electronic or mechanical, including photocopying, recording or by any information storage and retrieval system, without permission in writing from the publisher. This book is a work of fiction. Any resemblance to real persons (living or dead), events, or entities is coincidental.

Grey Gecko Press
565 S. Mason Road, Suite 154
Katy, TX 77450
www.greygeckopress.com

Printed in the United States of America

Also available as an eBook

Library of Congress Cataloging-in-Publication Data
Padgett, George Wright
Cruel devices / George Wright Padgett
Library of Congress Control Number: 2014951634
ISBN 978-1-9388216-9-1
First Edition

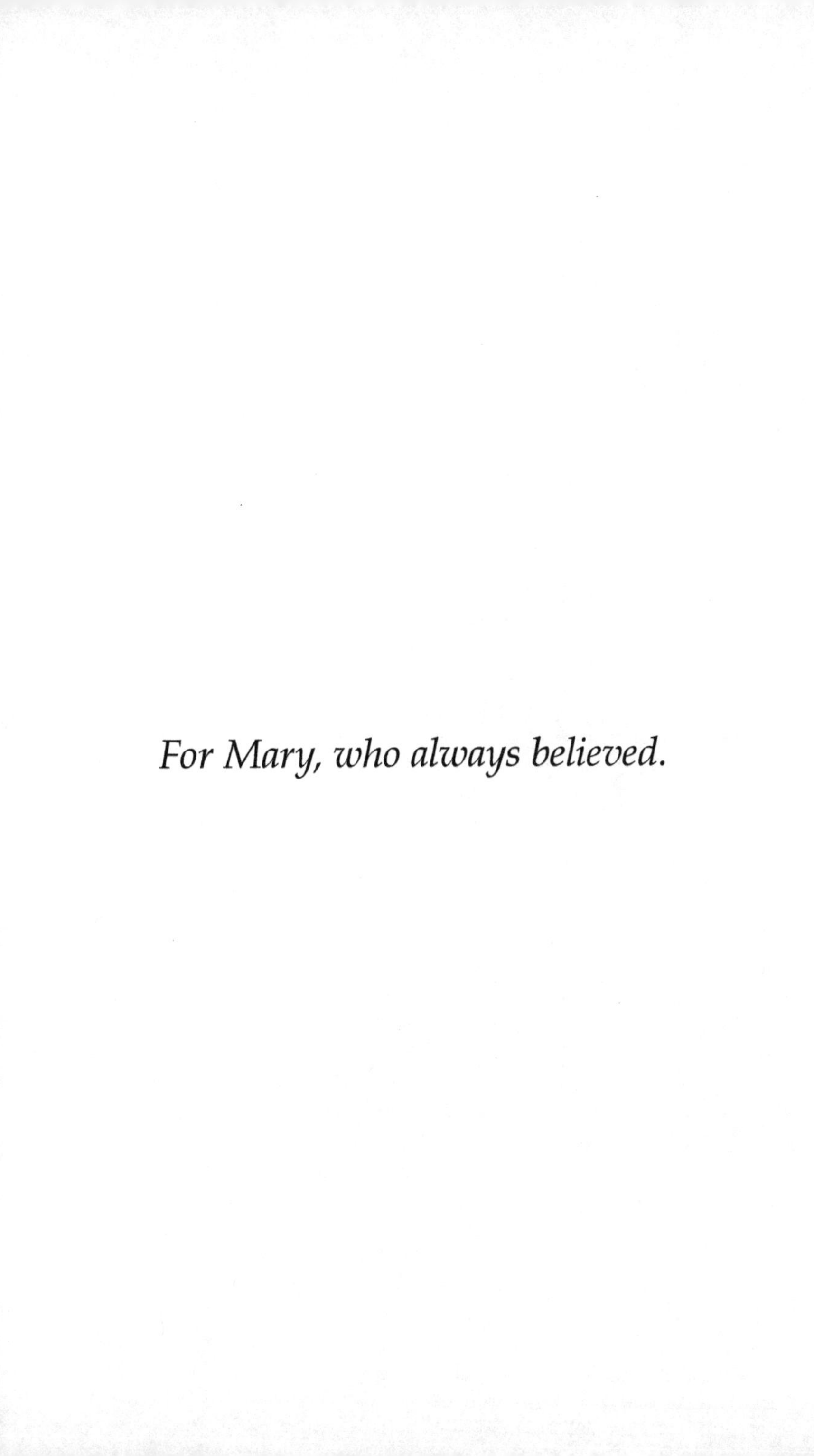

For Mary, who always believed.

ONE

IT HAD NOTHING TO DO WITH SEX, though the sex had been good at times. In fact, physical attraction had played an insignificant role in Gavin Curtis's brief affair with grad student Monica Garcia. It'd been about regaining the control that the bestselling author had felt he'd forfeited to his publicist and wife.

Josephine Garner had served as his publicist for two years before they were married, for the five years of their marriage, and ever since it had ended. They had managed to salvage the working relationship from the rubble of the divorce, and now Gavin had what he wanted—he got to make the rules again.

Usually.

"You *have* to get William something," Josephine pleaded over the receiver. "He's turning seventy-five."

Gavin glared at the picture of her on his phone and then back up at the line of people before him. He leaned back in the uncomfortable folding chair the store had supplied him with. The line went on forever, and the signing was just getting started. "I should? Why? Shouldn't he be getting me things by now? After all, my books put Regal Press on the map in the first place."

Gavin intended to get the old man something special. He just didn't know what yet. Goading Josephine was a bonus.

"Your manuscripts are the only ones that he edits since his retirement," the irritated voice on the phone said. "Look, I'm not going to argue with you about this." There was a brief pause before Josephine added, "I shouldn't have to remind you that he's your editor *and* a professional friend."

A gangly teenage boy with acne approached the table.

Josephine continued, "I know that you've got to get going to the event. I found a bottle of Cheval Blanc '64 online. We can both give it to him next week."

"Bad idea," he told her as he received the book from the teenager.

"Rick . . . uh . . . my name is Rick," the boy said with nervous awe.

Gavin nodded in acknowledgment but continued speaking to Josephine. "That's probably the worst gift you could get."

"But it's a six-hundred-dollar bottle of wine."

"That may be," he said, cradling the phone between his shoulder and ear to pick up his pen, "but Bill Cavanaugh is a recovering alcoholic. How is it that you don't remember that?"

Josephine sighed. "Jeez. I did forget that."

Gavin grinned in triumph as he signed the book. "Why can't you just buy him tickets to a Yankees game or a Broadway show? Or how about a cruise or something for him and Beverly?"

The teenager reached for the book, but Gavin dispassionately slapped his hand away.

"No, not that. He's more of a shut-in than you are except when he's doing his motorcycle thing. Oh, I'll think of something."

"Nothing too expensive. Unless I can write it off," Gavin said, watching the boy before him gnaw at a hangnail on his thumb.

"Gavin, he's your *friend*."

"Thanks, Mr. Curtis," the teenager said as he reached for the signed book for a second time. "I've read all of your work, but my favorites are the Damien Marksman novels."

Gavin raised his eyebrows and looked over his bifocals. "You've read everything and yet you favor warlock vampire detective stories?" His tone was acidic.

The fan's skinny body stiffened. He slowly pulled his hand away from the table as if he had accidentally roused a sleeping Bengal tiger. He stammered, "Y-yeah, even your short stories in *Vampyrous Magazine*."

"Everything? Ever hear of *The Serpentine Protocol?*"

"Gavin?" Josephine asked. "Who are you talking to?"

The boy tried to look away, but Gavin locked an unblinking stare on him that demanded eye contact.

"Is that something new?" Rick asked.

"Hardly," Gavin said, still ignoring Josephine's voice on the phone. "If all you've read are the vampire-detective novels of mine, you're missing out. Check out *Serpentine*. It's my espionage novel from a few years ago. It's kinda Ian Fleming with the edginess of a Palahniuk novel."

"Gavin!" the voice on the phone yelled.

He shoved his cell at the dumbfounded Rick. "Here, Nick. It's my publicist, Josephine Garner."

"Uh . . . hello, Miss Garner?"

After a moment, the teenager's face formed a smile as he relayed his full name and address to Josephine.

Gavin's smirk melted.

Gavin reached to reclaim the phone, but Rick pulled back. He respectfully held a hand up to the author while he told the woman on the other end, "Yeah, that'd be *so* awesome. By the way, I'm looking forward to the next movie adaptation, 'cause it'll be kickass to see all of the special effects done for Damien's slave demon from book six."

Gavin knew what was happening: the kid was caught in Josephine's irresistible energy field of excitement and affirmation. It's what she did—make lemonade out of lemons and all that crap. Every challenge was an opportunity in disguise to her and all those other cotton candy clouds of nonsense.

Gavin also possessed more than his fair share of charisma, but, unlike Josephine, who left a trail of rainbows and sparkly glitter in her wake, his ability to "captivate the masses" was more objective driven. His charm was an instrument to be utilized when he wanted something. "You could sweet-talk the horns off the devil," his mother used to tell him with a smile.

As true as that was, charm hadn't been enough when it really counted. It hadn't been enough to rescue his mother from the long death-spiral of breast cancer. No, this power was best used on things like cutting ahead in line at a show or getting the best table at a pretentious new restaurant.

The paradox of it was that even though he never really "got" people, he could quickly determine what they needed to hear from him to give him what he wanted.

Part of his fascination with Josephine was that though she shared this same rapid assessment of people, she never used it against them. Most people who knew her regarded her as the high priestess of spin. They thought that it was all an act, like his was. Gavin knew that deep down, at her core, it was 100 percent genuine. She was the real deal.

Rick uttered a series of *yeahs* and *uh-huhs* into the phone as if he were the only one in the store. Gavin watched helplessly as the boy was swept away by Josephine's siren song.

It's said that opposites attract, and never was that truer than between Gavin and Josephine. While they were together, she placed sticky notes by the kitchen phone. Printed on each square was a small image of a unicorn. Gavin went through every sheet and drew a stick man impaled by the steed's horn.

She'd laughed when she'd seen the crude stick figures and had quietly erased all of the victims except for one. She'd posted that last sticky prominently on the fridge with an arrow pointing to the figure and a note. "This one is you, Gavin.

Love, Jo." The note had stayed there for over a month, until the adhesive lost its tack.

That's what she was doing now—cleaning up his mess, fixing what he'd broken, making sure that this kid whom he'd battered would leave an even bigger fan than before.

He eyed the kid as Josephine's tiny, indiscernible voice leaked from the receiver. He tried to make sense of the kid's black T-shirt: "My Clone Other Found Superintendent and All I Got Was This Lousy T-Shirt!"

He read it again.

What did that even mean? Who were all these people? The long line made him grit his teeth.

"Oh, I'd say about two hundred of 'em or so," Rick answered, turning to face the line behind him. The back of the shirt made even less sense than the front. In big, white letters, it asked, "Got Hemlo?"

"What?" Rick now completely ignored the man whom he'd made a pilgrimage to see. "Oh, we're at the Buy-the-Book megastore in Droverton."

There was another pause. Then, looking up at the high ceiling, he answered, "I guess so. It's the one that's three stories tall. Oh, yeah, okay . . . yeah, that'd be so cool. Thank you, Miss Garner. Thanks a lot."

Rick turned back to face the table. "Yeah, he's still here. Thanks again."

Gavin snatched the phone back from the kid.

"That was awesome, Mr. Curtis. Thank you so much. I can hardly wait."

Gavin shoved the closed book across the table at him as he said with a scowl, "You're welcome."

Before the next devotee stepped forward, Gavin jumped up. He turned to face the wall behind him and whispered into the phone, "Jo, what did you just do to me?"

"Gavin, you're such an ass. Don't ever do that to a fan again. I'm sending him a box set of the entire second series and Blu-Ray DVDs of the three movies to cover for your little tantrum or whatever that was. These people love you enough to give up time on a Saturday to stand in line for an hour and a half to spend forty-five seconds with you. You need to give them your attention. This is a part of your job."

"No, my job is to write." He hoped that she wouldn't bring up that he hadn't written anything of any substance in over a year.

"This is a part of the gig—an important part. Now you listen to me. Stop sulking about your spy novel or whatever is bothering you and get with the program here. We tried something different, and I'm glad you took a chance on something new, but this tour is about the *Shadow Soul Tracker* series. Relax and enjoy yourself. The people there love Damien Marksman. They love you."

"Love me? Of course they love me. I realize that, but they don't even know me. They know *about* me, but that's very different from knowing me."

"I know, but I do . . ."

"What? You do what?" He waited to hear the words.

"Look, Gavin. We both have a job to do. If you're getting to where—"

"I did my part. I wrote the stinkin' book, didn't I?"

"I know you don't like these things, but an author has to do them. Give me a call later and we can talk about what to do for the *Serpentine* book, okay?"

"Yeah, yeah."

"I'm sorry that I called you at the event. I forgot you're three hours in front of the West Coast over there. I thought you'd still be at the hotel. Anyway, just call me when you get back to your room."

"I will. Thanks, Jo."

"Good. Now put on your best happy-author smile and go sell another million books for all of us, okay?"

"Wha-hoo," Gavin answered sarcastically.

"And Gavin, I *do* love you."

He thought of the sticky note with the stick figure being run through by a unicorn, now tucked in his wallet.

"Same here," he said as he gently tapped the disconnect icon on the phone.

Gavin did his best to comply with Josephine's request to "play nice." With a smile frozen on his face, he recited the words "thank you for your support" three dozen times or more. It was obvious that the hollowness of the phrase went unnoticed by the store's patrons. The fans were too gobsmacked.

He invented a game to distract himself and pass the time. With each book he signed, he imagined filling out the execution order of the person in front of him. This resulted in a more flamboyant signature, and for a few minutes, he genuinely enjoyed himself. None of the lemmings had a clue.

But reality found a way of seeping through the cracks in the foundation, and forty-five minutes later, he was ready to strangle the next person who dared to ask him where his ideas came from or if he was a practitioner of the occult because of his main character's affiliation with creatures from darker realms.

He could tell that they all believed they owned a piece of him just because they plopped $24.99 on the counter, as if they were entitled to a sliver of his soul. He was more than the blurb printed on the inside jacket flap.

Just when he could take no more, an elderly woman in a neon-blue jogging suit hobbled up to the edge of the table. He guessed that she was in her eighties and that it was unlikely that she'd ever run anywhere in the exercise outfit that swallowed her up. From the canvas bag slung over her shoulder, she produced a thick book. It looked heavier than she was. Her veiny hands trembled slightly as the book landed on the table with a thud.

She said with an embarrassed giggle, "Oh dear, I'm so sorry, Mr. Curtis. I didn't mean to do that, but it's heavy."

"It's okay," Gavin said, leaning forward to grab the book before it fell off the edge.

It was his first novel, *Blood Stained*.

"Well, hello, old friend," he said to the book as his fingers ran over the embossed letters. The cover was worn but in decent enough shape, considering it was a first edition printed nearly thirty years ago.

The old woman beamed as Gavin said, "I forgot how thick this thing was."

He cracked the book open, and the nostalgic smell of old paper filled his nostrils. Gavin was lost in his own world as his eyes scanned the page. Reading a few lines, he chuckled. "This is great."

He flashed back to the romantic time when he'd written it—all of that glorious anxiousness, the excitement of releasing something so close to his heart. It had been a time when he'd still had something to prove to himself and to the world. It had been exhilarating, the beautiful fear of pushing himself out there, depending only on himself, like a tightrope walker high above the circus floor.

He'd bet on himself and won. But was this the grand prize—forever sharing a literary cell with his creation, Damien Marksman? Was this all there was, becoming captive to his own success?

Back then, creativity had been a raging river that he'd let carry him away downstream. Now he faced a drought, and for the last four or five books, he'd just gone through the motions. He'd sell his soul for a fresh idea that didn't include everyone's favorite vampire detective.

Judging by book sales, the so-called fans were oblivious. Each release set higher publishing records than the one before. He *was* trapped, and he resented them all for it, every last one of them. They were the prison guards confining him to this gilded cage.

But this little old lady seemed different. Perhaps she knew his farce. Maybe she saw his plight. He decided that it didn't matter. At least she had enough discernment to present this book instead of the new Marksman book.

Gavin dipped his eyes back down to the book, gently gliding his fingers across the page as if reacquainting himself with the soft cheek of a former lover. "I can still remember what it was like . . ." He flipped more pages and added with a smile, "I wrote this paragraph sitting in the back of a city bus headed to work."

He paused and then spoke as if he was talking only to himself. "This novel saved me from a life as a ninth-grade English teacher. Or, better said, it saved thousands of ninth-graders from being my literary victims."

He adjusted his bifocals. "Not too good with kids, I discovered."

"What's your name, my dear?" he asked, flicking the flair marker to the side for the two-hundred-fifty-dollar Visconti pen in his shirt pocket.

"I'm Eunice," she said. "Eunice Hodges. But it's not for me. I want you to make it to a different name."

"For someone else?" Gavin asked.

"Yes, for my son," Eunice said, clasping her hands in the middle of her chest. "His name is Doyle . . . Doyle Hodges. He just had his birthday. He's the same age as you. You both have July twelfth birthdays."

"Ah, that's a good day. So we're both fifty. Where is he? I want to tell him something."

"No, he couldn't get the day off work."

"So he sent you to stand in line?" Gavin sensed the crowd growing restless, but he didn't care. This was a *true* fan, and, judging by the age of the book, a reader who had probably been with him from the beginning, when it was still good.

"He doesn't know I'm here. I took the book from his room. We live together." She grinned as she whispered, "It's a surprise for him."

Gavin opened to the title page with newfound purpose. "Doyle, right? His name's Doyle?" He read the inscription aloud as he wrote it.

Doyle, meeting your sweet mother has been the high point of my visit to Connecticut.

Happy belated birthday to you (we Cancer signs have to stick together).

~G.L. Curtis

The smile on her face grew as she heard the dedication. "Oh, Mr. Curtis, he'll be so pleased."

"Well, Ms. Hodges, I'm glad that I could help," Gavin said as he handed the book back. "And tell your son something for me. Tell him we share a birthday with Henry David Thoreau."

Eunice was still beaming. "Really? Oh, yes, sir. He'll like finding that out."

She tucked the mammoth book back into the burlap bag around her shoulder and then paused as if she had something more to say.

The bookstore's manager—a short, plump troll of a man with a dreadful comb-over—appeared from Gavin's blind spot. "Uh, miss, the other customers . . . if you could just move over there to the—"

Gavin raised his hand, making his handler for the event fall silent.

"Miss Hodges, is there anything else for you today?" Gavin asked, motioning for the little fat man to retreat into the wings.

"Well, actually, that was for Doyle. I have something to ask for me. That was his turn. This one's mine."

Gavin chuckled as he took the Visconti pen back out of his breast pocket. "You *are* a shrewd girl. What may I sign for you?"

"Oh, nothing like that . . . just a question for you."

Gavin braced himself for the most inane question one could ask a writer: *Where do you get your ideas from?* Just when things were going so well between the two of them.

He was relieved when she didn't. She asked something of relevance. "What makes good horror? The fear of the unknown?"

Gavin repeated the words as a professor would present a rhetorical question to an auditorium of students. "What makes for a good horror story?"

He let the words dissolve in the air like vapor. After a few seconds, he conceded, "Well, fear of the unknown *can* be a contributor, but think about it—you don't know what the weather will be like next Thursday, but that doesn't scare you. Or who'll win the World Series, but you're not afraid about it. Are we the only intelligent life in the universe? I don't know, but it doesn't frighten me that I don't know."

He tucked his pen snugly back into his pocket. "The point is, there are millions upon millions of things that are unknown to us, but that's not where the fear stems from. The unknown can contribute to horror, but the kicker is control. That's where it's at."

Gavin poked at the table with a stubby index finger, emphasizing his point. "Removal of control is the main thing. Whether they realize it or not, most people are afraid of not being in control. This is more powerful than the fear of the unknown or even the fear of dying."

The line of people behind Eunice moved forward slightly, encroaching on her space. The air was electric. About a dozen hands extended, holding cell phones—undoubtedly recording the moment to post later on YouTube or other social media.

He decided to play along. They had cast him in this role of Horror Messiah. He'd act the part, turning their literary water into wine or, even better, turning it into blood. It was time to activate that good 'ol Gavin Curtis charm. With a million-dollar smile, he decided to crank the charm up to full tilt boogie.

He looked beyond Eunice into the growing sea of cell phone cameras and spoke boldly. "Think about it. If I wrote a short story of a guy facing a firing line in the morning—a character facing certain death—that is not as scary as someone who is facing the prospect of being used by or taken over by a malevolent entity like a ghost or whatever. Stevenson recognized this and put Mr. Hyde in control of Dr. Jekyll."

Gavin stood from his chair, and the cell phone cameras followed his ascent. "There's a trend these days to put a character in a situation where they have no control, because a maniac killer is in charge of their outcome. We, as humans, have something basic at our core that makes us crave control any way we can get it."

A female voice from the crowd hollered out, "But what about the occult? You know, the devil?"

Gavin scanned the faces to place the voice with the person. When he couldn't, he answered in a matter-of-fact tone of voice, "Still, control . . . it's still all about control."

He moved out from behind the table as he continued. "See, with God, there's free will and all that—not very scary."

Gavin reached the other side of the table and leaned against its edge with his arms crossed. "Now, as for the devil and his minions, those guys are all about control. Controlling the human race and all, that's what they do, or at least try to do. Think back to the stories in your Sunday school class."

A wave of repressed laughter rippled through the crowd. They had abandoned the line and now formed a huddle.

"I know, I know, but hear me out on this, ya bunch of heathens!"

A catcall whistle erupted from the mob, inspiring more laughter, this time unrestrained.

Gavin put a bulky arm around Eunice's small, over-perfumed frame. The frail woman bounced with joy as if the two of them had just been crowned Homecoming King and Queen. It felt good to work a crowd again.

Yeah, it's no wonder they love me.

Gavin's handler—the portly store manager—buzzed around, snapping pictures of the spectacle that his little book signing had become.

Gavin released Eunice and scooted into a sitting position back on the table. "Here's the thing: control is just an illusion that we placate ourselves with. We choose to believe we have control, but that's a fantasy of the mind. What a good horror writer does is simply pull the curtain back to give us a peek inside. Removing control results in horror, and the more controlling a character is before the writer strips them of it, the more horrific the fall."

Removing his bifocals, he wiped his brow with the back of his free hand. "It really doesn't matter if the character dies or what the outcome of the plot is. The reader has to confront their own lack of control in the universe, even if it's only on some subconscious level. What horror writers do is expose this through a story."

A pouty-looking Goth girl of about twenty nudged her way through the horde. Gavin was taken aback by the abundance of piercings on her face. The human-voodoo-doll woman asked, "But can't the reader put down the book? Just close it up and tuck it away?"

Gavin regained his composure and looked over the top of the girl's head and addressed the audience. "Ah, now you're getting ahead of me. Yes, that's exactly it. They're scared, but they're in control of it. The reader turns the valve that lets the fear in at a manageable rate of speed.

"They tuck the book back into the nightstand beside the bed, and everything is okay again. They'll outlive whatever happens in the book. They come out victorious even if the protagonist of the story gets themselves snuffed out. The reader returns to the cocoon of this false sense of control, and everybody continues on their merry way."

A voice with a Vietnamese accent rang out from the crowd. "What about a horror master like you, Mr. Curtis? What scares you?"

The group noisily echoed the question.

Gavin tried, for a few seconds, to locate the originator of the question, but he couldn't. There were simply too many people.

"I'm afraid of"—he paused for dramatic effect—"not being able to find my car keys!"

In one swift move, he pulled the Crescent Car Rentals key ring from his jacket pocket to an outburst of applause. He had them eating out of his hand, just like charming the horns off the devil.

In between guffaws, the Goth girl made an unexpected joke. "So you *can* control your car."

This inspired a few more chuckles from the room and an honest laugh from Gavin himself as he jingled the keys with the ridiculous yellow moon attachment. "Yes, I guess so. Now you're getting the hang of it. And now, before we get back to signing books—"

Before he could finish, a fire alarm shrieked. Seconds later, water spewed from the overhead sprinkler system.

The show was over. It was time to go.

Pandemonium ensued throughout the bookstore. Gavin's portly handler abandoned him, scurrying around with plastic sheeting to cover product. Playful screams and laughter echoed throughout the cavernous area as customers stampeded out of the store like spooked cattle.

Store clerks yelled instructions back and forth to each other like ship pursers panicking aboard a sinking vessel. In contrast, Gavin calmly proceeded to the front exit, his head covered with his sports coat. The cold droplets of water hitting grey tarps sounded like an endless round of applause.

Even though the crew moved at lightning speed, Gavin suspected there would still be thousands of dollars' worth of damage. He resisted the temptation to uncover the end caps that contained his latest novel, *Blood Clot*. He suspected that if the books were damaged, the store would just order another lot, inflating the sales of that drivel.

Once safely outside, he removed his jacket from over his head. The hot July sun felt good for a change.

Some of the store's patrons had already made their way to their cars, only to find themselves in an equally chaotic exodus from the parking lot. Others took refuge in the neighboring Jamba Juice outlet to the left of the bookstore. The line poured out the door of the franchise. It was going to be a good day for their sales. Gavin wondered if the Jamba Juice manager had tripped the alarm to get all of that business. Then he smiled at his own cynicism.

The rest of the crowd—the majority of the customers—looked back at the bookstore from the sidewalk like schoolchildren anticipating the recess bell.

On the curb next to Gavin was a young, muscular black man whom he guessed to be in his mid-twenties. He wore a black Buy-the-Book apron.

"Shouldn't you be in there?" Gavin asked, pointing at the doorway.

"Nah, I'm only here for today . . . to stock. My store is 719. They had me here to help with the extra business today."

"Extra business?" Gavin asked. He was intrigued that the clerk hadn't looked at him yet. The man stared forward at the chaos inside.

"Well, yeah, 'cause of you," the clerk said as if stating a universally known fact.

"Oh, yeah. Sorry, I guess."

"It's cool, it's cool," the man said as he shifted his gaze to his apron pocket. He produced a pack of cigarettes and began to light one. "I don't mind. I get time-and-a-half." He paused for some short puffs to get the cigarette going. "Yeah, time-and-a-half, baby."

A few delinquent customers exited the building, including an older man and woman who were not amused by the ordeal, as demonstrated by a stream of swear words.

"You got another one of those?" Gavin asked, pointing to the cigarette.

The man paused and then reached back into his apron. "Sure. Here, you can have the rest."

"Thanks," Gavin said, counting the three Marlboro Reds remaining in the pack. He balanced one of them on his lips and took out the Zippo also in the pack.

"Sure. I need to keep the lighter, though."

"Huh? Oh, yeah, okay." Gavin gave the Zippo back to him.

Gavin closed his eyes and inhaled the smoke deeply into his lungs. He exhaled a few seconds later, relishing the moment. He opened his eyes and asked, "Hey, can I sign something for you . . . you know, for these?"

The young man took another long drag and looked back at the doorway. "Nah, it's cool."

Blaring sirens announced the arrival of a slick, red fire truck. The party was in full swing now.

"Where are the rest of the workers?" Gavin asked. "Shouldn't they be out by now?"

"Don't worry, I doubt there's any fire. Just some jackhole pulled the fire alarm is my guess."

Gavin nodded, thinking how grateful he was to be away from the signing table. At least this guy seemed authentic, not just some wide-eyed fanboy.

Four firefighters in cumbersome gear shuffled into the bookstore, looking like they hoped to find a battle they probably wouldn't.

Gavin studied the other man, who was exhaling a steady stream of smoke. "You're completely dry. How are you completely dry? A stocker would have been in the back of the store."

A sly grin escaped from him. "Yeah, well, about that—"

"You're the only one out here who doesn't look wet. If I had to guess about who pulled the alarm, I'd have to say—"

"Smoke break," he cut in. "I needed a smoke break. That and the fact that old man Hastings fired my cousin a couple months ago."

"Hastings? Bossy little Danny DeVito guy with the comb-over? Is that the manager?"

"That'd be the one, in the flesh. Sorry if I messed up your party thing in there."

"Hardly what I'd call a party," Gavin said with a snort. "Actually, I'm grateful."

"Well, if that's true, if you don't want to hang out with your loyal subjects, you should head through that alley there."

"Why?" Gavin asked. "What do you mean?"

The clerk pointed at the people who were starting to amass and move toward them. "They look like a zombie horde from one of your books."

"Vampires." Gavin sighed as he took a step behind him. "I write vampires."

"Whatever. But they've already seen you. Make you a deal: you don't narc me out on the fire alarm thing, and I'll buy you some time here."

"It's a deal."

"Cool. Like I said, you should cut through the alley over there. Behind the bookstore is a loading dock with pallets. Hide back there, and I'll come get you when this mob scene has died down."

Then the clerk shouted to the crowd, "If I can have your attention, please! Buy-the-Book apologizes for the inconvenience, but Mr. Cutter—"

"*Curtis,*" Gavin interjected from behind him.

"Mr. *Curtis* will be heading to the Buy-the-Book location at the intersection of Hearst and Glenbrook." The man went on with the authority of a traffic cop during rush hour. "Look for the red brick building about six miles east of here. Hearst and Glenbrook store at twelve fifteen. Don't be late."

Wow, this kid had a lot of moxy.

He turned to Gavin. "What are you still doing here? Go, dude. Go hide. I'll get ya in a few minutes."

Gavin was speechless. The crowd hurried to their cars like roaches running across the kitchen floor when a light is clicked on.

Gavin shook his head and laughed in disbelief. "Those people are going to be pissed when they find out."

The younger man didn't acknowledge that. Instead, he pushed Gavin firmly in the direction of the alley. "Remember, we have a deal."

"Yeah, thanks. And thanks for the cigarettes."

"Whatever. Five minutes. Don't come back in until I get you at the pallets." Gavin nodded and headed down the alley.

Two

AFTER A LOT LONGER THAN FIVE MINUTES, Gavin became restless. There was no sign of his getaway accomplice. His mind wandered through its familiar paths, ending up where it always did—Josephine. He knew that he had been a jerk to her on the phone, but he knew she'd forgive him. She had always forgiven him—almost always.

As the July sun beat down, Gavin scrolled through listings in his phone. He stopped at the old thumb-sized picture of her that served as her dialing icon.

How long would it take her to discover that he'd ducked out? He debated calling her and decided against it. If she found out that they'd had to exit the store, she'd arrange for a signing table to be set up on the curb or in the parking lot or something. Knowing her, she'd probably give away a bunch of free books or find a way to make Damien Marksman towels to dry everybody off to make it up to all of them.

The tiny digital image of her gleamed a million-dollar smile back at him as if she already knew somehow. Even worse, if he told her that he had hung out with the guy who'd tripped the alarm, she'd suspect that Gavin had put him up to it. The fact that he was hiding behind pallets at the back of the store wouldn't help his case either.

He slid her image downward with his thumb. The directory displayed the entry above hers: Monica Garcia. It figured that Monica's listing would come directly before Josephine's. He tried to remember the last time he spoke to the woman.

Six months ago? Maybe nine?

She had finally stopped calling when she had left Newport Beach and returned to college.

He'd done his best to keep the news of the divorce from her for fear it would start everything back up again. While Josephine had moved on, Gavin wasn't ready to start up a life with Monica Garcia or anyone else.

Even so, he hadn't deleted the number of his former mistress, maybe to spite Josephine, or maybe because he genuinely regretted how the two-month affair had turned out for the girl. She wasn't to blame, after all. He had propositioned her.

Though he'd never said it, he regretted hurting Jo. She had deserved better. He had been stupid.

He paced beside a long, blue trash compactor, the stench of it bringing him back to the present. He grumbled to himself, "How can that smell be so bad? It's only boxes and packing supplies." Then he remembered the bookstore's coffeehouse. The combination of milk, creamer, and other additives with the July heat made for a noxiously sour concoction.

Gavin inadvertently scraped his foot across the flattened carcass of a frog. He jumped back at the realization and fitfully shuffled the stiffened remains to the side. A disturbing childhood memory of a botched frog dissection flooded his mind. "Jeez, this is so gross back here."

Gavin stared back at the icon of Monica on his phone. Tapping a series of commands on the device, he deleted her entry forever and tucked the phone away. He sighed and resumed pacing. He considered peeking around the corner to see if everyone had cleared out but decided not to chance it.

Where was the stocker? Were there people still waiting out there? Maybe Hastings figured out that the stocker had tripped the alarm. It could be hours before he came back. Maybe he had forgotten him. That was entirely possible, maybe even likely. "Mr. Cutter"—sheesh!

When he could no longer stand it, Gavin snatched his damp jacket off the waist-high stack of pallets and shuffled down the narrow, fenced-in pathway in search of a book of matches or a lighter for the two remaining cigarettes.

Why didn't he offer to buy the lighter from the boy?

Before twenty minutes ago, it had been nearly two months since Gavin had smoked. His on-again, off-again battle with nicotine had been a fixture of his personality since he was a sophomore in college. It was the only thing in his adult life that he felt powerless over. He hated it.

Even so, when the cool sensation of grey ribbons of smoke swirled down in his lungs, it was intoxicating—an ecstasy that couldn't be negotiated with. When he *did* give in, it was always as delicious as the lips of a siren nymph, the bittersweet taste of a million broken promises to himself. He was prepared to break that promise two more times today if only he could find a light.

Behind the bookstore, there was a rusted-out maintenance truck for the strip center. As he came closer, he peered through the windshield at the dashboard. There was a mound of empty fast-food containers, a newspaper, and several plastic Starbucks cups, but no lighter in view.

He continued down the back service way and crossed the moderately busy street, noting his path in relation to the bookstore. This was easy to do, since the behemoth's three stories towered above the single-story structures along the way.

The last thing he needed was to get lost in Droverton, Connecticut.

As he passed an abandoned dry cleaner, a paint store, a jeweler, and a plate-glass company, he thought about how Josephine had been right about Billy. He should get the old fart something for his birthday, but what?

Billy Cavanaugh was much more to him than the editor of twenty-eight of the thirty-four Damien Marksman novels. The man had assumed the role of midwife to the stories, knowing exactly what to do when the birth had gone breech. He had talked the temperamental author "down from the ledge" every time an idea just wasn't working, which had occurred more times than Gavin would ever like to admit. Billy was a friend, perhaps Gavin's only true friend. He'd have to do something special for him.

The noonday sun beat down, and Gavin began to sweat. He daydreamed about how good it would feel to shower back at the hotel and then hit the bar. He was already tired of walking. The irony of getting much-needed exercise by trying to get a cigarette lit wasn't lost on him. He quickly rationalized it, excusing a lifetime of neglect by thinking that he did exercise—just in unconventional ways. Rolling a suitcase through airports counted, didn't it?

He tried to add up the number of airports that he had shuffled through over the last three and a half weeks. He couldn't remember the exact tally. The fact that there had been more than he could count allowed him to conclude that he had been getting enough exercise, despite what Josephine would say.

Around the corner, someone sat at the bus stop enclosure on the opposite side of the street. The bright, neon-blue warm-up suit was unmistakable—it was Ms. Hodges. He was delighted to see her. Here was a person he felt an authentic connection with, unlike the parade of mind-numbed fans who worshiped anything that had his name stamped on it.

What he'd give to go back to writing for people like her again—writing something new, something that he could take pride in again.

He started to call out to her, but then he realized that she was talking to someone and that something didn't look right about it. A Toyota nearly clipped him as he crossed the street to get to her. As he approached, he noted the scene. An unkempt man in tattered cargo shorts was talking to her. The imposing figure leaned in and gestured broadly at the elderly woman.

Gavin sped up to join them. The man, who Gavin guessed was a panhandler, didn't notice his approach.

Eunice looked up from the conversation. "Oh, Mr. Curtis, what are you doing here?"

The man turned to see whom she addressed.

Before he could speak, Gavin said, "What's your story, bud?" He glanced down and caught sight of bright white fabric peeking up incongruously from crusty, old sneakers caked in mud and filth. The socks were folded down, almost tucked into the tops of the shoes.

"What du-duh-do you mean?"

"Are you here to catch the bus or what?"

"Nuh-nuh-nuh . . . no . . . mu-mu-money," the man stuttered as he presented a flap of cardboard with crudely formed letters written in marker.

Gavin studied the man for a moment. "No money, huh?"

"Nu-nuh-nuh . . . no," the man answered with a more severe stutter than before.

"I can spare five dollars, Mr. Curtis," Eunice offered as she began to rummage through her tote bag.

Gavin moved over to the man, his overweight belly nearly touching the panhandler's stained orange T-shirt. "Don't give this clown one red cent."

"But Mr. Curtis, he told me—"

"He's a fake and a liar." Gavin stared into the man's hazel eyes. After a second, the man began to blink irregularly and then tried to look away. Gavin shifted, placing himself back into the man's line of sight.

"Miss Hodges," Gavin said, "I've studied people my whole life. That's one of the things that makes me a good writer." Gavin stepped back. "This chump's not for real. He probably lives in a nicer house than you and your son do, no offense."

"How do you know?" she asked. "How can you tell?"

"Socks," Gavin said, pointing down. "Those socks are perfectly clean. He's not committed enough to let dirt actually touch his skin."

"Hey, wait. You said 'writer.' Are you Gavin Curtis, the writer?" The man spoke without a trace of a stutter.

"Yes, he is," Eunice offered as if she were a proud parent. "Gavin Curtis."

"Oh, man, this is cool. This is awesome. I can't believe that it's you!"

Gavin switched his sports coat to the other arm and said, "I suggest you take your act someplace else."

"Huh? Oh, yeah, but can I get an autograph first?" He flipped the handmade sign over and presented it to Gavin for signing.

"Get lost, you jerk."

The man's elation melted to a scowl as he left.

From a safe distance, he yelled, "I think your new book sucks!"

Gavin raised his eyebrows and softly murmured to himself, "Yeah, well, that makes two of us."

Eunice, perched on the bench, was enjoying the show. She adjusted the canvas bag beside her, shrugged, and winked.

Gavin looked back at the man and shouted, "Hey, wait a second!"

He turned with a look of anticipation. "Yeah?"

"Do you have a light?"

The question was answered with the man's middle finger, lifted high.

"Well, that wasn't very nice of him," Eunice said with a disappointed frown.

Gavin waited until the man was safely out of sight before he reached into his jacket. "Miss Hodges, I forgot to tell you this earlier . . . "

A puzzled look formed on her face. "Yes? What is it?"

He produced a crisp hundred-dollar bill. "I was supposed to give you this special Gavin Curtis bookmark back at the bookstore."

"Oh, Mr. Curtis," she gasped as her veiny hands covered her mouth. "You shouldn't do that."

He shook his head. "I want to. I want you to take this and hail a cab before that creep comes back."

"Thank you." She waved her hands in front of her chest. "That's too much, though. I only live about—"

He butted in firmly. "I need you to get home safely with your son's book, okay? If there's change left over from the ride, buy him a belated birthday cake or something, from me."

Before he knew it, she'd given him a quick peck on the cheek. "Thank you, Mr. Curtis. Thank you so much."

He folded the bill into her cool, soft palm.

"You're a hero, Mr. Curtis." He was close enough to see tears welling up in her eyes as she said, "You're just like . . . like Damien Marksman."

Ughhh. Sucker-punched.

Again, always with Damien. Would he ever be free of him?

He forced a smile, wondering what it looked like from the outside.

"Thank you again," Eunice said, and then her expression shifted to puzzled concern, as if she'd seen something worrisome. She pulled back for a second and tilted her head, her thin eyebrows revealing an odd intensity. "You . . . You be careful, Mr. Curtis. I know it sounds silly . . . well, silly to my son, Doyle, but sometimes I . . . I get these *feelings* about people." She forced a smile. "Oh, I'm sure it's nothing. I'm such a ninny, but . . . please be careful, Mr. Curtis . . . for me, okay? I don't know why . . . it's just a feeling."

Something about the way she said it sent a shiver up his spine. "Yeah, okay, Miss Hodges. I am. I mean, I will be." He felt a little dumb and awkward. "I will," he promised again, dabbing the sweat from his brow.

Gavin watched from the bus stop as Eunice disappeared from sight around the corner. Moments before, he'd offered to walk her to a street with heavier traffic to hail a cab. She had graciously refused, thanking him again with another peck on the cheek. She'd even apologized for not having a light for his cigarette, but she told him there was a Quickie Mart several blocks over.

Now that she was safely on her way, he walked in the direction that she'd indicated.

He passed a quaint establishment called The Salad Bowl. Hand-painted images of cartoon vegetables parading about on the windows made Gavin snicker. The happy faces of carrots, celery, tomatoes, and other produce indicated that the vegetables had no idea what fate would soon befall them.

"Probably no smokers in there, just a bunch of health nuts."

Plastered to the connecting fence were various movie posters. He winced as he passed eight side-by-side advertisements for a July 4th release. The posters were for *A Chalice of Dragon's Blood*, the latest flick based on his Damien Marksman novels. Dissatisfied with the Hollywood interpretations of his books, Gavin had stopped attending the movie premiers years ago. They always focused on the gore, compounded with a ridiculous number of explosions, rather than the subtleties of character development or plot.

The recent casting of a Caucasian as Damien's love interest in book five had caused a controversy. In Gavin's version, the woman was a dark-skinned Haitian, and the producers opted for a skinny white girl from the Bronx.

The box office success of the films was bittersweet. It had made him a household name, but he felt dirty and couldn't convince himself that he hadn't sold out.

As he passed through the remains of what was once a used-car dealership, he found that he was still unable to shake the eerie feeling that had descended upon him at the bus stop when Mrs. Hodges had warned him to be careful.

He thought about it, trying to assess what had made him feel so queer, trying to understand it—to categorize it and maybe file it away for future use in some yet-to-be-written horror novel. He attempted to sort out the peculiar sensation hanging over him.

It wasn't her exact words. Everyone tells other people to "take care" and "be safe." No, there was something else.

He caught sight of his reflection in the dusty window of the abandoned dealership. He paused and tried to suck in his gut, but his gut wouldn't have it, his light-blue dress shirt still drooping over the cinched belt of his khakis. The glass was too far away for him to see the day-old growth of facial hair, but he knew it was there, that rough-as-sandpaper feeling on his chin and cheeks. He saw his dark hair, long overdue for a trim, blowing in the breeze and making him look like a mad scientist in training.

There had been a time when his appearance had mattered, but not anymore, not really. Except for his recently purchased pair of white tennis shoes, Gavin looked like he'd just been released from the city drunk tank.

He sighed and resumed his trek, and his mind returned to Eunice's warning.

He repeated her words aloud, trying to strip them of their power while simultaneously mocking himself. "'You be careful, Mr. Curtis. Please be careful for me, okay?'"

It took him a third of a book to begin to freak out readers, and she'd done it to him in eleven little words. He did need a smoke. He should just go back to the bookstore. Surely someone there would give him a light.

But, wait. In the distance, there was a red octagon blooming from a tree-trunk-sized metal pole. It read, "Stop & Shop Food Store." He picked up his pace.

Halfway to the store, he passed a rusted-out, mammoth, two-story metal building. The look of the place resembled a large house or lodge. Because of its great size and jumbled patchwork construction of older sheets of metal woven in with newer, shinier scraps, it came off as schizophrenic.

A single red maple tree in the overgrown yard bore a sign painted on a half-sheet of plywood. Gavin read the sign aloud. "Pawn, Antiques, and Things." As he moved closer, he read the inscription added at the bottom in parentheses. "And Small Equipement Repair."

"Misspelled *Equipment*," he told the tree.

At the end of the building was another structure made of the same oxidized siding, but this one looked more like a house. Although it was smaller in size and only a single story, the A-frame metal hut shared the other property's overgrown vegetation.

The house had a short, open deck made of two sheets of plywood laid on cinder blocks. Plopped down in one of two cast-iron chairs was a haggard-looking woman in a jaundice-colored bathrobe. One hand clutched a coffee cup while the other flicked ashes into a coffee can on a small, round table.

A cigarette!

Gavin moved swiftly toward his target. Hand-painted on a plywood sign behind the woman was the proclamation that "Madame Kovács Sees All / Solves All." He recognized the typography from the other sign. He smirked. At least there were no misspellings on this one.

He stepped up briskly as he compared the fiery image of the soothsayer with the creature slumped down in the chair.

He determined that if she was Madame Kovács, the sign must've been painted thirty years ago. Either that or the artist was being generous to avoid being hexed. Her face was as wrinkled as a crumpled paper bag—even her wrinkles had wrinkles. She flicked more ashes into the Folgers can.

He slowed down to avoid startling her. "Uh, Miss Kovács?" As he moved closer, it was clear that the artist had also edited out Madame Kovács' most prominent feature, a harelip.

Very generous indeed.

"Excuse me, miss. Can I get a light?" He waved the pack of cigarettes like a peace flag.

Her pupils rolled around wildly like black marbles. When they finally locked on him, she squinted and grunted. The hand with the cigarette scratched at her dark bird's-nest mound of hair. "What? What are you wanting?" She spoke in what Gavin guessed was a thick Hungarian accent.

Gavin was distracted by the faint sound of music—no bass, just a treble whine like a chorus of mosquitos. He quickly identified the source, a blue handheld radio propped up on the cast-iron table between the chairs. "Wow, I haven't seen one of those things since the seventies. I mean, that even pre-dates the Walkman. Did you get it from next door?"

Kovács dunked her harelip deep into the coffee cup.

If it was coffee.

When the harelip emerged, it glistened. "What you want?" She squinted at him with an even more curious look than Ms. Hodges had given. Then she gasped. "Torri?" She jumped to her feet, uttering rapid-fire shouts in Hungarian.

Gavin looked behind him to see what she had become fixated on, but nothing was there. When he turned back to her, she was trembling.

"Miss, are you—"

She shifted her attention back to him. "You leave . . . not good for no. Something bad, you."

He extended a cigarette and said, "Look, just calm down. I just want a light." He sighed. "Smoke, smoke?" he said as if by speaking in his own broken English, he could somehow meet her halfway. He advanced, stepping onto the sagging wooden deck. The plywood creaked and moaned beneath his weight.

"No! Leave this!" She motioned around as she shouted the order. "Leave now before too late!" With alarming speed, she bolted for the protection of the screen door.

"Well, hell's bells. What's gotten into this crazy old bat?" he said to himself while making a cursory search for her lighter or matches. He found nothing.

Her walnut-colored face glared at him through the mesh of the screen as she nervously stroked the gold links of her necklace. Gavin caught the glint of a green emerald in the shape of a pear.

Partly out of spite and partly out of frustration, he lunged at the door and yelled, "Boo!"

Madame Kovács jumped back, spilling some of the contents from the cup on her matted robe. She spouted some indiscernible phrase, which Gavin suspected was a string of curse words in her native tongue. He laughed as he moved to search the cast-iron-frame table for matches. Nothing.

The music from the transistor radio caught his attention again. He recognized the tune now. It had been at least twenty years since he'd last heard it.

> *. . . I'll have another piece of apple pie, you know it don't seem right*
>
> *I saw him at the sawmill yesterday on Choctaw Ridge*
>
> *And now you tell me Billie Joe's jumped off the Tallahatchie Bridge*

He picked up the radio and stared at it. From behind the screen door, Madame Kovács protested in a frenzy of curse words. Gavin had an idea and moved over to the screen door. He extended the radio, jiggling it at her.

"You want it?" he asked, pointing at it. Now that he was in striking distance, Kovács became quiet. Her glare burned through the mangled mesh of the screen at him.

> *. . . That nice young preacher, Brother Taylor, dropped by today*
>
> *Said he'd be pleased to have dinner on Sunday, oh, by the way*

"Yes? You want? Give me a light and you can have it back."

From behind her rushed a yipping, bug-eyed Chihuahua in full attack mode. Madame Kovács picked up the dog and shoved its barking face at Gavin from the other side of the screen door like a weapon.

This was getting absurd.

. . . He said he saw a girl that looked a lot like you up on Choctaw Ridge

> *And she and Billy Joe was throwing somethin' off the Tallahatchie Bridge*

Gavin sighed, disgusted with the whole affair. He stared at her for a moment, looking for the slightest hint of reconciliation. There was none, and the rat of a dog didn't show any sign of stopping either. Gavin shook his head.

As he moved to return the transistor radio to the table, he lost his footing on an uneven part of the deck. All 263 pounds of him came down like a sack of bricks. He caught himself with his hands, and the radio went silent. Returning to his feet, he saw the fragments of the blue AM receiver on the ground beside him.

Seemingly unaware, Kovács shouted, "You go! Not good to be here!"

Gavin mumbled, "Crazy old witch, I oughta just leave it here for her and her stupid dog."

He emptied the ashes from the Folgers can onto the ground and scooped up the pieces of the device. From his sports jacket, he produced a hundred-dollar bill and shoved it into the dirty can.

Carrying large amounts of cash while on book tours was a habit he'd started years ago. It was originally a way for him to avoid explaining his expenses to Josephine. If there was no credit card receipt for a high bar tab or a visit to a gentlemen's club, then everyone was the happier. Even though they no longer shared bank accounts, he continued the practice. Old habits die hard and all that.

Plus, cash was a great persuader, which allowed Gavin a certain amount of control. After all, no one's face ever lit up when he flashed a credit card, but smiling Ben Franklin knew how to party.

Gavin approached the door, and Madame Kovács shrieked.

"Look, all I wanted was a smoke."

Before Gavin could present the money as restitution, the woman cracked the screen door and the little dog charged out. The rat of a dog nipped at his legs as Gavin carefully moved backward. Then it ran in a frenzied circle around him, apparently interpreting Gavin's attempts to avoid crushing it as a retreat.

With a slow, steady, wide sweep of his foot, Gavin managed to gently push the dog off the deck. The dog landed on its back and yelped as it bounced. Back on its legs, it ducked under the safety of the deck, barking at him from beneath cover.

Gavin was relieved to hear that the dog still had fight in it. He didn't want to injure the little monster, just get it out from under his feet. He could offer money for a radio, but replace a broken Chihuahua? Even he understood people's attachments to their pets.

With the dog out of the way, Gavin returned to the screen door. Madame Kovács retreated in a panic further into the house. He slung his jacket over his shoulder, traded the can to the other hand, and grabbed the aluminum knob of the door. Then he hesitated for a moment, remembering Ms. Hodges's creepy warning to him.

Whoa, wait a minute! What are you doing, Gav? He released his grip on the knob and peered through the mesh of the screen. For all he knew, she was calling 911 . . . or worse, getting a gun or something. Bursting in uninvited could be considered trespassing. She'd be within her rights to defend herself from an intruder.

He immediately envisioned half a dozen headlines in whatever Droverton had for a local paper. No, it would be bigger than that. It would probably end up in the *Enquirer* or *Publisher's Weekly.* "Famous horror author shot dead by local psychic."

He stepped back from the door while warily scanning the entryway for signs of movement. He wondered why he'd attempted to be nice to the old hag in the first place. He could simply leave. But then he imagined retelling the story to Josephine. She'd find out—she always did eventually. She'd find out and then browbeat him for traumatizing an old woman. He didn't need that grief.

Then he remembered the "Small Equipement Repair" next door. "Miss Kovács, I'll be back in a few minutes, okay?" As he negotiated the plywood deck, he mumbled, "So don't turn me into a bat or anything."

A tin bell above the door announced Gavin's entrance into the dilapidated shop. The sharp smell of wicker, old wood, and mothballs filled the cluttered area. An assortment of stacked, mildewed trunks, suitcases, and ramshackle barstools inadvertently formed a makeshift corridor leading to the right half of the room.

Coffee can in hand and his jacket still slung over his arm, Gavin cautiously navigated the path. He took extra care so as not to bump anything that might bring the entire place down on him. His destination was a modern-looking cash register atop a dusty glass counter across the room. Above the register dangled a naked light bulb plugged into a socket. He glanced upward at an orange extension cord from the light that disappeared into the rafters.

"Hello? Is anyone in here?" Gavin asked, approaching the counter. To the right of the register, a figure slightly lowered a fully opened newspaper, exposing his eyes and the top of his nose.

"Oh, sorry," Gavin said with a nervous laugh. "I didn't see you there."

The man grunted a disinterested acknowledgement as the newspaper returned to its original height. Except for his fists holding either side of the paper, the man was completely concealed.

Gavin moved closer, resting the coffee can and his jacket next to each other on the counter. He waited a few seconds for the man to finish whatever article he was reading. When nothing happened, Gavin tapped on the newspaper as if it were a door and he was politely knocking. "Uh . . . excuse me, customer here wanting to make a purchase . . . purchase services."

The paper lowered, revealing an olive-skinned man who Gavin guessed was in his early thirties. The man's facial features were sharp and angular. Gavin caught himself admiring his appearance, the two- or three-day-old razor stubble, the perfectly shaped eyebrows. But Gavin's gaze stopped at the half-opened blue and grey Puma windbreaker, where copious amounts of dark chest hair swirled this way and that on the man's half-exposed abdomen. It was like viewing the overlapping patterns of trees from above a forest. Gavin smirked.

"You really should get yourself some gold chains to finish off the look there," Gavin said.

The man blinked slowly a few times before Gavin added, "You know, numba one gangsta and all that." Gavin mimicked throwing gang signs and squinted his eyes to indicate his street cred.

No response.

"All right," Gavin said, reaching for the coffee can. "Your sign says that you fix things. Can you repair this transistor radio?"

Without acknowledging the can, the man shouted, "Béla!"

Gavin jerked at the volume of the man's voice. "What do you—"

"Béla!" the man hollered again, timed to cut Gavin off. He stared into Gavin's eyes. This time, he stretched the syllables out, adding an inflection at the end. "B-ééééé-l-aaaaa."

The shout made Gavin realize that he had a headache. He closed his eyes for a moment while rubbing his temples. When he reopened them, another man, presumably Béla, was emerging from an opening behind a green flannel blanket tacked to the wall. The man looked at Gavin and then at the Puma jacket man. Béla clutched a clear, half-empty Starbucks cup that contained the darkest coffee Gavin had ever seen. The green straw of the cup found its way to the man's mouth, and Gavin heard a faint clicking sound.

There was a family resemblance between Béla and the Puma jacket man, but there were also significant differences. It was as if all of the leftover raw materials to make the Puma jacket man had been heaped together and left out in the afternoon sun: the ingredients were all there, but the baking directions hadn't been followed. Gavin also recognized a familiar weariness in the man, the kind of tired look that creeps in after turning forty.

Without any prompting, Béla took the coffee can. He produced a pair of spectacles from the breast pocket of his white dress shirt and jiggled the can around, tilting it toward him. A second or so later, he put it down. "Radio. It's parts for radio."

Gavin instantly took note of the Hungarian accent, though the man's English was far better than that of Madame Kovács next door.

"Yes," Gavin said, having a difficult time masking his frustration. "I know that."

The newspaper rose again, concealing the Puma jacket man's face.

"What is all this ash?" Bela asked as he eyed him suspiciously. "Where did you get this radio? I've seen it before, it's familiar."

"It's a long story," Gavin said with evenly measured words. "Can you fix it?"

Béla chuckled as he reached for the plastic Starbucks cup. "Fix? Sure, I can fix." There was the odd clicking sound again as the straw hit the man's lips. That's when Gavin realized that the almost-black liquid sloshing in the bottom half of the cup wasn't coffee at all. Béla spit into the opening of the straw and wiped a strand of tobacco juice from his chin with the back of his hand. "I can fix anything."

Gavin nearly retched, but he couldn't look away from the tiny bubbles of saliva that lined the inside circumference of the cup like a micro-string of spit pearls.

"I should not fix this, though believe me that I can," Béla said, looking over the rim of his glasses at Gavin. "You should buy something better for yourself." He punctuated the sales pitch with another spit.

"Here," he said as he bent to reach for something in the grimy glass case. Béla returned to Gavin's line of sight with a cardboard box the size of a lunch pail. Japanese or Chinese letters covered the package. It had graphics of radio towers and what looked like busy lightning bolts happily shooting from the structures. Béla eagerly removed the lid of the box and pushed it toward Gavin. "See? This is radio and clock. It's much better for you."

Gavin shook his head and carefully maneuvered the Folgers can away from the plastic cup of blackened saliva. "No, I want you to fix *this* one."

A dejected-looking Béla took the can, and, with raised eyebrows, asked, "Why? Why for this and not a new radio? It has clock, you know . . . tick tock, tick tock." He spat again. "I show you." Before Gavin could stop him, Béla plugged the radio into a power strip slung over the edge of the counter.

A cheery voice from the radio announced that they were listening to WHCN The River 105.9. "This is Tommy T, and I want to remind you to keep listening for when we play two bridge- or river-related songs in a row. You could win $1059 if you're the 105th caller when we play 'em."

Gavin found himself in something of a staring match with Béla as the overenthusiastic Tommy T rattled on. "We'll be doing this promotion right up until the 5k Fun Walk next weekend when the Thanatos Bridge restoration project will be complete."

Béla twisted the volume knob to make the DJ's voice louder while offering an obviously forced smile. With upturned palms, Béla nodded eagerly to Gavin as if there was no way he could refuse the radio now. Gavin stared at the device for a few seconds as it proclaimed, "Cindy Nakahara won yesterday by identifying 'Take Me to the River' by the Talking Heads and 'The River' by Bruce Springsteen . . ."

Gavin slyly reached across as if to examine the radio but turned the volume down at the last second, fading out the peppy sound of Tommy T's voice. That explained why he'd heard the Bobbie Gentry song. He noticed the wounded frown on Béla's face, but he pressed on. "How much to fix the blue one?" Gavin asked. "The one you have is very nice, but I need this one. It's portable."

Béla spit into his straw and then dumped the contents of the Folgers can out for closer inspection. He made an exaggerated grimace, showing his reluctance. For a few seconds, he used a stubby pencil to probe the ash-covered components with the visible distaste of a pathologist examining a multiple-gunshot-wound victim.

The silence made Gavin feel awkward, so he broke it. "I'm sorry, it's just that this one is sentimental to me."

"Sen-ti-mental, eh, but it belongs to someone else, no?" Béla asked as he arranged the radio fragments.

"Huh? Yeah, sentimental. How much?"

"Twenty-five dollars?" He looked over his glasses again with raised eyebrows. When Gavin didn't flinch, Béla repeated himself, this time more confidently. "Yes, fifteen minutes, twenty-five dollars."

Gavin grabbed his sports coat from the counter, saying, "Highway robbery. It probably didn't cost that much to begin with. Get it done in five minutes and I'll give you fifty."

Puma Jacket lowered his newspaper and eyed Gavin suspiciously.

Béla nodded in agreement. "You pay sixty and I do batteries for you, new ones."

"No, just the radio," Gavin said, removing the cigarette pack from his jacket pocket. "The batteries should be fine."

"But the sen-ti-mental," Béla protested.

Gavin ignored him and instead asked, "Hey, do either of the two of you have a light?"

Puma Jacket rested the paper on the counter and pointed to a small sign on the wall behind him.

No Smoking

Gavin did a double-take. Beneath the framed sign hung a picture of the two men with their arms around the harelip herself, Madame Kovács.

"It figures," Gavin said to himself. His headache was pounding.

The newspaper returned to its original position, blocking Puma Jacket's face. A voice from behind the paper muttered, "Nasty habit."

Gavin shook his head, deciding that he wasn't about to stand there and watch Béla fill his cup anymore. As he turned to wander about in the shop, Gavin waved his finger in the air, saying, "Five minutes."

Béla acknowledged the command with the wet sound of spit splashing in his plastic cup.

THREE

GAVIN WANDERED DOWN THE CLUTTERED AISLES feeling like he was strolling through Salvador Dali's flea market. With rows of junk stacked high on shelves, the area was set up more like a cluttered library than a pawn shop. It was a claustrophobic space, dense with knickknacks, furniture, and moldy clothing that had been out of style for many decades. He smirked, imagining himself transported into one of those TV hoarding shows, or better yet, the Island of Misfit Toys.

He moved slowly. The light was as dim as a carnival freakshow tent, and he certainly didn't need to bump something and bring all of this junk toppling down on him. Worse was how the uneven shelves of junk barricaded any airflow. The air was dank, and in this corner of the metal box of a building, Gavin felt the July sun roasting the top of the roof far above his head.

He turned the corner of the labyrinth of junk to see a white ceramic cat perched on a shelf at the end of the aisle. Amused, Gavin said to himself, "This must be what the sign meant by 'Antiques and Things.' This must be the 'and Things' part of the exhibit."

The cat was a typical mold-made piece like those found in any pay-to-paint shop in a mall. What made this one so bizarre was that someone had bored a dozen or so holes in it. Translucent marbles of every color plugged the holes. Examining the ceramic's underside revealed a fist-sized hole and a mounted forty-watt bulb with a cord. "Oh, man, it just keeps getting better and better," Gavin said with a snort. "Maybe today wasn't a total waste after all."

He looked around like a man on a mission. "I've got to plug this in. This is the perfect weird, tacky gift for Billy." He imagined the older man opening the gift box and, after the shock, politely smiling and thanking him for such a thoughtful present. The real fun would come later when Beverly would undoubtedly forbid Billy to display the monstrosity anywhere in their home and Gavin would act wounded. Gavin would be able to use the item as proof that the man was totally "whipped." He knew that Josephine would get a real gift on behalf of them both, but he'd rack up a lot of mileage with this little stunt.

"I've gotta see light shining through these marbles." He looked for an outlet to plug it into until he remembered the penlight on the rental car keys. The crescent-moon flashlight was a marketing item from Crescent Car Rentals. Gavin had taunted the rep at the counter until she had admitted that it looked more like a banana than a moon crest.

He wedged the ceramic cat under the arm holding his jacket and took the gaggle of keys from his pants pocket. He did his best to shake his own keys from the rental ones, but the curved "moon" had hooked through the ring. The keys jingled violently until his heavier set dislodged and, with brittle chimes, bounced across the cement floor. Gavin let out an exasperated sigh as he placed the rental keys with the penlight on the shelf next to a shoebox labeled "Classey Neckties."

As he bent to pick up his house keys, there was a rustling on the shelf behind him. He turned as the box of ties hit the floor. The keys were gone.

What the . . .

Gavin tried to peer through the opening left by the dislodged box of ties. He determined that whoever swiped his keys from the other side had been quick enough to block his view by placing a hot-air popcorn popper in the way. A sudden chill ran through him, manifesting in goose bumps. He stole a quick glance upward, but there wasn't any A/C ductwork in the rafters.

He called out to his unseen culprit. "Hey, whoever's there, the joke's on you. I walked here. The car is miles away." He scurried down to the end of the aisle, shouting, "So you'll never find it if that's your plan!"

As he lumbered around the corner of the labyrinth of junk, he was astounded that the pathway was empty.

No one could have run away that quickly, so they had to be hiding in one of the shelf nooks.

He hunched over, spying for crawlspaces in which the thief, or what he hoped was just a prankster, could have made their escape. A brief wave of nausea swept over him, causing him to shudder and break into a cold sweat.

"What was in those breakfast burritos I had this morning? Ugh . . . or what if it's the flu?"

He shifted the cat lamp to his other arm as he wiped his forehead with the back of his hand. If he were sick, Jo would have to cancel the tour for a couple of days. That actually wouldn't be too bad. He could use the rest.

He returned to his pursuit, though it was more of a brisk walk than a trot now. "Hey, whoever's out there, I'm not feeling so good here. Say I give you twenty bucks and you come out." He slowed down even more as another shiver crept up the back of his neck, making his neck hairs bristle. He swallowed hard to keep from vomiting. He was short of breath. He was definitely getting a day off from the tour. Jo wouldn't dare risk him contaminating the "Damien Marksman Faithful" with influenza.

He sensed someone watching him from the shadows, though the person was wise enough to stay safely out of sight. "Look, no harm done," he shouted. "I'm not mad or anything.

I've just got to get out of here, okay? You've had your fun. Come out where I can see you."

He stopped to listen for any trace of footsteps, breathing, giggling—anything. There was only the sound of his own panting. His stomach felt like it was somewhere far away. He tightened his grip on the ceramic cat in frustration.

Gavin closed his eyes to concentrate. There was a smell, a scent different from the mixed stench of mothballs and mold. It was a pleasant smell, the scent of . . . lavender.

The scent must have been from a perfume or body spray. *A woman.*

A strong gust of air brushed the nape of his neck, and the smell of lavender was overwhelming. Gavin opened his eyes and spun around, but he remained the sole occupant of the aisle. "What's going on here?" Gavin yelled. He swiveled back around in hopes of catching a glimpse of someone.

Another blast of air assaulted him, giving him the unnerving feeling of being caught in a vortex. The air that swirled around him was cold, but not like air conditioning or the chill of a freezer. It was as if someone doused him with a bucket of ice water, yet he was completely dry.

The sensation only lasted for a couple of seconds, but it was enough to cause Gavin to lose his footing. The cat slipped from his grip, shattering on the floor with a loud crash. Brightly colored marbles ricocheted in every direction, leaving only shards of the original piece on the ground.

The blood rushed to his face. "What the crap!"

Taking a few steps, he called to his unseen voyeur. "Let's stop this game now. I'll double it. Miss? I'll give you forty bucks. Just bring my keys to me . . . now." The last word soured as it left his lips, but he didn't care.

"Enough of this. I'm Gavin Curtis. Gavin Curtis, the writer! I'm a . . . celebrity!"

His anger smoldered as he resolved to make whoever was doing this to him pay. His steps became purposeful—defiant even—until a blue-tinted marble found its way under his heel. Though the tiny glass orb barely weighed an ounce, it brought all 263 pounds of the man down for the second time in less than an hour.

The impact of his fall shook loose an uneven tower of vinyl records, launching a domino effect of miscellaneous small housewares and junk until the entire aisle toppled behind him. Gavin let out a grunt because of the pain in his back, followed by a few choice expletives as the area cascaded down like a faulty mineshaft of knickknacks and rotten furniture.

He stood, surveying the piles of junk that blocked the way he'd come, and spewed out a venomous rant at the debris. "If there was *any* money in this dump, I'd sue Béla and his brother, or cousin, or whatever that Puma-jacket-wearin' freak of a welcoming committee is, and level this entire place to the ground!" He rubbed at the crick in his neck before adding, "And for good measure, I'll evict that old harelip of a witch, Madame Kovács, next door!" He picked his jacket up from the floor, dusted it off, and slung it back over his forearm as he continued his search. His tirade melted away into a whine. "Jeez, all I wanted was a cigarette!"

He made his way around another aisle. A small beam of light cut through the right side of a taller shelf. The light mockingly peeked through the spaces between the boxes and clutter as if signaling to him to come. "So, hide and seek, huh?" he whispered to himself as he trotted to the source. The light bounced in exaggerated motions from the other side of the wall of junk. "That's right, tease me all you like, but we'll see what happens at the end of all this."

As stealthily as he could manage, he navigated through a row of waist-high piles of clothes that lined both sides of this junk-infested corridor. The dingy fabric spilled out of overstuffed trash bags stacked two high and reeked of mildew.

Where did they get all of this junk?

When he got within a few yards of the light, it went off. At least he was close. He rounded the corner and was shocked to find that the path made a dead end at a cyclone fence. The barrier stretched up into the rafters. A metal sign posted on the gate warned "Keep Out," embellished with a crudely painted skull-and-crossbones in red. More rows of mismatched shelves of junk blocked the view of how far back the caged area went.

He examined a large padlock—opened—and the corresponding chain that had been tossed onto the concrete floor.

The chill and sickly feeling returned briefly with the fragrant reminder of lavender. He fought down feelings of confusion and panic as he peered between the links for any sign of movement. All was still.

She had to be in here.

The gate resisted at first but finally gave way and swung open with a long squeal.

Gavin moved inside, looking for the woman. "If you need a ride or something, I can help out."

He moved along the shelves. These were higher-quality items, though still eccentric in nature—a rack of antique muskets and bayonets; a stack of perfectly folded blue flags, bearing what he guessed to be the state emblem of Connecticut; and enough choir robes to outfit the Mormon Tabernacle Choir.

"This must be where they lock away the 'good stuff,'" Gavin huffed, heading down another alleyway of antiques. Deciding to call upon the old Gavin Curtis charm, he injected his voice with a friendly, melodic quality. "Like I was saying, I can give you a lift somewhere. I don't mind."

He made it to the end of another aisle. A large, rectangular object draped with a thick mover's blanket leaned against the wall at the end. He tugged at it, causing the heavy cloth to fall to the floor. It looked like an old western saloon mirror, and on its side, it was as tall as he was. He studied his reflection in the ornate mirror.

He watched himself as he lied, laying on even more sweetness. "I'll drive you, but I have to have my keys. I have to have my keys first, and then we can go." He had no intention of helping this person. This game had gone on long enough. As agitated as he was becoming, he was also rethinking the forty dollars. What were they going to do about it, anyway, if he didn't reward them?

With one hand, he tried to make himself more presentable, running his fingers through his windblown hair. As he did, the reflection showed a woman approaching from behind him, about ten feet away. He guessed her to be in her mid-twenties by the yellow sundress she wore, but he couldn't be certain since the dim light left her face in shadow. The soft fragrance of lavender filled the area.

A few more seconds—a few more steps—and he'd have her, whoever she was. He smirked at his reflection as he turned around. "Ah, so you wanna take me up on my off—"

He froze mid-sentence—he was completely alone. His mind reeled as if it had been sucker punched. "What's going on here?" Gavin's lip quivered as the question escaped from his mouth. After a second, he mentally snapped back, scanning the area for the woman, but there were only shelves of junk.

The return of nausea accompanied the unsteadiness of his stance. He staggered to lean on the shelf nearest to him, but at the last second, he decided against it for fear of it collapsing. "What are you doing here?" he finally managed to sputter out. "What is this? What are you doing to me?"

As he reluctantly turned to face the mirror, his entire body felt clammy. Most noticeable was the anxious look on his face in the reflection, but the image of the woman was gone.

Something on the opposite side of the row of shelves caught his eye. Nearly ten and a half feet up on a shelf shone a tiny light. "There it is!" he exclaimed, trotting down the row. He no longer cared about the woman or what she was doing to him or even about the radio. He just wanted to get his keys and get out of there as quickly as humanly possible.

Reaching the end of the aisle, he searched for boxes or anything else that could support his weight. Quickly slinging his jacket over a bundle of PVC pipes protruding from a nearby shelf, he dismissed the idea of shaking the keys down—that'd be too risky. He'd knocked over enough stuff for one day.

On the end of a nearby shelf was a stack of pre-war knockoffs of Samsonite luggage. As he grabbed one of the cases to test the loadbearing capabilities of it, he realized he was panting. Thankfully, the case didn't buckle beneath his weight. Any moment now, he'd have the keys and be on his way out.

He anxiously looked around to guard against a sneak attack from the woman. Seconds later, he'd formed a suitcase ziggurat and slid it against the shelf to steady it. Taking a deep breath, Gavin cautiously scaled his luggage construction. The cases were manufactured to be slightly bowed instead of flat. Sweat poured down his brow as he moved carefully to prevent the cases from sliding off one another. His heart raced.

Halfway to his destination, he saw it. Time slowed to a crawl as Gavin gazed upward at the fiery orange hues reflecting off a copper object. It had the circumference and height of a wide-brim pith helmet. At first, he hardly recognized what manner of device it was, but then he remembered photos of turn-of-the-century typewriters. That was before the machines were shaped like rectangular boxes, back when the design trend involved semicircular keyboards sprouting from a base. The QWERTY keyboard layout hadn't even been accepted yet. Though Billy was the expert on that type of antique hardware, Gavin knew this was something special.

He guessed that the flat, round, nickel-sized pads attached to the twenty or so metal tendrils were the keys of the contraption. Even from his vantage point, the overlapping, spoke-like stems weaved in and out, twisting like pipe organ tubes before disappearing into the midsection of the typewriter. A tiny wireframe cage extended three or four inches from the top.

Thrilled with his discovery, he ascended the remaining levels of the precarious luggage staircase. "Now, that's something Billy *will* love," he said aloud.

There was a noise from behind him down the aisle, and Gavin caught a whiff of lavender again. He carefully twisted his head, but the only motion was his reflection in the mirror at the far end of the aisle. He looked like King Kong laboriously scaling the Empire State Building.

The middle suitcase shifted slightly, causing him to flail about for a second. He instinctively grabbed for the edge of the shelf but connected with the outermost typewriter keys instead. The machine responded with four rapid-fire snaps. *Clack-clack-clack-clack!*

Gavin caught his breath and steadied himself. He was intrigued with how the metal keys were unexpectedly warm to the touch. "Well, at least it still types." Gavin cautiously took his final step, bringing him eye-level with the device.

A rush of confusion washed over him as he read the four letters on the page.

OUCH

At the precise moment that he grabbed the sides of the machine, a spring released with a click and thrust the carriage back into the starting position. The crisp ding of the mechanism's internal bell acknowledged the swift reset. A perplexed Gavin was helpless as the shift in weight made him wobble on the stack of suitcases. The world moved as if in slow motion again as he let go of the device. He attempted to gain a handhold on the shelf, but it was too late—he was already falling.

He hit the ground hard, landing flat in a sitting position. Pain exploded up his spine as he let out a wail. With his head cocked back, he saw the machine teetering on the edge of the shelf above him.

Uh oh . . .

He watched in horror as the device broke free from the shelf's edge and came tumbling down to meet him. There was a painful flash of light and then darkness.

Gavin dreamed of a memory from when he was ten years old. The boyhood version of him left the cramped two-bedroom apartment that he and his mother occupied on the south side of the city. They often found it necessary to relocate in an attempt to find her a better-paying job or to avoid creditors that always seemed to hunt them down eventually. Sometimes, the two of them would move two or three times during one school year. The nomadic existence sentenced Gavin to a world of social awkwardness—forced into a perpetual state of flux, doomed to the role of the outcast wherever they landed.

So it was no surprise that when the boys in the apartment complex hollered for him to come and see what they were doing, Gavin eagerly ran to them in the hopes of establishing new friendships. Maybe it'd be different this time.

The two older boys were crouched over something on the sidewalk, studying it with an uncommon intensity for pre-teens. As he approached them, the bigger of the two said with his back still turned to him, "Hey, come here and check this out."

The dream played out exactly as it had in real life. The other boy asked, "You're not squeamish, are ya?"

At that moment, young Gavin noticed a dissected frog on the ground and gulped, saying, "No, I'm fine." He forced himself to take a step closer. If this was what it took to establish a friendship with the boys, he was willing to do it.

"I'm Gavin," he said, bending to the ground. He positioned himself next to the larger boy, who repeatedly doused a cotton ball in a flimsy, disposable plastic cup and then mashed it on the frog's head for a few seconds. Next to the frog was a small, slimy mound of what Gavin suspected to be the creature's entrails. He noticed an odd, pale bubble beside the frog. The small sack, about the size of a nickel, was connected by a sinewy tangle of innards that came from within the jaggedly cut abdomen. The bubble expanded and contracted slightly.

It only took Gavin a second to realize that the frog was still alive. Though the sight was disturbing, he was determined not to look away, not to "wimp out" in front of the older boys.

His mind raced. He barely heard the second boy return his introduction. "I'm Troy. Troy Bridges. And this is my brother, Des. You just moved into the second-story apartment on the corner, right?"

"Uh, yeah," Gavin said, masking his distaste. "Me and my mom, three days ago. Is that chloroform you're putting on it?" The fumes made his eyes water.

"Nah, I wish. Where would we get any of that? You watch too many spy movies." Des spoke in a matter-of-fact manner. "This is bleach and acetone. You get acetone from fingernail polish remover."

Gavin nodded as if this was the obvious chemical alternative, the substitute that he'd have chosen to keep a frog unconscious if he were fresh out of chloroform. He paused before asking, "That mucus-lookin' bubble there—that's his lungs, right?"

"Well, Troy says that he read frogs breathe through their skin, but that sack sure looks like it to me." Gavin was alarmed at the boy casually probing the frog innards with a stubby pocketknife.

"I guess there's only one way to find out," Des said, plunging the blade into the soft membrane of the sack. The bubble deflated.

To Gavin's surprise and disgust, the unconscious frog began to spasm wildly as if attempting to escape. To make it worse, the other two boys laughed, saying, "Look, it's swimming. It's trying to swim away."

Troy added, "I got bad news for you, Kermit. You're not going anywhere like this."

Gavin watched in horror as the swimming motion slowed and then ceased entirely. His own breathing sped up.

"Pretty cool, huh, kid?" Des asked, cleaning the pocket-knife on the grass.

"Let's get another one from the ditch," Troy said with enthusiasm as he sprang to his feet. "Comin', Gavin?"

Tears welled up. He forced himself to say in as calm a voice as possible, "Nah, I'm cool. I wanna stay here with this one . . . you know, to look at its guts and all."

"Suit yourself," Des said. "We'll be back in a few minutes with more. Don't spill that cup. We don't have any more fingernail polish remover."

"Yeah, okay," Gavin replied, transfixed on the lifeless thing before him.

When the brothers were a safe distance away, he ran at full speed back to his apartment. He returned with a shoebox and scooped up the frog's remains by hand into the makeshift coffin. With tears streaming down his face, he carried the box to the drainage opening at the curb. Gavin crammed the box into the opening between the grates before returning to the scene of the crime. He violently stomped the cup, splashing the mixture in every direction. Doing this was certainly going to get him in trouble with the older boys. He might even get a beating, but he didn't care. His mind was filled with the image of the frog struggling to swim to freedom.

A high-pitched sound punctured the bubble of the dream, rhythmically stabbing at Gavin's semi-conscious mind like a tiny dagger. After a few moments, the sound took form. The bursts of noise were the barking of a dog.

Dog . . . what is that dog barking at? Gavin questioned, still unable to open his eyes. Through the fog of his mind, he felt something pushing his left thigh. Was the dog doing that? He didn't even have a dog. No, the barking was farther away.

There was another nudge, more forceful this time.

It felt as if his brain was on fire. He struggled to open his eyes, but the most that he could manage were thin, sleepy slits. Bright, orange splotches on a background of black hovered in the haze before him.

A man's voice commanded, "Get up."

Something heavy was in his lap. He tried to look down at it, but he stopped short due to the blinding pain that throbbed in synch with the barking.

The orange splotches came into focus. They were a print of flowers on a drape or something.

There was another nudge on his left, even harder than the previous ones. The man's voice, more clear now, ordered, "I said to get up!" It came from the side of the pushing.

"Where . . . am I?" Gavin slurred out to the orange flowers. The barking changed from annoying shrieks to a constant rumbling growl. As the image of the flowers sharpened, he strained to open his eyes to a half squint.

It was a dress worn by . . . Madame Kovács? What was she doing here? Wait—was he in a hospital? How could a dog be in a hospital?

"Get out of here." This time, the nudge was a kick. Gavin rolled his head to the left. The Puma jacket man was there, ready to administer another blow. "Stop it! I'm hurt!" Gavin instantly regretted yelling at him when the effort compounded the pressure in his aching head.

"Get up or I'm call the cops," he said with an accent thicker than even Madame Kovács's.

"Cops?" Gavin did his best to comply, but his arms and legs were like lead. He was slumped in a half-reclining position with his shoulders and head propped against the fallen luggage. Instinctively, he shoved the antique typewriter out of his lap and onto the floor to the right of him. The impact of the device rang out with a loud, metal clang. Madame Kovács answered it with a loud gasp.

With his vision more in focus now, Béla came into focus behind her, holding the dog. The man moved forward and handed off the Chihuahua to Kovács, never slackening the death grip on his Starbucks spit cup.

Kovács stroked the dog, placing her harelip atop the animal's tiny skull for a kiss, and then pointed at the device next to Gavin. When she said something in Hungarian, Puma Jacket shook his head in defiance.

Kovács repeated the command with more authority.

Gavin studied the man's reaction. Even through the throbbing of his head, he noticed Béla's thin-pressed lips and bulging eyes. A bead of sweat trickled down the Hungarian man's forehead.

He wasn't angry.

He was afraid.

Béla jumped into the fray and shouted in Hungarian at Puma Jacket. His shouts stoked the fire of Gavin's headache. Béla's yelling went on for what seemed like forever. The man's face reddened from screaming. Puma Jacket settled for shaking his head in refusal.

These people are nuttier than an outhouse cat. Oh, my head.

Finally, Puma Jacket yelled something, and the area went quiet. Even the dog hushed its growling. Everyone standing shifted their eyes to Gavin on the floor.

This can't be good.

Béla spit into his cup and ordered, "Stand up! Stand up now!"

Feeling nervous about being the punchline of an impending joke, Gavin went on the offensive. "I oughta sue every last one of you." He rubbed his head, stopping when he found a tender spot that made him wince. "I'm sure I've got a concussion or something." He pulled his hand back, surprised that it wasn't covered with blood.

"He said for you to be getting up!" Puma Jacket shouted, adjusting his stance as if to show he was prepared to kick again.

"Gimme a minute, will ya?" Gavin grunted as he rose to his feet. He made the mistake of moving his head too quickly, sending his world swimming again. He waited a moment for the throbbing to return to a manageable level before continuing. "How much for the typewriter?"

Even in his dazed state, he caught the three of them trading peculiar looks. Béla stepped forward, pointing at the typewriter on the floor. His eyes were wide. "Pick that up," he said. He paused to spit. "Put it on the shelf there."

"Did you hear me? I want to buy it."

Madame Kovács chimed in, still speaking Hungarian.

This time, Béla offered a translation, ignoring Gavin's request. "Yes, and be careful not to touch keys—dangerous here. No typing. Put it back."

Gavin scoffed as he retrieved his keys from the floor and his jacket hanging on the PVC pipes. "Put it back? I'm going to *buy* it." He produced his wallet from the coat pocket.

Béla nervously spit into the cup. "No! Not possible. Not for sale."

"My dear Béla, everything's for sale." Gavin snapped a single hundred-dollar bill from the wallet as if he were a magician performing his signature trick. "You just tell me how many of these you need for me to take it off your hands." His head still felt awful, but he relished watching Béla squirm, regardless of the reason.

Gavin looked at the old woman in the black dress with orange flowers and wondered how long he'd been unconscious—obviously long enough for her to get dressed. The shining, emerald, pear-shaped necklace she wore matched the dress better than the bathrobe from when he'd first seen her. He wondered why anyone would willingly choose to wear a pear necklace. Maybe it was a Hungarian thing.

She shot him a contemptuous look while placing another wet kiss atop the dog's head.

He took another bill out, less flamboyantly this time. "Two hundred dollars. That's a bargain. I doubt this old clunker even works anymore, but I want it for a friend."

"Two hundred?" Béla scoffed. "Two hundred for stuff you broke, but not that."

Gavin answered in a belligerent tone, "Look, I didn't break anything. Your girlfriend, sister, or wife, or whatever threw all of that stuff down when she stole my keys." Of course, this was a lie, but they didn't know that he was the one who had knocked everything over in the other aisle.

Béla looked genuinely surprised.

Score one for Team Gavin.

Béla spit and asked, "Girlfriend? A woman?"

"Uh, yeah, a girlfriend *would* be a woman." Gavin shifted to Puma Jacket, then back to Béla. "Don't play dumb—the chick in the yellow dress?" His side of the conversation gained traction, though he didn't know why. "Come on. What kind of a rube do you take me for?"

Béla's blubbery face looked puzzled.

Madame Kovács nudged the man. "See? I tell you."

Gavin pressed his theory. "You have her lure people back here so you can mug them, right? Isn't that the game?"

Béla spoke softly. "You saw it?"

"Her. I saw *her.*"

Béla nearly dropped the Starbucks cup from his trembling hand.

These people are nuts.

Béla spun around to Madame Kovács. The two began speaking frantically in overlapping whispers. They reached a consensus of sorts, and he said nervously, "Just put on the shelf, and we'll let you go. Just put it up, but not typing."

"Let me go?" Gavin huffed. "Am I a prisoner here? Have you kidnapped me?" He shoved the bills and his wallet into the coat pocket and quickly snatched his cell phone. "The first rule of taking a hostage is to take their communications from them." His head felt like it would explode from pressure, but he wasn't backing down, not one inch—not from these clowns. He tapped in three numbers, pressed send, and then activated the speakerphone setting. "See, two can play at that little 'I'm calling the cops' game. The difference is, I never bluff."

Right on cue, a voice from the phone said, "911. What is your emergency?"

Béla, almost pleading, said, "You're not understand. There are things you don't know. It's something—"

"You want the cops sniffing around here or not?" Gavin brandished the phone like a crucifix from one of his novels.

"911. What is your emergency?"

Then the knife came out.

"Hang up!" Puma Jacket howled with the blade in his hand. "Hang up now!"

"Whoa, hold on there, Slick," Gavin said, lowering the phone.

"*Baszd meg*! Shut up! Turn off now!"

Gavin focused on the knife. The entire universe shrank to the size of a single switchblade, and that knife was aimed at his neck. His breathing became labored. The blood flowing to his head made his skull feel as if it would explode at any second, but he had to remain calm. The unwelcome image of Eunice Hodge's worried expression flashed in his mind. "Okay . . . I'm doing it, doing it right now."

"This is not joking! Turn it off!"

Gavin's hands shook from the adrenaline surge. His index finger quaked as he pointed at the disconnect key. He demonstratively tapped the screen, holding it up in surrender. "It's off. I hung up. Let's just dial it all down a little. I'm putting it back in my pocket. No more cops, no police. Let's all just be cool here, okay?"

The man with the knife wiped his forehead with his free hand. "Now, do what my brother said. Put the machine back, there." He pointed at a low shelf.

There was no room on that shelf. It was full of multicolored porcelain cats wearing sombreros. Gavin cleared them two by two, arranging the Mexi-cats on the floor beside the fallen luggage. When one of the figurines slipped from his shaking hand and shattered on the floor, Béla screamed, "Don't break them!"

Gavin was grateful that Puma Jacket held a knife instead of a gun. The man would have likely discharged a gun by accident by now.

"I'm sorry! I'm just a little freaked out right now. I'll pay for them."

Gavin methodically moved the Mexi-cats from the shelf one at a time to avoid any more mishaps. His palms were slick with sweat, but he didn't dare stop to wipe them.

Geez, there must be like fifty of these crappy little things. Though they were only the size of salt and pepper shakers, a flash crossed Gavin's mind—if he could throw them hard enough, he could make an escape. *Who am I kidding—what if I missed? I'd never be able to outrun Puma Jacket. Maybe Béla, but not Puma.*

"That's enough," Béla said. "Now put it in there."

Gavin squeezed the final Mexican cat figurine tight in his palm. *I'm Gavin Curtis. I don't deserve this.* But he put that cat down, too.

Béla nervously spit more tobacco juice into his cup. "Just put it away and then you leave."

He bent down to the typewriter. The mechanism was just as strange looking from this angle. The stems fanned out of the top like metal plumage, and four brackets held a paper scroll that disappeared into the base of the machine. Everything on it appeared to be hand crafted, making some areas disproportionate from others, like a kid's science-fair project. It certainly wasn't mass produced.

How Billy would've loved this piece of junk.

"Just put it away so we can get away from here," the Puma jacket man said. "Not safe for us."

Gavin picked it up with both hands, intrigued again by the metal's warmth. *How can it be warm? Is that what freaks them out? Bunch of superstitious bumpkins, what do they think this is?*

Gavin gently placed it on the shelf. He wasn't sure why, but he paused while still holding the antique typewriter. He observed a puzzling phenomenon of feeling exhausted and refreshed at the same time. He stared at the device, and for a few seconds, he forgot about how badly his head pounded, how his heart was racing, and how his shirt was drenched with sweat. He forgot about how a crazy man with a switchblade stood waving it at him just a few feet away. He forgot about the fortuneteller and her dog and her busted radio. He forgot about Béla's spit cup.

Except *forgot* wasn't the correct term. He was aware of all of these things, but he was conscious of them in the way someone reading a magazine or newspaper article would be aware of what was happening in the story. He marveled at the sensation of somehow being disconnected from where and when he was. The sound of rushing wind beat against his ears, but there wasn't so much as a faint breeze against his body.

Béla asked behind him, "What is he doing? Why is he just standing, not letting go?"

The intoxicating smell of lavender enveloped him, except he wasn't smelling it. The scent was more like it had been transformed into a light.

The dark-grey warehouse faded to a scene of a brightly lit room—a kitchen. The entire area was bathed in ruby-red light, as if he were looking at it through a plastic sheet of red filter gel. The image of a young girl in cutoff shorts and a T-shirt appeared in Gavin's mind. His vantage point was over the shoulder of the child as she playfully mashed the keys of the antique typewriter on a kitchen table. He guessed the girl to be about five or six. She giggled with delight each time the antique responded to her touch with percussive strikes.

The image in his mind zoomed in closer. The girl stopped typing and slowly turned. Shaking her head from side to side, she pointed at Gavin.

The hate-filled grimace on her face stunned him. Her mouth formed the word "no" as the scene jolted back into reality. He heard a woman's voice scream a single word: *adulterer*. But it wasn't the voice of Madame Kovács, and he wasn't certain that he'd heard it with his ears at all.

He let go of the device, and his thoughts returned to normal. The dreamy euphoria instantly subsided into the pain, anxiety, and physical sensations of where he was. All of these things rushed at his mind as if he were looking down into a geyser the moment it erupted. His body felt heavy and lethargic again.

What was that?

Madame Kovács stared at him with her black irises as she placed another harelip kiss atop the head of her rat-dog.

Gavin cautiously put his jacket on despite the fact that he was sweating buckets. "Béla, sir . . . if you dislike this typewriter thing so much—"

Kovács sharply cut him off. "It is not for sale! Cannot leave here. Not safe."

"Four hundred dollars! That's my final offer. That works out to be a hundred bucks apiece, three for you and one for the yellow-dress lady."

"No lady! *Szellem*! You go now!" Madame Kovács said through tight lips. She pointed the bug-eyed dog at Gavin and commanded the two men with a single word. "Boys!"

Béla and his brother instantly sprang into action, and before Gavin knew it, the switchblade was at his throat. A shudder of fear ran through his body like he'd never experienced.

All at once, he realized that no one knew where he was. He was keenly aware that these men could do anything to him and no one would know. *Be cool, Gav. Just be cool.*

Before he knew it, the men had positioned themselves behind him and were manhandling him through the maze of junk down a new pathway for him.

"All right," Gavin said as he stumbled from the shoves to his back. "You can keep the lady's hundred. I don't care what you do with it."

They were heading for the emergency exit of the shop. There was no exit signage, but he recognized the panic bar mounted on the metal door. "Look, guys, wait a minute," he said, short of breath. "Let's try this all again." His head pounded with every step. "Please wait a—what's the problem here?"

With a final shove—Gavin guessed it to be from Puma, since Béla still clutched the spit cup—he was sent stumbling toward the door. He barely managed to get his hands up in time to the push bar before slamming into the door full-on.

The metal door sprang open, and Gavin's momentum carried him spinning another twenty to thirty feet. The unexpected brightness and heat of the sun were disorienting. When he finally stopped, he looked back at the brothers laughing just outside the doorway. Puma waved the knife as he shouted, "If you ever to come back here, I'll cut the balls for you!"

Feeling confident that he was at a safe enough distance, Gavin converted his embarrassment and rage into mockery of the man's English. "'Cut the balls,' eh? 'Cut the balls' for me? Yeah, I guess they *could* use a little trim."

"You come back, I cut you! *Baszd meg.*"

"If I were ever to come back to this rat hole, I wouldn't come alone! I'd bring the entire—" Gavin paused to remember where he was. "I'd bring every Connecticut state trooper with me, ya bunch of sick—"

He saw it, but it was too late to move out of the line of fire. The most that he could do was to block with his arm to avoid being hit full in the face. Even so, Béla's Starbucks cup of a spittoon exploded across Gavin's midsection. The warm juice sprayed like a paintball hitting the bull's-eye. His chest was soaked, and his hair was damp, but what did him in was the sweet taste of mint that had found its way into his mouth.

"Béla, you son of a—" But it was already too much, and his stomach emptied a yellow and pinkish paste-like substance that vaguely resembled breakfast burritos and hot sauce from a few hours before.

On hands and knees, Gavin stared with watering eyes at the slop he'd made on the cement a few feet from his nose. The pungent aroma of sick mixed with the smell of sour mint and teased at another heaving.

He heard laughter but couldn't look up. He hated these guys. He concentrated solely on restraining his gag reflex from sending a second wave of puke through his burning esophagus. His head pounded hard enough for him to hear his pulse in his ears.

Hold it together, Gav.

As he worked at steadying his breathing, the triumphant slam of the metal door rang out from across the lot. Gavin tilted his head.

He was by himself.

An aftershock rumbled through sore stomach muscles, beckoning his gag reflex back into action. Closing his eyes tightly, he fought it down.

He suppressed the urge to cry, and the emotion surprised him. "I don't cry," he told himself. The idea was comically foreign to him. He concluded that this emotional treason was his body's release, the aftereffects of the adrenaline surge now that he was out of harm's way.

Crazy Gypsy bastards. Why were they so afraid of that thing? What kind of crazy story did that harelip witch concoct for them to act that way?

Still sweating profusely, Gavin stripped off his jacket and clutched it in his fist while it hung behind him on the pavement. He spat to clear his mouth of vomit and any remaining trace of Béla's juice. He wiped his mouth and returned to his feet.

Why is this happening to me? I'm Gavin Curtis! I just need to get back to the resort, take a shower, change clothes, and hit the bar.

He slid his hand into his pocket, careful to avoid the dark, reeking stains of tobacco juice that had already soaked into the tweed fibers. The cell phone screen displayed: 1 Missed Call—Josephine. "Not now, Jo," he said to himself, activating the phone's GPS feature. When it came online, he clicked an app to summon a local cab and plugged in the address.

A minute later, his phone rang. A peppy female voice from Red Dot Taxi confirmed the request and said that her closest driver would be there in five to ten minutes.

He checked the time and looked for a spot in the shade where he could hole up until the cab arrived.

Across the way, there was a click followed by the squeak of the metal door partially opening. Gavin's heart raced as he scanned the empty lot for cover from Béla and his brother, but they never came out. He eyed the cracked-open door suspiciously for a long moment. Was this a trap? Were they trying to lure him closer so they could really do some damage?

For some reason that he couldn't explain to himself, he took a curious step toward the door. *Nah, think about it, Gav. They had you in hand. If they intended to rough you up, they would've done it inside, in private.*

He took a few bewildered steps closer, ready to flee at the first sight of the men. The faint scent of lavender hung in the air.

The woman . . . did she do this?

He paused for a few seconds, searching for any sign of movement.

Maybe she was waiting just inside the doorway to hit him on the head again to get his wallet. Maybe they really didn't know her after all.

Gavin chided himself for whipping out his wallet so casually during the confrontation. That had been stupid. If the woman was hiding behind a stack of junk, she'd undoubtedly heard—and even possibly seen—him brandishing hundred-dollar bills.

Against his better judgment, he slowly advanced until he was peeking in the doorway. There was no sign of the woman, the men, or Madame Kovács. Gavin's throat burned with stomach acid and bile.

As he crossed the threshold, the all-too-familiar musty smell assaulted his nostrils. It took a moment for his eyes to acclimate to the darkened area inside, and his heart rate climbed again.

If I make it through this day without having a coronary, it'll be a miracle.

He hadn't noticed the sound of his tennis shoes squeaking on the cement floor before, but now it was unbearably loud. He was sure it would give away his location. Gavin stopped and, as quietly as possible, slid them off and cradled them under his arm.

The cement floor of the warehouse was cool through his nylon socks. Each step filled him with dread, but something inside of him wouldn't allow him to turn back, not yet. He moved stealthily, ignoring every rational thought in his brain like a moth drawn to a campfire.

Gavin's spine stiffened at a nearby noise. It sounded close, but perhaps it was deeper back in the warehouse. He wasn't sure. He froze in place and strained to listen. He wasn't able to determine if the sound was real or if his imagination had gotten the better of him. After a few tense seconds of absolute silence, he edged onward, taking even smaller steps than before.

His heart thumped punishingly in his chest as if to remind him that he wasn't well suited to this type of work. Technically, he was trespassing now, though it would have been their word against his. He warily scanned the area for any sign of foul play or his former captors or the woman in the yellow dress. There was still no sign of anyone.

The creative hemisphere of his brain invaded his thoughts, as it was prone to do. As he crept along, caricature-like images of Béla, Puma, and Kovács bombarded his mind. He imagined a grotesque two-headed beast that wielded a massive broadsword. One of the heads was severely misshaped and spewed venomous, armor-melting acid at regular intervals. The other rambled on about castration. The demonic twins were controlled by an equally gruesome abomination: the cave troll queen of the damned, evil in its purest form—a creature who took her orders from a barking dragon's skull that she obediently carried at her breast.

That's not helping right now. That's actually making the situation worse. He bit the inside of his cheek to regain his focus, and the images blinked out of sight.

On the verge of hyperventilating, he paused to regain control over his breathing.

He wasn't sure what had compelled him to come back. He could have walked away—should have walked away—but now Gavin had a new objective. It was mostly payback, but it was also loyalty to his old friend. He had decided to take the antique typewriter for Billy as an act of retribution for what they'd done to him.

Anxious about the time, he checked the display on his phone. To his astonishment, maneuvering through the area hadn't taken very long at all. By his estimate, there were a few minutes before the cab would arrive, but he needed to hurry.

Gavin's heart leapt when he turned down the aisle and the typewriter was waiting on the shelf, although it should have come as no surprise that it was exactly as he had left it. The storeowners wouldn't even touch it.

What a bunch of superstitious, inbred cretins. That annoying little dog probably has a higher IQ than the three of them combined.

Gavin quietly placed his shoes on the cement and wiggled his feet into them. He moved to the antique but froze in place when indistinct voices echoed in the distance. His heart raced, but he kept his cool.

Was it the woman?

No, it sounded like Béla's voice giving orders.

Cleaning up that mess would likely take them a while, and he doubted that Madame Kovács and her little dog would offer any help. She had probably returned to her fortunetelling hut by now. The only one unaccounted for was the woman in the yellow dress.

Gavin looked around, feeling vulnerable to attack, but he saw no one. The fragments of the sombrero-wearing cat crunched beneath his shoes as he reached for the typewriter. It felt good to hold the device again. Though he didn't experience the sense of euphoria as strongly as before, there was an undeniable energy coursing through his body. He was sure that he could run a marathon at that moment if he had to. He attributed the sensation to the release of endorphins. Not getting killed by the Hungarian versions of Tweedle Dee and Tweedle Dum certainly was a boost to the ol' ticker.

Looking at the scroll of paper spilling from the top of the machine, he noticed a new line of type. Below the word "ouch" was the sentence:

I'M COMING THROUGH.

It struck him as the oddest thing he'd encountered all day. The three Hungarians were terrified to even touch the machine. For one of them to type on it must've been a major breakthrough.

Béla probably made Puma do it, but why?

He tucked the device under his arm and headed for the exit. The fear of being caught was gone. He felt invincible. With the typewriter balanced on his hip, he fumbled in his jacket for his wallet. Gavin was many things, but he wasn't a thief.

He wadded up four of the bills and tossed them on the floor. Then, after several brisk steps, he returned and snatched up two of the hundreds, tucking the crumpled bills into his pants pocket.

Gavin effortlessly negotiated each twist and turn through the maze of junk to the exit. He swiftly shut the door, being careful not to slam it. There was no reason to risk alerting anyone to what he had done. The way they had reacted to him barely handling the antique, they'd blow a gasket at having the device out in direct sunlight.

Boogeyman never goes out in the daytime.

He convinced himself that taking it was actually doing them a service. They were free from whatever morbid fixation they had with the machine. Even more than that, he'd deliver it to a nice home where it would be treasured, not locked away in some junk-heap dungeon. Wherever it came from, whatever it was, those lunatics wouldn't need to worry about it anymore. As peculiar as it was, he felt a little like a hero of sorts.

Across the vacant lot was a silver Town Car with a Red Dot logo on the side. He tried his best to move inconspicuously to the cab without sacrificing any speed. After a few seconds, he abandoned acting casual and broke into a trot.

The driver got out of the cab as he approached.

"Are you okay?" she asked, opening the passenger door.

He wasn't sure if she meant because he was running or if she was commenting about the condition of his tobacco-stained clothes.

"Yeah, I'm fine. Uh . . . I need to go to the bathroom really badly."

It was a lie, but it instantly shut down any further questions.

"Take me to the Droverton Convention Center Resort," Gavin said, bracing the antique typewriter on the seat next to him. "There's a big tip in it for you if you get me there quickly enough."

Four

GAVIN SHOWERED LONGER THAN USUAL when he returned to his room. He scrubbed vigorously until even the slightest hint of Béla's mint-flavored tobacco juice was just a bad memory. The luxurious room's trash bin overflowed with the shirt and jacket he'd worn. He knew it was wasteful to throw the clothing away—a good dry cleaner could've treated the stains—but even if every disgusting molecule of Béla's spit had been purged, the items would carry the humiliation and shame of it. His pride alone would forbid him from ever wearing them again. He knew he wouldn't even allow himself to replace them with anything that looked similar, because it would remind him of his defeat.

Though, in some perverse way, he *had* won. The antique typewriter on the plush bed of his hotel suite was like a trophy. For everything that those three had put him through, he'd come out of it with a prize: the perfect gift for William Cavanaugh. No one would be able to outdo this present.

As Gavin dried himself, he looked across the enormous suite at the device perched on an oversized pillow. He recalled dozens of times that Billy had boasted about how he had outbid Tom Hanks at a Sotheby's. They had been neck-and-neck, bidding for a 1904 prototype typewriter designed by François Lambert. Billy had stolen the auction from the actor for a few thousand dollars and had put the artifact on permanent display in his study. To Gavin, that machine had looked like the brake drum of a car in miniature, with button-sized lug nuts positioned around the circle—in other words, a rusted piece of junk. Even so, it made the old man happy, and Gavin's prize was ten times stranger.

Wrapped in a bath towel that threatened to unknot itself at any second, Gavin moved to the device. He tore off the exposed section of the paper roll, the part of the scroll with the sentence "I'M COMING THROUGH" typed below the word "OUCH." He frowned, remembering the tender spot atop his head that he'd been careful to avoid in the shower. What were the odds of accidentally typing "ouch," or any other comprehensible word for that matter?

He tried his best to determine how much of the paper scroll was left in the machine. It wouldn't do well to give it to Billy without a healthy amount of paper. The coarse, dingy, beige roll of stock curved out of sight into a locked undercarriage, making it impossible to tell how much remained. He placed the clunky relic beside the laser printer on the suite's massive oak desk.

Gavin marveled over the layout of the typewriter. He recognized the function of many of the components. The couplers, the platen and knobs, the clapper, the bail arm, and the carriage release were all there, but they were twisted, curved, or fastened in a different area of the device than that of a conventional typewriter. The absence of plastic meant it was constructed a century or more ago. Nearly the entire machine consisted of copper, steel, brass, and even lead in places.

The only exception to this was a cobalt-blue piece of felt affixed to what appeared to be the space bar. It jutted out further from the base than the other keys and had the peculiar shape of a comb. Gavin delicately ran his finger over the felt, careful to avoid putting enough pressure on it to make it strike.

Stranger still were the keys themselves. Far from the conventional QWERTY keyboard system, Gavin counted only twenty keys in all. Every letter was accounted for, but the embossed metal top of the round pads had an odd pairing of *T* above *D, G* above *O, Y* with *H, Q* with *4, Z* with *1*, and so forth. Each character set was displayed in bold uppercase letters. Thinking of how he could send text messages from a modern device that fit in the palm of his hand, he mused, "What a long way we've come."

Gavin cracked his knuckles and said, "Okay, let's test this baby out. Can't have any keys sticking, now, can we?" He dictated as he typed, "'The quick brown fox jumps over the lazy dog.'" On every letter, the device's tiny hammer against the paper made a hard cracking sound. "Wow, this is *really* loud."

He leaned forward in the desk chair to view his handiwork. A smudged parade of crooked, oily, black letters presented themselves across the top of the page:


```
TYE QUI3K BUOWN FGX JUMMS OVEU
TYE LA1Y DOG.
```


He discovered that the felt-covered space bar also served as the register key. When struck normally, it functioned as the spacer, but when struck with slightly more pressure, the machine rewarded the user with a satisfying clink and the bottom character of the pad activated. Gavin scoffed, "The learning curve to work this thing must have been horrendous." He straightened in his chair, preparing for a second attempt. "No wonder this thing never made it to market."

He typed with determination, expecting the loud cracks this time.


```
THE QRICK BROWN FOX 5UMPS OVIR
THE LAZY DOG.
```


"Spellcheck, where are you when I need you?" He surveyed the page. Despite his inability to master the quirkiness of the typewriter, all of the letters appeared boldly on the page. "He's gonna love this. It'll be the best gift at the party. Nothing else will even come close."

Inspired, Gavin reached for his cell phone and dialed Billy's number. As it rang, he continued to play with the typewriter. "'The five boxing wizards jump quickly.'" He viewed the faulty result:

```
DHE FEVE BOXISG WEZARTS JUMM
QUECKLY.
```

Just as the other party picked up, he exclaimed, "Crap!"

A confused-sounding, elderly voice on the other end replied, "Hello?"

"Hey, sorry, Beverly. It's Gavin Curtis."

Relief came into the woman's voice. "Oh, yes. How are you? You're coming next week, right?"

"Yeah, sure. That's kinda why I'm calling. Is the old man around?"

"What's that noise?"

"It's nothing," Gavin said as he typed. "They're doing some construction where I'm at. That sound is a nail gun or something." He pictured Beverly on the other end of the phone, probably wearing her trademark checkered apron. She always wore an apron. In fact, he couldn't recall any event where she hadn't been wearing one.

She also couldn't keep secrets, which was why he had just lied to her. He had learned that the hard way with his proposal to Josephine. It was easier for him to fib than to risk telling her anything.

"You're coming with Josephine, right?" Beverly asked.

"We'll both be there, but we're coming separately," he said absently, continuing to type.

"You know that she's available again, don't you?"

The words hung in the air like a fog. Gavin stopped typing.

"Are you still there, Gavin?"

The question made him snap to. "Uh . . . yeah, yeah, I'm—"

"Did you hear me?" Her voice was downright cheery to deliver the news. "She broke it off with that photographer guy. Oh, what is his name? It was something like—"

"Ray," Gavin volunteered a little too quickly.

"Oh, yes, that's right. You used to call him 'X-ray Ray.'" She sounded giddy with gossip. "I guess he really is 'Ex-Ray' now."

As she giggled at her joke, Gavin pictured the man. Raymond Salazar had elevated his status from paparazzi to coffee-table–book photographer. His crazy idea to superimpose X-ray images of C-list celebrities over their pictures had been a wild hit. It had snowballed into the mainstream until the gag was a listing of Who's Who in Hollywood.

Major stars clamored to pose for Ray's *Celebrities Over-Exposed* book series, which was enjoying its fifth volume. Ray had been transformed from a lowlife outsider to a mega sensation. He was like the doorman of an exclusive club, determining who was desirable and interesting enough to get through the velvet rope.

Gavin's only encounter with him was after the divorce. Josephine had served as publicist for both men and had begged Gavin to attend Ray's first gallery opening. He was appalled that Ray's gimmick would be considered art and had told him so. The photographer had said that he'd considered taking Gavin's picture until he realized that he wouldn't be able to find anything inside him to photograph.

In true Gavin Curtis form, the first victim of his next book was a sleazy peeping-Tom photographer named Raymond Salamander. Months later, he found out that Josephine and Ray were secretly dating at the time of the opening and hated him even more.

"How did you find this out, Bev? How do you know that it's true? I mean, who told you?"

"She did, my dear boy. Josephine said so. You two make such a nice couple."

Gavin's mind flashed back to the bookstore. She had admitted to still loving him on the phone.

"Be nice to her, Gavin. She's one of the good ones."

"Yes. Yes, she is." A lump formed in his throat.

Beverly must have sensed it, because she said, "Let me go get William for you, sweetie. We'll see you next week, okay, love?"

Gavin nodded but couldn't utter a response. It was all too much. To occupy himself while Beverly searched the townhome for her husband, Gavin resumed his typing. As his fingers moved across the keys, he mumbled, "'The crazy expert in woven pajamas quickly stabbed a ghost frog.'" He paused, remembering the dream of Troy and Des that he had in the warehouse. This time, he didn't check his sentence but quickly typed another of his practice phrases: "'Twelve ziggurats quickly jumped a finch box.'"

"Hey, Sport," a grizzled voice said from the receiver. "Is that the music of a Remington 16 that I hear?"

Gavin couldn't resist smiling. "No, not quite. How are you doing, old man?"

"Breathing," Billy answered as if the one word should be an ample sentence. He was a true editor.

"That's good," Gavin chuckled. "Maybe I should try it some time."

"Whatcha working on, kid? Something new for me?"

"Pangram," he answered without a break in his typing.

"What? A pangram?"

"Yeah, you know—a sentence that uses every letter of the alphabet at least once."

"I know what a pangram is. I'm your editor, remember?" The response sounded like a rebuke. "What I don't know is why you're typing a pangram instead of a manuscript for me to read."

"I'm in a rut," Gavin admitted, pulling his hands away from the keyboard. "I'm done with Marksman. I'd just about give anything for a fresh idea."

"A rut? No such thing," Billy chided him. "'When zombies arrive, quickly fax Judge Pat.'"

"Zombies what?"

"Pangram," Billy said with the curtness of a drill sergeant. "'When zombies arrive, quickly fax Judge Pat.'"

Gavin obediently typed the words. He was getting used to activating the lower register and locating the keys, and the result was slightly better than before. He paused a moment and then said, "Here's a new one I came across the other day. 'Joaquin Phoenix was gazed at by MTV for luck.'"

```
JGAQUIS PHGENIX WAN GAIED AT BH
MTV FOR LU3K.
```

"What's a Ja-quin?" Billy sounded like a ref citing a foul. "They have to be actual words, Sport, or it doesn't count."

"Joaquin Phoenix? He's an actor." Gavin waited for Billy to rescind his accusation, but there was only silence. "He's been nominated for several Academy Awards. He played Johnny Cash. He was in *Gladiator*!"

"Never saw it. Sounds stupid, though. Johnny Cash as a gladiator?"

Before Gavin could offer a rebuttal, Billy added, "Ah, hang on a second . . . " A few seconds of silence passed before he said, "'Question: Just what unexpected horrors befall a very crazy Mr. Gavin Curtis?'"

"You just did that in your head? Very funny." He tried to think of a rebuttal using Billy's name, but nothing came.

"I don't hear you typing anything over there, Sport."

The antique device complied beneath his fingertips as Gavin begrudgingly typed the line.

Q: JUST WHAT UNEXPECTED HORRORS
BEFALL A VERY CRAZY MR.GAVIN
CURTIS?

He proofed the line. For the first time, it was error-free.

"Hey, wait," he said. "It doesn't work." He read the line again, this time searching. "Nope, doesn't count," he said with great satisfaction to his editor and mentor. "You left out the *K*. There's no *K* in that sentence."

The phone went silent. Gavin imagined Billy scribbling out the sentence to check him, but he was right. A moment later, the wet sound of a raspberry came through the line followed by good-natured laughter. "Guilty as charged, but at least I didn't make up words. Anyway, how's the tour going? Where are you?"

"It's going as well as can be expected, I guess. I'm in Connecticut for the next day and a half. I think I encountered the entire cast of David Lynch's next movie an hour or so ago."

"Is this to be another episode of the misunderstood artist?" There was a pause followed by an even longer raspberry.

"Why do I put up with you?" Gavin pushed the chair back from the desk.

"Because I tell you the truth no matter how much it stings to hear it. I tell you when your prose is too longwinded or self-indulgent. I tell you when a plot point is meandering or ridiculous. But I also affirm you when you get it right, and you get it right a lot."

Gavin caught himself nodding in agreement. The adulation was short-lived. Billy said, "But about retiring Damien Marksman, you're dead wrong." The older man quickly added the equivalent of a verbal left hook. "You're not doing another one of those *Serpentine* stories, are you? I'd rather clean Beverly's aquarium than read that stuff again."

Gavin was reduced to the role of an ex-con presenting himself to his probation officer. "No, but what does it matter to you anyway?" He stood and paced the length of the suite. "What do you get out of all this anyway? Who cares what I write?"

"What do I get? Beverly gets new furniture, and if there's any dough left over, I buy new toys for my Harley. That's what I get—that and the satisfaction of giving something exciting to your readers."

"Furniture, huh?"

"Well, actually, she's got her sights set on some type of high-tech washer/dryer combo thing, but you know what I mean."

"So, furniture and appliances? You should go on tour instead of me. After all, the big finale lighthouse fight scene in *Beware the Hemoglobin Hemo-Goblin* was all your idea anyway."

"Yeah, nice try, Champ, but you're the superstar. You have to do it. It's a necessary evil."

"'Evil' is the right word for it, all right, but why is it necessary? If someone likes the book, they should just get it. I just find it strange, this whole preoccupation with wanting to meet the guy who made it."

Gavin plopped down on the bed and stared at the ceiling texture. "Let me ask you, do I have to meet the chef that prepares the porterhouse at the steak restaurant? Does it make it taste better somehow? What of the cattleman or whoever raised it? Should I meet them, too? What is this lunacy?"

There was a pause before Billy calmly replied, "Art is different. We allow art to touch us inside our hearts. It touches us in a deeper way than a hunk of meat in the belly. If it's good, it stays with us."

Gavin jerked up to a sitting position. "Art? Hmph! You know what I should've done? What I should've done from the very beginning? I should have hired a surrogate and placed his picture on the back of the book. Then I'd pay him, the actor, to come out once every couple of years to prance around like a prize pony and do all of this traveling as the wonderful Gavin Curtis."

"Yeah, that would've been the way to do it, but you didn't, Sport. And why would you want to inflict being Gavin Curtis on anyone else when you don't even want to do it yourself?"

Gavin moved over to the window and stared at the parking lot far below. An SUV crept through the lot, looking for an empty spot like a shark circling the water for prey. "Is that some more of the hard-edged truth that you say I like so much from you?" Before the older man could answer, Gavin said, "I ought to kill Damien off. I'm done with vampire warlock detectives. I'm written out. I have no more ideas left for him, no worlds or dimensions for him to conquer, no mysteries to solve."

"But he's immortal," Billy offered, as if Gavin needed any reminder.

"Yeah, my mistake." He watched the SUV circle the lot for the third time and found himself morbidly curious about whether or not a fall from his room's height would kill a person or just maim them.

Billy snapped him out of his morbid daydream. He shifted to his wise sage voice. "Alas, it's the cruelest device of all to betray one's self into abandoning who or what they really love."

Gavin scoffed. "What does that mean?"

"Just that it can be a nightmare when your dreams come true."

"Why can't you just say 'Careful what you wish for' like everyone else?"

Billy ignored the question. "There was another popular writer—an author of detective stories, in fact—who tried to kill off his main character, but the fans wouldn't let him."

Gavin was pacing again. "How could fans keep the writer from telling the story that he wanted to?"

"Happens more often than you'd think. You've got to dispel this idea that you're the artist and start to see that you and I are in the entertainment business. People like what you've done with Damien Marksman. They're good stories."

"They're tripe. I want to do something important."

Gavin reached for the typewriter keys but pulled back when Billy stunned him by shouting, "Important? Entertaining *is* important!"

The old man abandoned his scholarly professor voice. "What you—what *we* do is important. We help readers escape their humdrum existence into fantastic worlds where they don't have to worry about their mortgage payment or light bill for a few minutes before going to bed at night."

Uh, oh . . . he's on a roll now.

Gavin was the only child of a single mother. There was no father around to lecture him through adolescence, but over the years, William Cavanaugh had come to fill that role. Today, the chastisement meter was set to "stun." There would be no reprieve now until Billy got it all out or Beverly interrupted him for some "honey-do" that couldn't wait. Gavin would just have to weather the storm.

"My dear boy, do you think that a cabbie wants to drive to his patron's destination if they're not in the cab? Of course not. He's providing a service. Everyone has a job to do—a role to play. The cab driver's job is to deliver people where they want to go. You and I are in the same sort of business. We get to take people places, places in their minds, places maybe they can't go or don't think to go by themselves. It's simple. Don't overthink it, and *don't* screw it up. It's not just about you."

Gavin returned to the chair and looked at the antique on the desk. In an attempt to regain control again over the conversation, he asked, "Who is it?"

The question succeeded in derailing Billy's rant. "Who's what?"

"The writer, the one who wanted to kill his lead character, the detective."

"Doyle," Billy answered flatly. "Sir Arthur Conan Doyle."

"Sherlock Holmes?" Gavin scoffed. "He tried to kill off Sherlock Holmes?"

"He *did* kill him off in a short story entitled 'The Final Problem.' Doyle ends both Holmes and Moriarty by plunging them down Reichenbach Falls. He said that writing the stories was distracting him from more serious literary efforts. Sound familiar?"

"Reichenbach Falls?" Gavin said the letters aloud as he typed.

REEƷHEŞBAƷH FVLLŞ

"Arrgh, crap!" Gavin exclaimed.

"What are you doing over there?" Billy asked.

"Nothing. How do you remember all this stuff, anyway?"

"It's a good read. You should look it up. Anyway, the fans were so outraged, they formed a letter-writing campaign to the editor of *The Strand Magazine* demanding that Doyle bring him back. He did, and it's a good thing, too, because after that, he went on to write *The Hound of the Baskervilles*."

"Well, aren't you a wealth of knowledge, Mr. Cavanaugh, sir?"

"Be as sarcastic as you like, but just know that you should 'be careful what you wish for,' kiddo."

"That's what I love about you. You have the most eloquent way of telling me that I'm completely wrong about stuff. You even managed to work in one of the UK's most beloved novels, *Baskervilles*, while delivering the literary equivalent of an elementary schoolyard wedgie."

Billy chuckled. "What can I say? I'm a good editor, and you know you love it. So if you didn't call for help on a new story, what did you call for? Everything okay?"

Gavin ran his index finger over the warm copper hub of the machine. "I just wanted to tell you that I found the perfect gift."

"Should I be worried?"

"No, it's a *real* gift this time—something really special, better even than the retirement present. I think that it's handmade, so it's obviously one-of-a-kind."

"This is for real, not some gag gift? My grandchildren will be at the party, so no X-rated stuff."

Gavin pictured Billy waving an admonishing finger in his den hundreds of miles away. "No, nothing like that. You'll have to get that type of stuff from Beverly."

"Hardy har har."

"No, it's something you'll really want. It's probably the best gift I've ever given anyone. That's why I called. It's going to be great."

"Hmmm." The skepticism in Billy's voice was without apology. "Well, we'll have to just wait and see, won't we, then? By the way, Beverly is going to make those cake ball things for me. It took an act of Congress to get her to consent, since she wanted to do a big three-level cake, but she's going to do it for me."

Gavin pictured her in the apron again. "You did that so you could eat more. It's harder for her to keep track of how many you eat if they're cake balls."

A long laugh on the edge of turning into a raspy wheeze ensued. "You know me all too well. I'll set some aside for you in case you're running late."

"Running late? I won't be late."

"It's okay, but you're always late."

"Whatever. I'll be there on time, you'll see."

"Bye, Sport. Keep typing. Beverly really wants that new washer/dryer."

"You're awful. Bye, Bill."

Gavin made his way out to the balcony with the two cigarettes and a book of matches that he'd bummed from the cabbie. The warmth of the July sun felt good. The suite was too cold after his scorching shower. He could never regulate the thermostats of hotel rooms. He existed in a perpetual state of annoyance, the pendulum swinging between "stuffy" and "meat locker cold."

He sat in one of the loungers for a few minutes as more cars vied for empty spots in the crowded lot below.

Yeah, a person would definitely die if they fell from this height.

He lit his second and final smoke. *Ah, yes, and what of Ms. Garner?*

Toward the end of the marriage, he had developed a theory that he had a relationship shelf life of only five or so years—the exception being Billy, of course. He figured that after half a decade, the other participant would have heard pretty much every original thought that he'd ever have. After that, they'd be sentenced to endless reruns of witticisms that had grown stale long ago. Like a carton of milk, once it expired, there was no going back. But now he wondered, was it the other way around? Had it been his interest that had diminished?

Like someone sifting pebbles from a bucket of sand, thoughts like these bounced around in his mind for a few minutes.

Finally, he stood, tossing the cigarette butt over the rail. It twisted in a series of acrobatics on the way down until it disappeared from sight.

In the end, Josephine had gotten the house, which was fine by him. It had always been too gauche for his tastes anyway, though he did miss his writing area in the study. She also took a car and various other prizes that her attorney had won for her.

Gavin was awarded the beach house in Santa Monica, his current meager residence, his book library, the new sports car, and the busted motorcycle that he had tinkered with since before they were engaged.

But the main thing that Gavin had gotten from the divorce was the opportunity to get his way again, specifically in the arguments the two were prone to having. He got to be right. He was granted complete control of himself again, and it felt good.

After half a decade of having every decision challenged by her, the final confrontation was over salad dressing. The relationship had ended rather anticlimactically. He had chosen to take a stand over Ranch dressing. He had protested that he didn't want some kind of lite Ranch or yogurt custard imitation, but the real stuff—nice and fattening.

The night that Josephine stormed out of that restaurant, Gavin ate the most delicious salad of his life. That meal came to symbolize the turning point. He'd taken back control and could do what he wanted when he wanted and go where he pleased. That was also the night that he met Monica Garcia. Had it been out of revenge against Jo that he'd slept with the young, unsuspecting woman—an act of defiance to prove that he could do what he wanted? What seemed clear in the moment had become muddled over time. Now, here he was a few years later, in complete control, but in control of what? Had it been worth it?

Should he approach Josephine at Billy's party to say something about her break-up, or would it be better just to leave it alone? He missed being with her. He even missed being annoyed by her. But was he willing to try and reconcile things, to give up being a bachelor, forfeit what he wanted to do for the sake of being with her? Would it be different this time?

He decided this was too much to contemplate fully sober and returned to the room to dress and go to the resort bar.

F ɪ v e

THE DREAM GAVIN HAD THAT NIGHT was unrelenting. He was drowning. He opened his eyes under water as a mouthful of air bubbles escaped. The river water tasted bitter, and he coughed, expelling more bubbles.

This isn't real! he screamed in his mind as he thrust toward the surface. *This is a dream!* Despite the effort, he sank again as if he were being sucked downward. The flickering light through the top of the murky water grew faint as an unseen force pulled him deeper.

I've gotta wake up!

Panic took control of his limbs. As he flailed about, sinking ever downward, his arm snagged something like a vine or rope. He managed to grab onto the slick, rubbery line, twisting the vine around his arm, and stopped himself with a jolt. His heart pounded, and his lungs felt as if they were on the brink of exploding from the lack of oxygen. Gavin saw spots.

Though the undertow no longer pulled at him, the weight of his waterlogged clothing added to the strain of pulling himself up the rope.

After a few agonizing moments, Gavin burst through the water's surface. He gasped uncontrollably as rain pelted him.

When he came to his senses, he saw that the rope, which turned out to be a green extension cord, was tethered to the support beam of a nearby bridge. He pulled himself along the cord toward the steel structure.

The distance between the low bridge and river was a mere three to four feet. If he could grab on to the steel under-girding, it'd be a refuge until the storm passed. Gavin heaved toward the structure with all of his might. A few strenuous moments later, he made it under the bridge. His lungs burned with exhaustion as he tried and failed to grab the support beam.

The extension cord wound tightly around the column, and something that looked like dark seaweed floated atop the water next to it. He carefully rotated himself to the side of the cold concrete pillar. He reached for the stringy object that bobbed about. Fear seized him as he realized that it was a mound of jet-black human hair. Trying to free his hand from entanglement, he pulled back, lifting a young Asian woman's head from the water in the process. He gasped in shock and let the head hit the water with a splash.

The extension cord encircled the young woman's body below the surface, crisscrossing her form. She was strapped to the column with her arms against her sides.

Gavin was petrified with dread. The anxiety of being in close proximity to a dead body was almost more than he could bear. Maybe he could free her and let her float away. Holding tightly to the extension cord with one hand, he grasped her hair with the other. The dead woman's eyes were closed, and large, plastic earrings dangled from her ears an inch or so above the surface. The design was of two turquoise dolphins swimming opposite each other in a circle. He lowered her head and cried.

Gavin tried to move away, only to discover that he had become entangled in the hair again. He splashed frantically to get loose, but he couldn't break free. Out of panic, he let go of the extension cord. Now his only lifeline was the dead girl's perm.

He tried to grab the cord around her neck but instead snagged one of the dolphin earrings. The hoop ripped through the flesh of her lobe. An instant later, he was floating backward away from her under the bridge.

Hard rain struck his face even more fiercely than before as he emerged from under the bridge. A figure looked down from the edge. She wore a yellow dress.

Jo, is that you?

Gavin shook the raindrops from his eyes for a better look. "You're not my Jo," he mumbled in confusion.

The scent of lavender filled his nostrils. The woman held something above her head the size of a small suitcase, something shiny. He couldn't make out the unclear shape.

Then, with a voice that boomed like thunder, she said, "I'm coming through, and you're going to help me." She threw the object, hitting Gavin squarely on the head, and then everything went dark.

Gavin awoke to the sound of his own screaming.

Even after the initial shock of coming out of a sound sleep lifted, he continued to breathe heavily. The details of the dream faded like fog subjected to the heat of a new day.

He took a moment to acclimate to his surroundings. The bedclothes were a damp, tangled mess, and he was drenched in sweat. On the far side of the room, an elongated shard of morning sunlight escaped through the suite's drapes onto the floor.

Gavin's mouth tasted like a burned tire. He grunted, "Coffee," and shambled in his plaid boxers across the plush carpet to the small percolator. Moments later, the single-cup maker was dutifully brewing a small foil packet labeled House Blend as he headed to the bathroom.

Returning to the main area of the suite, he promised himself to never again get as drunk as he'd been the previous night. He didn't even remember how he'd made it back to his room. Cup in hand, Gavin took long, measured sips of the steamy liquid. Not even a river of coffee could wash this headache away. He remembered how Josephine would have a fresh pot of his favorite blend waiting for him each morning. She joked that the aroma warded off the evil fairies that caused writer's block.

If only that were true. Gavin hadn't written anything new in over a year and a half, not since the divorce. The book tour he was on was for a manuscript that he had completed while he was still with Jo. Except for an essay written for *TIME Magazine* comparing vampirism to a distorted version of the Eucharist, he hadn't done anything of note for over nineteen months, fairies or not.

He opened another single-serving packet and set another cup to brew. Across the room, something caught his attention. At first, he thought that one of the white curtains was off the rod and on the floor, but that wasn't it.

Across the suite, a long, beige sheet of paper curled out of the typewriter and onto the floor like a thousand-year-old ribbon. It reminded Gavin of the classic images of St. Nicholas holding a spiraling parchment with the names of every child in the world. He moved cautiously toward it, hoping that he hadn't damaged the device during his bender from the night before.

To his astonishment, the winding scroll was covered in typewriter text. Expecting clumps of nonsensical type on the paper, he was shocked to find coherent sentences. Of course, each paragraph contained random occurrences of words with wrong characters, but that was the fault of the machine's peculiar keypad.

It smelled like the pages of an old book. He held the midsection of the roll of paper to his nose and took in the aroma. Closing his eyes for a few seconds, he imagined himself in a cramped cottage bookstore, holding a first-edition Faulkner or some other classic work. The scent eased a fraction of the pounding that was his head.

With exuberance, he traced the scroll back around to where it started on the floor, back at the beginning. The story began with the abduction of an erotic dancer of Asian descent on her way to work at a men's club. Written from the perspective of the killer, the opening chapters showed his blasé attitude in selecting a victim as if he were choosing a ripe tomato from a fruit vendor's cart.

Gavin's eyes raced across the sheet with unmitigated delight. He remembered the classic Hemmingway quote: "Write drunk; edit sober." Maybe the old codger had been onto something after all.

He continued as the text masterfully described the character forcing the girl under the boardwalk and tying her to a support beam with an extension cord. As the killer applied another layer of duct tape to the victim's mouth, he told her that when the tide came in that night, she wouldn't drown through her mouth, but her nose. He kissed her on the forehead while tearing one of the dolphin-shaped hoop earrings through her left lobe. The killer examined it like a trinket that washed up on the shore of some lonesome beach.

The last thing the perp said to the crying girl was the single word, "Souvenir."

Then the story unfolded with the typical aftermath of the detective genre—an early morning fisherman spotted the body, there were descriptions of the goings-on at a crime scene, and a crotchety old detective worked the manhunt with a newbie partner. Even though these segments were not nearly as intense as the crime, they were still first-rate. The best part of it was the absence of the Damien Marksman character.

As he prepared to remove the paper from the typewriter, something on the page caught his eye, or rather something *not* on the page. The pangrams he'd typed the afternoon before while on the phone with Beverly and Billy were gone, except for one—the one that had left out the letter *K*. He shuddered when he looked at it.

> Q: JUST WHAT UNEXPECTED HORRORS
> BEFALL A VERY CRAZY MR.GAVIN
> CURTIS?

But those words hadn't been the last ones he'd typed before heading off to the bar. Those had been "Reichenbach Falls." Was he losing his mind? Everything he'd typed before and after that sentence was gone, yet the blank space was still there on the page where those words had been. He ran his finger across the coarse paper stock and was slightly relieved to feel indentations in the blank areas on the paper. But why did all of the other phrases fade or disappear and the text about him remain? Even more alarming was the possibility of the story of the murdered Asian dancer dissolving into nothingness. Using the camera feature of his cell phone, he took snapshots of the writing, thirteen pics in all.

Gavin delicately tore the paper roll from the top of the machine and grabbed his pen for markups. He re-read the story as the long scroll trailed behind him on his way to the edge of the bed. The writing was sublime. It was perfect, superb in the classic Gavin Curtis style. It was chock full of what a leading horror critic from long ago had classified as "Curtis's poetic flourishes of gore."

Gavin placed the pen on the bed beside him. He didn't need it. Other than the mistype errors caused by the quirky machine, there was nothing to change. It was a flawless piece. He marveled at the notion that he'd written a first draft that required no revision—and written it stone-drunk, no less. Usually, Billy Cavanaugh only looked at his stories after the third or even sometimes fourth draft, but here was something that Gavin could proudly send to press without any editing.

Giddy with excitement, he made a fist pump in the air. "I'm back! Oh, God, this is gonna be so huge. I'm *so* back." It felt like he was twenty-five again, despite the awful hangover pounding at his head. The aches brought on from the night before would pass, but this thing was his emancipation from the rut he'd been trapped in. The disappearance of the pangrams didn't matter.

He shot a glance at the alarm clock display. It read 10:38 a.m. in dark red characters. Gavin fumbled for pillows to prop himself up for his third self-indulgent reading and clicked the television remote. The Dodgers and the Reds had been tied 1-1 at the end of the fourth inning last night when he was in the bar. At least that was what he last remembered of the game. Cycling through the channels to get the final score, he came across an overly chipper morning show. He decided he could endure them for the sake of the scores. The hosts cackled away for a few minutes about the latest celebrity mishaps and gossip.

Finally, they broke to the scheduled local news segment. There was an aerial shot of half a dozen police cars and emergency response vehicles parked along a fishing pier. The crawl at the bottom of the screen relayed the grim message: "Local resident, Misa Kawaguchi, abducted near Pier 719, bound to support column until drowned. Police Chief Taylor: 'The most inhuman thing that I've ever witnessed.'"

Gavin rose slowly from the bed and stood, remote in hand, feeling his mind turn inside out. His blood ran cold while a distraught-looking man in uniform, who Gavin guessed was the police chief, concluded his final comments about the murder. A high-school yearbook photo of a smiling young girl replaced the image of the man. It must've been the most recent photo the media could get by airtime, the graduation date being from four years before. The text under the picture read, "Victim—Misa Kawaguchi." Gavin gasped, noting the girl's Asian features.

The floor beneath him felt as if it had fallen away. He slumped to the floor with his back against the bed, crumpling part of the paper roll in the process. *What's going on here?*

He chewed his lip as the report continued. The newscaster bore a solemn expression as he encouraged viewers with any information regarding the case to call the station's tip line. Gavin sprang into action, nervously jotting the number down in the margin of his story.

As the program shifted to a brief recap of weather and sports, Gavin stared at the widescreen in frozen silence. The Dodgers had beaten Cincinnati 4-1, but he barely registered it. Internally, there was a firestorm swirling in his mind as he struggled to force the pieces of the murder together.

How could this be? Was this for real?

The channel returned to the annoying clamor of the morning show, prodding Gavin from his trancelike state. He turned the television volume low.

Think, Gav! Think about it. What's happening here? Concentrate. Just work through it like a puzzle.

As crazy as it seemed, there had to be a logical explanation.

He paced even before being aware of doing so. When he passed in front of the full-length mirror, he caught sight of his hair spiraling in all directions.

"Where did the story come from?" he asked, patting his hair down. A few wild strands defiantly stood back up. One thing he knew was that he couldn't take this horrible thing that happened to the girl and market it as fiction—not without altering some of the details, at least.

He looked down at the phone number scribbled on the parchment. Of course he didn't have a Crime Solvers tip. How could he? But maybe he could get some information about the case.

Gavin grabbed his cell phone from the nightstand only to discover that the battery was dead. It'd been a stroke of luck that there'd been enough of a charge to snap pics of the story. He set it to charge and picked up the hotel phone.

Then he lowered the phone to its cradle as if placing a sleeping rattlesnake back in its terrarium.

How could he be so stupid? He wrote detective and spy novels! It'd be child's play to send a trace back to where he was.

He stared at the cord, taut between his twitching fingers. Until he had all the facts, and most importantly, until he was able to prove his own innocence, he couldn't tell the cops what he knew. He couldn't tell anyone.

But what if the police already knew about him? The notion made him feel like he'd been kicked in the chest. It was undeniable that someone out there knew what was happening.

What if the police concluded that he was involved? What then? How could he prove he wasn't? What if someone accused him?

Gavin rushed to the window, half expecting to see squad car lights. There were no patrol cars, only the parking lot and the blocked-off bridge in the distance. "Stupid, stupid, stupid!" he chided himself. Of course there were no police. This thinking was merely the result of an overactive imagination, right?

Be cool, Gav. Be cool. Gotta get control of this before it goes off the tracks.

Frustrated, he repeatedly slammed his palm against the wall next to the curtain. "This is ridiculous. I haven't done anything wrong."

He glanced down at his stinging hand. "It's impossible! I couldn't have done what's on the page."

He turned from the window to face the antique typewriter on the desk. Gavin swallowed hard and approached the device.

But could he have done the things on the page, things that he'd written about?

The news reported that the murder scene was only a couple of miles from the resort. Gavin massaged his temples. This was the mother of all hangovers. Could he have been drunk enough to have been there and not remember it?

Even if he had walked two miles stone-drunk—murder? Why would he kill anyone? It was impossible. He just needed time to sort it all out. Equal measures of confusion and panic flooded in like a tsunami, making it difficult to breathe. He began to hyperventilate. He thought of the suffocating frog from his childhood. If he didn't settle down, he was going to pass out, or worse, have a heart attack.

He stopped at the edge of the desk, transfixed on the machine as if he were waiting for it to move. Had it moved? He was certain that it'd been in the center of the desk when he tore the story from it. Now it was slightly over to the left.

He reached ever so slowly to touch it. Before his fingers made contact with the keys, a knock from the door startled him. Gavin jumped back from the desk as if a cannon had been fired in the room.

Cops!

Without thinking, Gavin rushed to unlatch the sliding door to the balcony opposite the entry. The glass was a quarter of the way open before logic kicked in and he recognized the obvious flaw in going that way. There was no escape, and he couldn't very well hide from the police out there.

More knocking at the door rang out across the vast suite, this time more forceful.

He faced the paper roll with the story opening—*evidence!* The chapters might as well be his confession. He scrambled to wad up the scroll and shove it between the mattress and box spring. A few seconds later, the dreadful click of a key card disengaging the door lock made the hairs on the back of his neck stand up. They were coming in.

The metal swing-bar latch prevented the door from opening all the way.

The unexpected voice of a woman announced, "Housekeeping?" with an inflection that sounded more like a question.

Was it a trick? Were the police behind her, waiting to pounce on him?

"Uh, just a minute," Gavin managed to blurt out. "Uh, I'll be right there."

He bounded for the door and shoved it closed. Looking through the peephole didn't reveal as much as he'd hoped. There was the fisheye distortion of a tired, thirty-something-year-old woman waiting to come in. She tapped on the door. "You want me to come back?"

She leaned forward until an almond-colored eye filled the peephole. "I've got other rooms. I can come back in a half hour."

"No," Gavin answered abruptly through the door. He had to be cool. If the cops were out there beyond his view, he needed to appear normal, and the normal thing would be to let her in to clean. And why not? He hadn't done anything wrong. "Gimme a sec to get my robe on."

"All right." She pulled away from the peephole and adjusted the cleaning bottles on the cart behind her.

He grabbed a plush robe from the bathroom along with a couple of oversized towels. After draping the towels over the typewriter on the desk, he checked the bed to ensure that none of the scroll peeked out from under the mattress.

He tried to calm his breathing. *Be cool, Gav. Be cool.*

With trembling fingers, he unlatched the door. "Sorry for the wait."

The woman pushed the cleaning cart past him without a word.

Gavin peered down the hallway for any trace of an ambush. It was empty for the moment.

Already in the bathroom, the housekeeper began her duties. When she saw Gavin watching her in the mirror, she turned to face him. "Are you feeling okay? You seem a little out of breath. I could radio someone if you need a nurse."

"No, I . . . when you knocked . . . well, I was . . . running in place." He knew this was a weak explanation, but now he had to go with it. "For exercise. You know, jogging in place? Yeah, here in the room."

"You know that we have a gym on the third floor, right? And you can schedule a time with a trainer."

"Yeah, but I like self-led exercises." The lie's credibility was crumbling faster than he could spin it. "I don't like using equipment that people have sweated on." Gavin felt like an idiot, but he had to keep it going. "It's working pretty good for me, in fact—five pounds in two weeks."

It was obvious the woman saw through the lie, as demonstrated by her new interest in cleaning the toilet rather than speaking with Gavin.

He studied her. He wanted to ask if she knew anything. Were there any police in the lobby? Was anything out of the ordinary happening?

Looking over her shoulder at him, she asked, "Do you need to use the commode? Because I can make the bed if—"

"Huh? Oh, no, it's fine. I just wanted to ask you something."

She turned back to the toilet and scrubbed at it more vigorously. "What?"

"I wanted to ask if you'd heard anything."

"About what?"

"The murder."

She stood up and flushed the toilet. "What murder?"

Was she bluffing? Was it a trick to get him to let his guard down before the cops burst in?

"There was a murder—a drowning—a couple of miles from here. A young woman."

The woman peeled the rubber gloves from her hands and tossed them into her plastic bucket. "Nope. I 've been making my rounds." She offered a polite "Excuse me" as she passed by him into the main area of the suite. Pointing at the mound of towels on the desk, she asked, "Do you need me to replace those?"

Gavin quickly skirted by her and placed a hand atop the concealed device. "No, they're fine. They're not wet or anything. I wouldn't put wet towels on wood." As absurd as it was, he felt like his mother had found a stack of Playboys in his dorm room.

"There's not an animal in a cage or something under there, right? One time, a fella tried to keep an injured bird that he—"

Gavin cut her off. "No bird, no animal, nothing like that."

She turned slowly. Without a doubt, she knew he was lying about the exercise. Why should she believe anything else he told her? Even so, he was compelled to keep the machine hidden from her, even though he didn't know why. She was just a maid.

She resumed her work—adjusting the couch cushions, straightening the room—and only paused when emptying the soiled sports coat from the trashcan.

Gavin sat in the desk chair next to the covered typewriter. Maybe she really was only here to clean the room. He studied her reflection in the mirror when it came time to change the bed sheets. Would she discover the story hidden between the mattress and box springs? What would he say? He readied himself to spin around in the chair and run to snatch it from her.

As it turned out, he'd tucked it far enough in that she didn't find it.

The maid twisted a large beach towel into the form of an origami swan and arranged it on the middle of the bed. Monica Garcia had loved those silly towel animals. Steamy afternoons in hotel rooms were commonplace during their two-month fling. Often after lovemaking, she'd gently attempt to deconstruct the terrycloth creation to learn how it was formed, but she was never able to master the art.

What an awful mistake she had been. Their relationship had been as doomed as a towel swan in a tornado, unable to sustain itself under the weight and strain of real life. All that was left of them was the wadded-up, cautionary reminder of something that should have been avoided from the start.

Gavin decided to officially apologize to Josephine at Billy's party. He'd approach her in private, maybe by the pool or on Beverly's patio, and tell her he was sorry for everything he'd put her through. He'd never actually said it before.

The high, shrill sound of the vacuum assaulted Gavin's brain like a million needles. He made his retreat to the balcony, closing the glass door behind him.

Plopping down into one of the cast-iron chairs, he saw a boy doing bike tricks in the parking lot below. Where was the resort security to stop this hooligan? The kid's parents were probably on the golf course or at the spa or something.

Gavin leaned his head back. As he rubbed his eyes to relieve the tension in his head, the unwelcome image of drowned Misa Kawaguchi's yearbook photo crept in.

The biggest question that remained was *why*. Why would anyone do this? Why would anyone do this to *him*? Someone had gone to a lot of trouble to orchestrate this. He knew that he had some crazy fans—some real nut jobs, in fact—but this took it to a whole new level. If it *were* a fan or fans, then why not reenact a Damien Marksman storyline? How would they even have known that he was working on a new story for the first time in months?

No, it was something darker. He was sure of it.

He was being set up.

The idea made his blood boil. Since he obviously wasn't the killer, someone else must have been. And that someone had set him up, or at least they were trying to implicate him.

It was simply dumb luck that he'd seen the news broadcast about the drowning. The killer—or killers—wouldn't know that. This gave him an advantage. He'd have to play it smart, though. No more mistakes like almost calling the cops. He blamed that error on his raging headache. He'd need to act more methodically from this point. His career and his life depended on it.

Who knew he was at the resort? It only took a second to realize that anyone with any skill could narrow down where he was staying in Droverton. There simply weren't a lot of five-star accommodations here. His mind flashed back to the hundred or so faces at the book signing yesterday.

The boy on the bike weaved through the parked cars of the lot below. *Who lets their kid bring a bike to a hotel?*

The whine of the vacuum faded. A few seconds later, the maid tapped on the sliding door. "Is there anything else, sir?"

"Yeah, there's a kid down there on a bike, in the parking lot."

"Sir?"

"He's just riding around and around. It's not safe."

"Did he do something to your car?"

"No, but he's—"

"You just don't like him riding his bike out there, right?"

"Like I said, it's not safe."

She paused. "Okay, I'll report it."

"For his sake."

"Yes, for his sake."

"Of course."

"Is there anything else, sir?"

"No, I'm good."

Gavin returned inside. "Wait . . . who knows I'm in this room?"

She looked puzzled. "Sir?"

"Is there a way for people to find out the guests of the resort, the rooms that they're in?"

"No, sir. That's *very* confidential. Only the front desk would have that, and they don't release that information, but you could leave a message for someone there if you're needing to get in touch with—"

Gavin waved off the reply impatiently. "No, no, nothing like that. *Me,* does anyone know about me, that *I'm* in this room?"

He attempted to manage his bird's nest of crazy hair and forced a smile like one of the pictures on the inside flap of his books. "Do you know who I am?"

The woman looked nervous. "Sir?"

"I said, do you know who I am?"

With a saccharine-sweet smile, she answered, "Sure, I do." The sarcasm was as thick as a two-by-four. "You're the guy who runs in place in his room for exercise and who definitely doesn't have an animal hidden under a stack of towels."

With that, she rolled her cart out of the room.

Gavin unwrapped and ate the mints from his pillow as he peeked into the hall. The end of the maid's Rubbermaid cart disappeared into a room further down the corridor, the door closing behind it. There was still no sign of cops.

Guess I'm in the clear after all, at least for the moment.

Gavin examined the swing-bar door latch while opening and closing the door to determine whether it could be unhooked from the outside. He was baffled.

There were only two possibilities that came to mind: Either the killer came in while he was passed out or asleep, read the opening of the story, and then went out to re-enact the crime verbatim. Or else the killer committed the act and then snuck into his room to type it up.

Both theories had gaping holes in logic. For starters, as loud as it was to type on the machine, how could he have slept through such a racket, no matter how drunk he'd been? That and the fact that someone would've had to mimic his writing style at his best. The notion that someone could write Gavin Curtis better than Gavin Curtis was ridiculous. *Nobody* was as good as he was.

It had to be the alternative, that someone had come in after he had finished writing the opening and used the story as a script.

"Okay, then—motive," he said, rubbing his forehead. "What would be the motive?" What was the endgame for someone framing him for murder? Was it blackmail? Cold, hard, cash? Was someone trying to bag fat cat Gavin Curtis, this generation's greatest author?

He removed the towels covering the typewriter. Clicking on the desk lamp and squinting, Gavin bent to examine the machine. Were there fingerprints that the police could use to implicate the real killer or killers? He'd have to come up with a better explanation before he involved the police. Even he found his current theories too hard to swallow.

Was someone out for revenge? Sure, he'd made plenty of enemies along the way, even a few "frenemies"—colleagues that would like to take his place on the bestseller lists. But would that have warranted this? Taking away his life and using his own writing as a weapon against him? He seethed with anger at the prospect and determined that whatever was happening here, whoever was doing this, he'd prosecute them to the fullest extent of the law.

One thing was certain: he must act quickly. The time to solve this and exonerate himself was ticking away. At any moment, the culprits could spring the trap. He had to hurry, and the first thing to do was to get away from this room.

Gavin dressed quickly in a pair of khaki slacks, a golf shirt, tennis shoes, sunglasses, and a blue LA Dodgers ball cap. Before leaving, he took the wadded-up story from under the mattress and stowed it securely in the room safe.

The elevator ride from the seventh floor was quiet, since Gavin was the sole occupant. The reflective panels showed how awful he looked.

He emerged from the elevator and made his way to the concierge station. A slender, uniformed black man, who looked to be in his thirties, finished giving directions at a dizzying pace to a resort guest, a large woman in a pastel muumuu. The concierge disappeared behind the counter and then popped back up a second later with a handful of trifold brochures. "Here you go, miss, and I just sent a copy of your spa itinerary to the printer in your suite. Just call down here if you need anything else."

Gavin waited, then gave the woman a wide berth as she vacated the area. He moved forward, crossing some invisible boundary that activated the man behind the counter.

"Hello, sir. How may I help you this fine morning?"

Gavin leaned in, lifting his shades to read the man's nametag. "Listen, Thad? Is that your real name, Thad?"

"Yes, sir, it is. Short for Thaddeus." He replied as eagerly as a puppy's wagging tail.

"Your parents must've hated you," Gavin mumbled.

"Sir?"

"Look, in order for us to conduct business here, I'm going to need you to dial the *Good Ship Lollypop* routine down—I mean, like *way, way* down, okay?"

"Understood, sir. A little hair of the dog for you this morning?"

"Yeah, but first I need to understand something about your door locks around here."

Thad looked bewildered with an almost comically pouty expression. "Did somebody lose their door key?"

"No, I didn't, but can anyone get into a room once the swing-bar latch is closed?"

Thad thought for a second. "No, there's not really a way around those. That's why we use them, for the safety and protection of our guests."

"But there has to be a way to jimmy it, like if a kid was too short to reach it and was locked in a room. What would you do then?"

Thad shook his head, crinkling his brow in the sincerest look of concern. "We'd send a maintenance worker to go through the sliding door on the balcony—very dangerous." The concierge thought for a moment more and then added with a knowing smile, "But wait, if the child was too short to unlock it, then how could they latch it in the first place?"

"Okay, never mind," Gavin said in frustration. "I need some help with something. I think someone is trying to . . . to prank me. Thad, I need your help. Do you have records, like cab call records, of me leaving the resort, or if I left the bar with anyone?"

Thad leaned in discreetly. "Is this about a female guest, Mr. Curtis?"

The question took him by surprise. "Why would you say that? Why did you ask if it was a woman? Did you see me with someone?" Gavin removed the sunglasses to get a better look at the man's eyes. "And how do you know who I am?"

"Mr. Curtis, I assure you that the Droverton Resort guards your privacy with the utmost care and discretion."

Gavin noticed that Thad looked away from him as he said this.

Something's up.

"We go to great lengths to help you avoid troublesome encounters with paparazzi and tabloids during your stay." Thad's eyes met Gavin's again as he showed a mouthful of perfect teeth. "And how do I know you? You're my favorite author. I'd recognize you anywhere, despite the ball cap and shades." The man was practically gushing.

Gavin raised a hand in surrender. "Okay, all right, but is there any record of anyone visiting my room or of me going out last night? Or the video cameras in the hallways—can you look at the recordings to see if anyone came into my room? It's important."

Thad playfully clicked away at his console keyboard. "Um . . . yes, uh-huh."

"What is it?"

Thad raised an index finger, and the clicking resumed. Finally, the concierge stopped and confided, "I'll have to get with security about video, but I can establish a timeline for everything else for now. You authorized your tab at HWBG at a quarter 'till ten, then ordered room service from your suite a little after eleven. The tray was picked up on the twelve-thirty sweep."

"What is a HWBG?"

"Sorry—Hungry Waters Bar & Grill." Thad gestured to the bar entrance across the far side of the lobby. "So according to *this*, you were here all night, but like I said, I'll get with the security crew to review the video." A few final punctuated strikes of the keyboard signaled that the search was over.

"But what about after room service? I hate to admit it, but I was pretty zonkered. I need to know if I went anywhere after that." Gavin spoke in shamed tones. "I can't really explain why."

"Oh, but I can vouch for you," Thad said in the peppy voice that Gavin had warned him about using.

"You saw me after eleven?"

"Heard you." Thad smiled with glee. After a pregnant pause, he motioned to one of the other workers. "Theresa, cover my station for a moment while I help this guest."

Thad ushered Gavin behind the counter into a boxy staff break room adorned with federal wage posters and employee-of-the-month memorabilia. When the two were seated in wobbly metal folding chairs, he continued. "Okay, so . . . I'm a little nervous, because of our privacy policy and all." Thad closed his eyes as he took in a breath. His eyes popped open like a jack-in-the-box with a smile to match. "Ms. Garner, your publicist, was worried about you when she couldn't get you on your phone, so Mr. Edwards, the on-duty GM, went by your room. This would've been about eleven-thirty. Though you didn't answer the door, he heard the sound of typing."

Thad's eyes were as wide as saucers. "When I came on at midnight, the staff was busy comping the rooms on your floor because of all the noise." Thad stopped to pantomime typing. "Mr. Edwards made sure that all of the guests knew the noise was Gavin Curtis writing—hopefully another Damien Marksman novel being written . . . here . . . at the Droverton Resort, so exciting!"

Gavin's eyes wandered the small area. It came as no surprise to him that nearly every employee-of-the-month Polaroid on the wall was of the man across from him.

Thad couldn't be less aware that he was losing his audience. "Everyone on the floor got their stay for free as long as they promised to tell everyone they knew that you were here writing."

The statement brought Gavin back. "So I'm part of a publicity stunt?"

"Well, it isn't a stunt. We're just excited to have you here. It's like Fitzgerald writing Gatsby at the Seelbach Hotel in Kentucky. It's an event! It is a novel, right? Please tell me it's another novel."

He ignored the question. "So your privacy policy isn't worth squat."

Thad stopped smiling. Gavin prodded the man's chest with his index finger. "This Edwards guy, I oughta bust his ass. I want to talk to him." Mumbling under his breath, but loud enough to hear, he added, "I should sue the whole lot of you."

"But . . . he's gone. I could get Mr. Templeton if—"

Gavin heaved a sigh. There was no point in fighting about it now. "Screw it. I guess I am Gavin Curtis, after all."

Thad seemed relieved.

"So, Thad, you came up, too, as a part of the big author-stalking party?"

He eased into the answer as if testing the waters. "Well, yeah, Mr. Curtis. I took an early break. Like I said, you're my favorite author." He was back speaking at full speed. "There was a crowd of people in the hallway when I went up, mostly staff, but a few guests standing outside. You were really going at it. Do you always type on a typewriter? You see, I do a bit of writing myself, not anything like you, but—"

Gavin extended his hand again to reel the conversation back in. "You say there was a bunch of people around. Did anyone—anyone at all—come in while I was writing? Any staff or guest?"

"Uh, no, sir. I don't think so. I mean, I'll know from the security tapes, but I don't think so. That would seem—"

"Did anyone hear me speaking? Were there other voices in the room? I need to know. It's *very* important for me to know, Thad. What you say could determine what, if any, action I take against the resort."

For the second time, he stopped smiling. "I promise I'll check, Mr. Curtis, but is everything okay?"

"I can't go into details right now, but something's going on. I don't want anyone in my room for any reason. Understood?" Gavin stood and shook Thad's hand. "I'm counting on you."

The concierge beamed and acknowledged his new assignment with a nod as they left the break room.

Returning to his post, Thad motioned to Theresa to remove herself from the counter. "Post a Code A-4 on room 719."

"No one goes near my room until you find out who has been in there. And I'd like to get a printout of all the activities we discussed with timelines, the video notes, everything. When you get that compiled, just slide it under my door in a sealed envelope, okay?"

Gavin turned to head back to the bank of elevators.

"Okay, but Mr. Curtis, I can just—"

"What is it?" Gavin turned to face the man and didn't attempt to mask his annoyance.

"If you'd prefer, I can just print it to your room. Print it to your printer."

"The one on the desk in my room, you can send it there?"

"Of course. It's all connected. I can send a printout directly to it using the network."

Gavin stopped in his tracks. "*Transmitted*—that's it. Thad, you're wonderful." He removed his shades and sprinted back to Thad at the counter, laughing. "I need a cab as fast as you can get one!"

Six

"CAN'T YOU GO ANY FASTER?" Gavin asked.

"Sorry, sir, but the light is red," the cabbie said in a Pakistani accent.

"Run it. I'll pay for a ticket. Just go."

"Can't do that. There are cameras on the lights up there. And by the time the ticket came through the mail to me, you'd be long gone."

Gavin slammed himself backward into the backseat of the cab. "Have it your way. Just don't expect a tip."

"A tip is not necessary, but I have a perfect driving record, and I do not wish to have a ticket on it."

"Whatever." Gavin sulked for the remainder of the ride. When the cab passed the bus stop where he'd seen Ms. Hodges the day before, he leaned forward. "Okay, now, listen. When we get there, I want you to stay parked outside. No matter what happens, stay there. Keep the meter running if you like, but stay there until I release you to go. You understand?"

The cabbie sounded unimpressed. "Stay there. I understand."

"Even if a bunch of cop cars descend on the place, *you* stay."

That statement got a look over the shoulder at Gavin. "Are you robbing the establishment that I'm driving you to?"

The cab slowed, nearing the curb.

"What? No, you're not my getaway car. Get back on the road."

"Promise to me that my cab won't be used in anything illegal or dangerous."

"It won't, I promise. Just drive, please."

A few minutes later, they arrived at the destination. Gavin psyched himself up and then bolted from the car. "Don't drive away. I'll be right back."

The cabbie nodded indifferently.

Gavin made his way up the sidewalk and burst in the door of the antique shop. The familiar stench of mothballs and mildew accompanied the ringing tin bell above the door. He bounded down the dilapidated corridor of junk, this time unconcerned about knocking over the stacks of antiques. "Béla!" Gavin shouted as he advanced to the counter. "Béla, where are you?"

Puma Jacket—wearing a black tank top this time—was obviously startled to see Gavin. This was good. Gavin would get him to confess before he knew what was going on. He clicked on the recording app on his phone. "I know what you and your brother did. Where is he? Where's Béla? He needs to hear this, too."

Gavin waited for the man to appear from behind the curtain as before.

"He is not here, you *pöcs*. He's at jail!"

Gavin was stunned. Had the police already picked him up as a suspect? He had to regroup. "Uh . . . good . . . then. It's just me and you!"

"Get out of here, little man," Puma Jacket commanded as his hazel eyes burned through Gavin. "You call the 911 for cops to come yesterday, and they take him. They take my brother—his warrants."

"No, wait . . . they came for that? Outstanding warrants?" *If Béla's in jail, that only leaves Puma.*

"What about the dancer, Misa Kawaguchi? Look, I know that you two have some type of transmission device hooked into that typewriter and that you killed that girl to make it look like I did it. But I have an alibi! I have a half a dozen people on my hotel floor that can attest to my whereabouts last night, so your little scheme to blackmail—"

Puma yelled, "*Anyád picsája!*" as he produced a sawed-off shotgun from behind the counter. Gavin stumbled backward at the sight of it.

"Hey, man! Put that down, the cops are due at any—"

Puma pumped the gun as he shouted "*Baszd meg!* No more cops!"

Anticipating the blast from the shotgun, Gavin stumbled backward the length of the store to the doorway.

He ran down the steps to the cab as the cabbie put away the car's CB radio. "See, I'm still here," the driver boasted in a deadpan voice through the open window.

"Shut up and drive!" Gavin yelled, ducking deep in the backseat. "Get us outta here!"

The cab driver was all too eager to drop Gavin at the place where he'd left his rental car parked at the bookstore from the day before.

As he promised, Gavin gave the man no tip. In return, the driver muttered something under his breath about karma as he drove off.

Gavin sat in his rental car and collected himself. Within the last twenty-four hours, he'd gotten wet from a sprinkler system, been knocked unconscious, had a knife pulled on him, been spat on, gotten involved in a murder that he didn't commit, had a shotgun aimed at him, and started smoking again. He decided that he hated Connecticut.

He had to regain control over the situation, and quickly.

After a few minutes, he came up with a plan. He put the car in drive and headed to a pharmacy.

Ten minutes later, he returned to the car with a plastic bag containing a carton of cigarettes, a lighter, a pack of latex gloves, and a box of mint-flavored Nicorette gum.

Upon returning to the resort, he made his way quickly through the lobby in hopes of avoiding people. He was nearly to the elevators when he felt a tap on his shoulder. He turned and saw Thad.

The man ushered him discreetly over to the side of the lobby and whispered, "Sorry, Mr. Curtis, I didn't want to shout out your name and draw attention to you."

"Uh, thanks, I guess. What did you find out?"

"The security officer hasn't met with me about the surveillance tapes yet. Sorry. I stopped you to say that Ms. Garner called the front desk again and they relayed the call to me. I told her that I'd spoken with you a little while ago and that you were doing fine."

Gavin had completely forgotten about checking in with her.

Thad passed a quarter-size sheet of hotel stationery with a note and number. "She wants you to call."

"I got the number," he said as he wadded up the note. "You didn't tell her about anything that we talked about, did you?"

Thad regarded him with confusion.

"How I asked about the door locks or anyone going into my room?"

He sounded relieved. "Oh, none of that, but—"

"What? But what?"

"It might have slipped that I was excited that you were writing a story here at the resort."

"Is that all? Don't sweat it." Gavin pulled a hundred from his pants pocket. "Thad, it is of the utmost importance that no one—I mean *no one*—interrupts me today for any reason." He slipped the bill into the man's lapel pocket. "Don't want to chase away the muse and all."

The concierge responded as if he were taking a solemn oath. "Mr. Curtis, I fully understand. I do a bit of writing myself, and when I get started, I tend—"

Gavin extended the index finger of his free hand and pressed it against Thad's lips. "Shhhhhhh."

Thad shrugged as he pulled back from the finger with embarrassment. "Uh . . . Yes, sir."

As Gavin moved to the open elevator and pressed the button for the seventh floor, he called out, "Maybe I'll name a character after you if you don't mess this up!"

The elevator slid closed with Thad beaming like an expectant father.

The room was noticeably colder than it had been when Gavin left a couple of hours before. Tossing the keycard and plastic bag onto the dresser, he made his way to the thermostat. The temperature displayed an even seventy-eight degrees, but it was much cooler than that. He aggressively mashed the arrow key until the digital readout stopped at eighty-five. Next, he slid open the balcony door at the end of the suite to allow the warmth of the July sun into the room.

The kid on the bike was back at it again. Gavin didn't know why, but this teenager doing stunts in the parking lot annoyed him to no end. Gavin contemplated filling the latex gloves with water and tossing them like water balloons at the little punk. He only needed one pair, and the package contained an even twenty-four. On any other day, it would have been an amusing way to spend the afternoon, but right now, there were more pressing matters.

Focus, Gav, focus.

He tore open the package and snapped a glove onto his left hand. Obviously, his fingerprints already covered the outside and keyboard, but he was taking precautions for what he hoped to find inside. If Béla or his jackass brother had installed a transmitter in the typewriter, their prints would be all over the device. He'd simply pluck out the radio or whatever it was, present it to the police, and be in the clear.

The only problem he foresaw with the plan was that the antique would be impounded as evidence, leaving him without a gift for Billy's party. There was no way around this. It had to be done in order to implicate Puma Jacket.

He sighed as he wiggled his fingers into the second translucent glove.

Gavin approached the desk, and his heart skipped a beat as he saw the sentence typed at the top of the page.

DON'T LEAVE THE HOTEL AGAIN.

He turned and slowly looked around the room. After checking under the bed, in the closet, and in the bathroom, Gavin finally returned to the desk.

Was this some elaborate prank? He scanned the area for concealed miniature cameras. The only thing that he couldn't resolve about it being a hidden-camera show was that no one knew he'd taken the typewriter. He wasn't even certain that Béla and his brother knew, when he thought of it.

But they had to know.

His heart beat wildly as he typed.

WHO ARE YOU?

The machine was ice cold to the touch. He retyped the question, this time without mistakes.

WHO ARE YOU?

Gavin stared at the letters, awaiting a response. After a minute or so, he strained to listen. He put his ear near the device, expecting to hear a modem, a hum, or something—anything. All he heard was the sounds of kids cheering on the stupid bicycle boy from the lot below.

Gavin proceeded with his original plan: locate the transmission device, remove it, and take it to the cops. He tilted the machine on one side and then the other, searching for a way to gain access to its inner workings. It felt like a block of dry ice through the latex. How could it be that cold?

With every seam heavily welded, there was no way for him to peek inside. His million-dollar imagination placed him in a dimly lit bunker at the height of the Cold War. Pictured there were Russian spies—make that Hungarian spies—transmitting top-secret launch codes and the like from this heap of metal.

He lifted the machine above his head for the light of the desk lamp to shine inside the circular opening of the paper feed. He shook it several times in hopes of dislodging a piece of it. The keys swayed as they made jangling noises, but they revealed nothing.

Gavin remembered the banana-shaped flashlight on the rental-car key ring and wished that he'd detached it instead of giving it to the valet. He had to get a better look inside.

The midday sunlight beckoned to him from the balcony. At least it would be warmer out there and have better light.

Grabbing the device and clumsily sliding the door open, he made his way to the cast-iron furniture. He placed the typewriter on the small table with care. Even in the natural light of day, the machine gave up no secrets.

Gavin was perplexed. There had to be a way to change out the roll of paper if nothing else. He cautiously tilted it onto its back, looking for a latch.

He wished the bike kid would shut up. There was a congregation of delinquents below now. "What a little punk." He tried to ignore the distraction, but it was too much. The teenage crowd was chanting something—probably the boy's name—and Gavin needed to concentrate. He had to figure this thing out before the blackmailer or blackmailers lowered the boom on him.

Where were all of these kids' parents?

"Concentrate," he ordered himself, returning the type-writer to its level position.

Somehow, the bicycle boy was doing figure eights while standing on the hub of the front wheel. The stunt was impressive enough for Gavin to stop and watch for a few seconds. More hoots and hollers came from below.

Gavin returned his attention to the typewriter. The whip-crack strike of the keys filled his ears as he typed a pangram.

```
TWELVE ZIGGURATS QUIC6LY JUMPED A
FINCH BOX.
```

He retyped the line, this time making sure to activate the shift register in the proper places.

```
TWELVE ZIGGURATS QUICKLY JUMPED A
FINCH BOX.
```

Upon completing the line, he pressed his ear to the device, hoping to hear something. He remembered the static and electronic gurgles of his first fax machine from years ago. There was nothing like that here, just silence except for the stupid bicycle kid and the ruckus from the kids down below.

"Shut up!" Gavin yelled, but the command either went unheard or was ignored by the teenage mob.

He pressed his ear to the cold metal of the machine—still nothing. He typed.

```
THE CRAZY EXPERT IN WOVEN PAJAMAS
QUICKLY STABBED A GHOST FROG.
```

He tried to listen, but the little stunt show in the parking lot grew louder. "Shut up, you stupid punks!" Exasperated, he snapped off the gloves and tossed them on the ground.

He thought he heard something within the machine, but he wasn't certain. Gavin lifted the device and held it to his other ear.

More applause, with added whistles.

"Argh!" He furiously pounded at the keys.

```
THE BIKE KID SHUT UP! SHUT UP!
SHUT UP!
```

This time, the carriage return snapped back as quickly as a bear trap, ringing an unseen metal bell from within the antique. Out of reflex, he pulled back from the abrupt retort of the mechanism. The smell of lavender returned. "Warm," Gavin mumbled. "The keys are warm."

Bewildered, he reached for it. He stopped short when he heard a scream.

The high-pitched shriek of a young girl's voice from the ground level pierced his psyche. Gavin jumped up and made his way to the rail of the balcony. Other voices joined the screams below. There was a figure on the ground. The entire crowd of teenagers shouted at once in a cacophony of sound, the music of panic.

The bicycle boy must've hit one of the other kids—no, wait. It *was* the kid on the bike. He was the one sprawled out on the ground. Had a car hit him? No, the cars were perfectly aligned in their spots. Was it a stunt gone bad?

"Hey!" Gavin shouted. "Up here!" It took a moment for a girl in the crowd to determine where the voice came from. She blocked the sunlight with her forearm as she looked up at the seventh-story balcony.

"What happened to him?" Gavin yelled.

She cupped her hands and shouted back, "Glen had a seizure! Call 911, mister!"

Gavin rushed in and dialed 911. He got a woman at the front desk instead, who took forever explaining how the phone system routed emergency calls to them. She told him that she was alerting the EMS team and would also dispatch the resort's on-site nurse to the scene.

Gavin rushed back outside. There were already a couple of adults hunched over the boy. The shiny BMX bike lay on the pavement outside of the huddle of people working to revive the kid.

Anxiously tearing open the carton of cigarettes from the drug store, he unwrapped a pack and shoved a cigarette into his mouth. He paced the length of the L-shaped balcony for a better look, but he had a poor vantage point. He contemplated going down to the lot, but what could he do there? He dismissed the idea moments later when the flashing strobes of the ambulance appeared. The vehicle's siren added to the symphony of chaos already in progress.

He sat back in the deck chair, watching the show through the balcony's metal guardrail.

He hadn't noticed it before, but the two lines that he'd typed were different in color from the greasy, black characters he was accustomed to from the machine. They were just as oily, but the letters had a dark burgundy tint to them. He inspected them, running his thumb over the words, "$HUT UP."

"Owww!" Gavin quickly yanked his hand away as if he'd accidentally touched a live burner on a stove. "Son of a—"

Out of reflex, he stuck his thumb between his teeth and sucked on it. Then he pulled it out and examined the small, red mark on it.

He stared at the typed lines of text. The color of the sentences grew darker, transforming to the blackened characters he was familiar with.

"That's impossible," he said. "And how could it burn me?" Even more outlandish was how the kid had fallen from the bike at the exact moment that Gavin had typed the line.

Had he made that happen, or was it a coincidence?

It had to be a coincidence, but somehow, deep inside, he knew it wasn't. He'd unintentionally caused this.

Gavin warily stepped away from the machine. Retreating into the coolness of the hotel room, he slid the door shut and studied the device through the glass.

Unlike whatever had happened to Misa Kawaguchi, the female dancer, Gavin had seen this unfold before his own eyes. There was no involvement of Béla or his stupid gangster brother on this one. It was just him, the boy, and the typewriter. As crazy as it was, he had to face the fact that the kid had been fine until he'd typed the line of text.

He lit another cigarette and locked the latch on the sliding door.

There was no reasonable explanation for any of this. It was impossible. Nevertheless, the evidence was below him on the asphalt.

Was this what the Hungarian trio had feared? He tried to remember waking up in that dank warehouse—the way they had acted when he had thrust it at them. What had they said? They weren't afraid of him. They were afraid of *it*. Why, then, had they typed the phrase "I'm coming through" on it? *Who* was coming through?

He'd never given much credence to Ouija boards, tea leaves, and the like, but something was happening here.

Was the device like sticking pins in some voodoo doll? What would happen to Puma Jacket if Gavin typed in, "The thug stabbed himself"? Could it reach that far? He fantasized about watching a news story about a Hungarian man fatally slipping and falling on his own switchblade.

Gavin knew he'd never do such a thing, even though he hated that jerk. He was no killer. He could imagine a thousand and one deaths for him, but to actually do it or cause it to happen was way out of bounds.

Then he remembered Kawaguchi on the television. That had been real. There was a sickening logic to everything now. Suppose that he'd typed the first chapters of the detective story while he was drunk, and the machine, as preposterous as the idea was, had made his words into reality. It was irrational, and yet it eerily made sense at the same time.

He considered an alternative explanation as a pit formed in his stomach.

Am I going crazy?

He didn't feel like he was insane, but did any madman ever know that they were crazy? Wasn't that a part of the sickness, thinking that you were fine? Wasn't it like a dreamer in a dream believing they were awake? How does one verify reality within a dream? How do you check to see if it's real?

As the ambulance doors slammed shut and the vehicle sped off with its teenage occupant, something stirred within Gavin. He needed to do something, but what?

For the first time in longer than he could remember, Gavin didn't know what to do. By his very nature, he was a person of action. Being frozen by indecision wasn't who he was, but he only stared out the sliding door, dumfounded. It was as if he were an actor who'd forgotten his lines and the entire play had skidded to a halt.

Should he follow the ambulance to the hospital? No, it was too late for that, but he could certainly find out where they'd taken the boy. He could check on him, but how would he explain being there to the boy's parents? "Hello, I made your boy go into a seizure with a magical typewriter that I stole from some gypsies." That sounded even more ludicrous than it was.

Gavin tore open the pack of Nicorette gum on the dresser and shoved two pieces into his mouth.

"I could just tell them that I saw the boy fall and that I was concerned about him," Gavin said to himself. It was true, after all. He'd just leave out the crazy parts. Nobody needed to know those bits.

Still feverously chewing the gum, Gavin lit another cigarette. The crowd on the ground level began to disperse. It felt good to have a plan. He could sort all this out later.

As the last spectator moved out of Gavin's view, he formed an even better idea. He'd visit the kid, and while he was there, he'd toss the antique typewriter in a hospital dumpster and be done with it. Let it end up wherever they store medical waste. It didn't matter to him. He'd be in the clear. Supernatural or just two remarkable coincidences—either way, it would all be over.

Gavin unlatched the sliding door and approached the machine. He stopped as he reread the command at the top of the page.

DON'T LEAVE THE HOTEL AGAIN.

He nearly swallowed the wad of gum. No, he was confined to the resort at least until he learned how to work this thing, whatever it was.

After a minute or so, he had an epiphany, which he whispered to himself. "If negative statements result in bad things happening, then what if I type something good?"

He inched forward, deciding he would write a line—maybe even an entire paragraph—about the boy getting better. He rationalized how a butcher knife, wielded as a gruesome instrument against a victim, could also be used to trim pork chops. "It's all in how you use it," he mumbled, trying to convince himself.

Gavin flicked the half-finished cigarette to the side and psyched himself up to touch the keypad. Would it burn or shock him? He was willing to endure a little pain for the sake of the kid.

He cracked his knuckles. He'd need to pay attention to the shift regulator to type correctly on the first attempt. This was especially important because if it did zap him again, he didn't want to tough it out any longer than necessary.

Gavin's hands hovered inches above the keys.

He felt clammy, and his heart pounded as if he were on the verge of a heart attack. What if he made it worse? What if merely typing something more about the boy moved him into greater jeopardy?

Stupid kid. Why was he riding around in the parking lot, anyway?

He wiped his sweaty palms on his pants and then returned them to the ready position above the keys. It was up to Gavin to work this out. He must set it right to fix what he'd broken in the bratty teenager.

It felt like a game of chicken with a semi truck with him in a Subaru. He couldn't afford to type the wrong thing, but something had to be done. At the last second, he impulsively decided to perform an experiment. Eighteen rapid strikes later, his test phrase displayed in eerie burgundy letters.

THE WOMAN LAUGHED.

Gavin read the line aloud. While the keys had been warm against his fingertips, he hadn't been burned. He resisted the urge to touch the text this time as the characters darkened on the page, noting that the change happened much faster than before. He also noticed the absence of the lavender smell that he'd expected.

He'd typed the most innocuous phrase he could think of. It was completely safe and had no connection to the bike boy.

Gavin waited, pausing to listen for screams or sounds of chaos. As expected, everything was otherwise peaceful. There was no activity from the lot below. He sighed in relief, though his heart thumped wildly. Now he only needed to type something to help his accidental victim.

His hands hovered above the keys as before. It took a minute for him to will himself to touch it again.

As he reached to type, a noise from within the suite startled him. Gavin jumped back from the machine and folded his arms. The jolt of adrenaline forced a gasp from him. The front door of the suite was still closed.

What was that?

After surveying the area, he realized that the mechanical click and brief churning sound was the suite's laser printer starting up.

"Argh, crap! Nearly had a heart attack." He moved to the desk.

Seconds later, the printer delivered two sheets to the document tray. Gavin snatched them up and scanned them for any new information that the concierge might have discovered. There wasn't any. It read just as Thad had told him: his bill for HWBG—Hungry Waters Bar and Grill—applied to his room at 9:47, a room service delivery at 11:19, meal containers picked up at 12:43, and a footnote about a disturbance on the seventh floor around 11:24, which he assumed to be about his typing.

There was a friendly note at the bottom.

> *It's an honor to have you writing here in the Drover-*
> *ton Resort. I'm looking forward to reading your new*
> *book.—T. Williams*

It was easy to guess that the *T* was for Thad. He crumpled it up.

"Thaddeus. Who names their kid Thaddeus? That's even worse than Theodore."

After Gavin reread the printout, he tore the sheets into thin strips and tossed them in the trash with the wad of stale gum. He didn't need Thad to help him investigate. The answer was clear to him now. Gavin was certain that no one had visited his room while he was unconscious. It had been him, though he didn't understand how his typing had killed the girl.

His stomach knotted up. A wave of nausea overtook him, forcing him into the bathroom. Then the moment passed, and he knew what he had to do next. It was the only thing to do.

With tears streaming down his face, he moved to the suite's safe. He entered the code that he'd designated, the same code he used for everything—his and Josephine's wedding anniversary. A few electronic chirps later, a metal click allowed him to slide the panel open. Gavin delicately withdrew the opening chapters. The long scroll of paper quivered in his twitching fingers.

Why? Why is this happening to me?

He bit his lip as he crumpled the paper and shoved it into a metal ice bucket. It overflowed the container, looking like the leaves of an exotic plant spilling over the sides of a flowerpot. Wiping away more tears, he grabbed his new lighter.

Gavin had the presence of mind not to burn it in the room and set off the sprinkler system. No, he'd had enough fire alarms and sprinklers from the day before at the bookstore.

He should have stayed there and waited. He should have never taken the device from the Hungarians. All of this would have been avoided.

He would end it now and destroy the infernal device once and for all. He'd erase every trace of it, including this.

Gavin placed the metal container on the far end of the balcony, away from the antique, and lit the protruding ends of the paper on fire.

"Are you happy now?" he screamed at the device. "Huh? Are you? Are you happy now?"

A woman pushing a stroller in the lot below sped up, no doubt thinking he was addressing her.

"Pffft. Hell's bells. This whole place is going to think I'm going nuts."

Watching the flames in the ice bucket, he said, "Who knows? Maybe I am."

Flakes of black ash lighter than air floated about the container, making playful somersaults before falling back into the fire. The bitter smell filled his nostrils, and fumes stung his eyes, but he didn't blink. Gavin stared at the ruin of his first substantial writing since his divorce. His return to greatness had been short lived. While he watched, he deleted the snapshots of the story on his phone.

When the flame finished devouring the sheet, he looked over to the machine with hatefulness beyond anything he'd ever experienced. Something primal awoke within him. If not for resort guests routinely exiting from below his balcony, he'd have thrown it over the edge and broken it into a million pieces. But he couldn't take the chance of hitting someone and bringing a nice manslaughter charge against him.

Moving at a snail's pace, he approached it.

The length of paper flowing from the top waved like a sail in a breeze, the lines about the boy on the bike and the woman laughing swaying in the wind.

Gavin had an idea—an admittedly bad idea, but something he had to try.

He leaned in to light the top of the paper scroll with his lighter. The device began typing.

```
YOU DON'T KNOW ME YET, BUT YOU
WILL.


I'M COMING THROUGH.
```

His rational mind kicked in. This was impossible. After a few more unsuccessful attempts to catch fire to the paper, he decided on a different approach. Tucking the lighter in his shirt pocket, he reached for the sheet, ripped it free in a fury, and leapt backward.

With his back pressed along the outer wall, he folded the jagged sheet into quarters and threw the paper into the metal bucket. Expecting the ashen stench of burning paper, he was surprised by the sweet smell of lavender.

A gust of wind knocked him to his knees. But, to his astonishment, the gale didn't extinguish the fire. The contents of the bucket smoldered as before.

All went quiet on the balcony.

Bird sounds in the distance carried on the breeze as if it were a normal July afternoon. He wiped his brow and let out a sigh as tiny embers flickered in the bucket.

The embers crackled and began to form an unnatural flame. Gavin felt cold as his eyes were transfixed on the image before him. Within the small, flickering flame, he saw the image of the little girl, the same vision of the child at the kitchen table playfully tapping on the antique typewriter. His eyes watered, but he was helpless to close them as the image of the girl transformed into a woman of twenty or so.

A jolt of fear shot through him. He knew this image. This was the woman in yellow from his dream. The image grew, first to the size of a doll, then double.

A paralyzing fear gripped his heart. The realization that something otherworldly was happening to him was almost more than Gavin could handle. The apparent alternative was equally as grave—if this weren't actually happening, then he was losing his mind.

As the image in the fire grew to nearly full size, Gavin shuffled past the table with the typewriter. He slammed the sliding door, nearly shattering it, and locked it. The woman of the fire was gone—for the moment.

His cell phone clamored for his attention, rattling impatiently on the nightstand. He unplugged it from the charger and returned to his post at the door. Still nothing.

"Hello?" Gavin whispered, his eyes shifting from the typewriter to the nearly extinguished fire and then back to the device.

"Hey, I've been trying to get ahold of you," Josephine said. "Why haven't you been answering my calls?"

"Jo, I'll have to call you back."

"But, Gavin, I need to—"

"I'm in the middle of something here. I gotta go."

"Why do you sound out of breath? Everything okay there?"

"No, I mean . . . I don't know. Look, give me five minutes. I'll call you back in five minutes, okay?"

"But Gavin, you—"

He hung up, lit another cigarette, and waited.

Seven

FOR SEVERAL MINUTES, HE PEEKED FROM BEHIND THE DRAPES at the machine's last message:

```
YOU DON'T KNOW ME YET, BUT YOU
WILL.


I'M COMING THROUGH.
```

He chided himself for not burning that, too, but what did it mean? Who or what was coming through? And why? Why did it want him?

He was still trembling from seeing the image of the woman in the fire. Was she the one typing? Was she attempting to communicate with him?

He had to put an end to this. He had to stop this before his mind snapped in two. Whatever this was didn't matter. It was time he got rid of it.

Tiptoeing out the front door of the suite, he hung the plastic "Do Not Disturb" sign on the door. For good measure, he also took the signs from two other rooms down the hall and hung them on his door handle as well. "Can't be too safe."

On the ground level, Gavin made his way across the lobby to the concierge stand, annoyed that Thad wasn't in sight.

A woman in her early sixties with a short, mousy hairstyle looked up to greet him. Her smile pushed her cheeks high, almost obscuring her eyes. "May I help you, sir?"

"I'm looking for Thad." He remembered the name at the bottom of the printout. "Thad Williams."

"I'm sorry, sir. He left a few minutes ago. Is there something that I may help you with?"

He pointed at her nametag. "Vicki?"

She nodded. "Yes?"

"When is he coming back?" He motioned to the break room. "Is he back there? 'Cause it'll only take a minute for me to get what I need."

She was already shaking her head. "I'm sorry, sir. Thad's gone for the day. He worked a double and won't be back until Tuesday. Would you like me to take a message for him?"

Scraping at the stubble on his face, he answered, "No, nothing like that. I need a big box. The size of box that something like a microwave would come in."

"Yes, I see," she said, thinking for a moment. "Your best bet is from the HWB Grill. That is, if you don't mind it smelling like produce. Otherwise, we could order a special shipper from FedEx. They'll deliver in the morning around—"

"No, no, I'm in a hurry. I need it today. I don't care what's been in it or what it smells like. It just needs to be the right size."

"Understood. I'll send a message to the manager on duty at the grill to let 'em know. Who should I say is coming?"

"Mr. Curtis."

Her face lit up even more. "I heard that you were staying with us, and the entire staff knows not to interrupt your writing for any reason."

He nodded out of reflex.

Taking a notepad and pen from the drawer, she said, "Normally, I would never do this, but my grandson, Dylan, is such a big fan of the movies, and he's getting into the books."

Gavin stared at her. With everything he was going through, she was going to make him sign something? He didn't have time for this.

"Look, I really have to—"

"He was in line yesterday at the bookstore, but there was a fire that forced everyone to evacuate before he could meet you." Her smile was infectious.

Well, he *was* Gavin Curtis, after all. He rubbed his temples and then autographed the pad with liberal flourishes, to Vicki's delight. "Thank you so much, Mr. Curtis, and ask for Christy at the grill."

The lobby was a frenzy of activity. New arrivals scurried like ants to make a 3:00 p.m. check-in. The noisy clusters of guests seemed eager to jettison other family members in order to maximize their time at the resort's golf course, waterpark, or day spa.

Gavin navigated through the swarm of people to the bar and grill where he'd spent the better part of the night before. Returning to ground zero of his epic hangover didn't appeal to him. Even though the after-effects were lifting, the very thought of booze made him queasy.

He was anxious to get the machine out of his room. It wasn't clear how, but it was apparent that the machine had some connection with the "ghost woman."

Get rid of the typewriter, get rid of the woman in the yellow dress.

He'd get the box and be done with it and leave this town for good . . . except he felt peckish. The last thing he needed to do was to drop the thing due to being weak from low blood sugar levels. He decided to get a sandwich or something light on his stomach. He would have ordered room service, but he didn't want to risk the safety of the hotel staff with the antique. Who knew what that thing was capable of? He remembered the bicycle boy. He thought of the dead female dancer on the news. He thought of the threatening message it—or *she*—had typed—"I'm coming through."

As he reached the doorway of the grill, his shirt pocket vibrated—he had a call.

"Hey, it's been more than twenty minutes," Josephine said. "You told me you'd call back in five. Where are you at?"

"Yeah, I know. I'm at the resort. Sorry, I'm just a little pre-occupied today."

What an understatement.

"I've called you like a dozen times since yesterday. Mr. Hastings said the fire department came on site—that everything was going great, that you even gave some speech or something, and then the fire alarms went off and you disappeared. Are you okay?"

Gavin stroked the high gloss of the faux-wood cabin siding. He guessed that the décor was intended to make it appear as if a lodge had miraculously appeared on the side of the hotel. "Yeah, I'm all right now."

"Now? You're all right *now*? What happened before? Did you lose your phone or something?"

"Look, Jo, something's happened. I can't really go into details . . ." His voice trailed off.

"Like what? Are you okay?"

"Yeah, well, sorta. I got a little hurt, just on my head, but it's okay now. At least I think it is." He gently massaged the injury and winced. "Anyway, the point is, I had some stuff happen and I couldn't call you back, but I'm fine now. I'll tell you all about it later." This was a lie. No one would ever believe any of this. Hell, he didn't know if he believed all of what had happened within the last twenty-four hours.

There's a ghost typing messages to me, and she says she's coming to visit?

"I gotta do some stuff today, and then we can talk."

"You're sure you're okay? You don't need to get your head checked out?"

"I'm peachy."

"Peachy? Now I know something's up. You never use words like 'peachy.' You're sounding a little weird. You promise you're okay? When I couldn't get you on the phone—"

"Fine! I'm fine."

Two female retirees exiting the grill hurried to get out of Gavin's range. He covered the phone and explained, "It's my mother. I have to yell so she can hear me."

The elderly women nodded, offering fake smiles as they escaped to safety.

Gavin moved from the doorway threshold to the far corner of the log structure. "I'm okay. I just need to deal with something, but I'm okay. Sorry about the missed calls scare."

He had to get her off the phone, grab a bite, get the box, and be done with this whole mess. Every minute that machine was in his possession was bad for him.

"I almost took a flight there, but I had the manager send somebody by your room instead. It took some arm-twisting, but I finally convinced them that I am who I said I was."

"You almost came here?" he asked in a panic. "Don't do that! Whatever you do, don't come and see me. You can't come, it's not . . . " He knew not to use the word "safe." That would instantly trigger alarms, and she'd be on the next flight out.

"Gavin, you sound weird again. What's going on? Is there something wrong there?"

He had to conceal his panic. Josephine wasn't one to be left out of the loop. She considered anything on tour her responsibility. Any negative he encountered was her job to fix.

"No, everything is fine, but I need you to stay put." He did his best to mask his anxiety, trying to sound warm. "Please do this for me—promise me that you won't come out here. Promise."

"Okay, you were supposed to check outta there today anyway. You're due at The Book Mark at six, remember? It's forty-five minutes on the turnpike from where you are now."

"I need you to reschedule that. Tell them I have the flu or something."

Though her words were fine, the tone of her voice betrayed that she felt defeated. "All right, we can reschedule. I'll just tack that stop on the end of the tour."

An awkward silence hung between them for a few seconds. Finally, Josephine said, "You sure are quiet. What are you thinking about over there? Tell me."

He hesitated, attempting to frame what he wanted to say. "I need to ask you something—something crazy, something completely off the wall."

"Yeah, what?"

Exhaling a deep breath, he attempted to ease into it. "If you had something, an artifact or something, that when you made a wish it came true, what would you do?"

"What do you mean? What would I wish for? Are you kidding? How hard did you hit your head?"

"What would you do? Just answer me."

Her voice perked up. "Wait, is this for a new Damien Marksman story? The front desk told me they heard typing coming from your room. Is that why you've been dodging my calls? I'm going to call the other bookstore as soon as we get off the phone. I can even cancel the dates after that if you need me to in order to keep your muse going. Gavin, I'm so excited for you!"

"It's not a story. Just tell me what you'd do."

"Sure." He could tell by her happy tone that she didn't believe him. "I don't know. Are we talking some genie-in-a-lamp kinda thing?"

He thought of the apparition of the woman in yellow. Had *she* given the bike boy a seizure? He hadn't considered it until now. Is that what this was?

"Gavin, I asked if it's like a genie."

He recovered. "Uh, yeah, in a manner of speaking. What would you do with it?"

"Destroy it."

He was shocked by the speed of her response. "Really?"

"Absolutely, I would. Those things always screw over the wisher. If you wish to live forever, the genie transports you to a tiny deserted island where you fall into a deep well and can't get out for all eternity or something like that. Why? What's your story plot?"

"I don't know. That's why I'm asking."

She scoffed. "Master storyteller, Gavin Curtis, doesn't have a dozen ways to plot out the genie-with-three-wishes conundrum? It's a red-letter day. Call your buddy, William Cavanaugh. Doesn't he always help you when you're painted into a corner?"

"Yeah, I guess."

"What's wrong? What did I say?"

"Nothing, I'm just trying to figure something out is all."

"Okaaaay, but with ancient artifacts, it always ends with some Twilight Zone-ish twist that leaves the wisher in the lurch. The best thing is for the character not to wish for anything selfish. He or she should make a request from a pure heart. It's even better if it's for the benefit of someone else, something good for other people, for mankind or something. Then trap the genie or demon or whatever back in the bottle and bury it deep enough that no one will ever find it again."

Gavin thought of the last line that he'd typed. "The woman laughed." That had been good, something without malice like his fantasy about stabbing the Puma jacket man. It'd been pure, and nothing had happened. If the woman in yellow only responded things that were malicious in nature, he was set—no more typing. He'd get the box and go.

"Does that help any?" she asked.

"More than you know, Jo. More than you know."

Her voice sounded sexy as she said, "Ahhh, so you are working on something." Immediately, the tone changed back to business, and he heard her tapping computer keys in the background. "Listen, I could extend your stay at the resort for another few nights if you'd like. For that matter, I could book you there for another week if things are really flowing for you. Gavin, I'm so excited for you. It's just like old times."

"Speaking of, I heard you were done with the photographer."

There was a long pause, and Gavin instantly regretted bringing the subject up so crassly. He was in the business of stringing words together, making millions of dollars out of putting sentences together in novel form. Why, then, was it so hard for him to hold conversations with her in real life?

Josephine's reply was as sharp as barbed wire. "Beverly Cavanaugh should learn to keep her mouth shut and mind her own business."

"Jo, I'm sorry. I shouldn't have said it like . . . Maybe we can talk at Billy's party next week. Look, I shouldn't have brought it up."

The response was curt. "No, no. It's fine. I'd rather not talk about it at the moment. Plus, you've got a story or whatever to write."

Another silence.

"We're good, right?" Gavin asked.

"Peachy."

The sarcasm slapped him across the face. He waited a few seconds, hoping that the conversation would return to friendly territory. Still feeling the chill, he forced out, "Promise me that you won't come out here."

"Wouldn't dream of it."

Wow, it must have been a bad breakup between her and Ray.

"Okay, it's just that you said before you were going to hop a plane and—"

"Gavin, I said I wouldn't. Do I have to swear to you that I'll leave you alone?"

"Yes. I need to hear you say it. I need to know."

"Fine. I promise that I won't fly to Connecticut to check up on you. Now, bye, Gavin. Get back to work on your secret little project."

"Okay, you can call me tomorrow. Everything should be sorted out by then. I just need some—"

Click.

The grill was considerably more crowded than when Gavin had visited the day before, when, if what Thad had reported was accurate, Gavin had taken up residency on a barstool for over six hours. He could mostly reconstruct the first two or three hours of watching the Dodgers game while he did his best to empty the bar's scotch, but after that, his mind was paste, remembering only a blur of images.

A hostess who looked like she might still be in high school finally directed him to a booth. "Sorry for the wait. We're a little shorthanded today." She offered a glossy menu. "Your server will be right with you."

As the girl turned away to tend to some other duty, Gavin stopped her. "Hey, why is this place named Hungry Waters?"

The girl's eyebrows raised half an inch. "I dunno. Some urban legend or something. It has to do with the bridge suicides. Theo gives tours sometimes."

"Theo, huh? His name is Theo? Does he work here?"

A waiter with a noisy, sizzling plate of beef fajitas moved quickly past her with a nod. The steaming meat smelled good.

She laughed. "Sort of. He's supposed to be here now, but he claims he has 'car trouble.'" The girl made air quotes while simultaneously rolling her eyes as if she'd practiced the gesture her entire life. "That's partly the reason we're so busy, because he didn't show up." The girl turned to leave again.

"Oh, one more thing. I need to see the manager, Christy."

"Something wrong?"

Now Gavin had her full attention. "No, she's supposed to be getting something for me."

"Oh, okay." The girl looked relieved. "She's unloading the truck, but I'll send her to you." She didn't wait for him to thank her or ask any more questions as she hurried from the booth area.

Growing antsy while he waited for his server to come, Gavin doodled on a paper napkin, writing the phrase "I'm coming through," scribbling several question marks, and underlining it. He had to get back to his room, and quickly. Maybe coming to the restaurant had been a mistake.

After a few minutes, a waitress approached. "Hi, sorry for the wait. My name is Katelyn, and I'll be serving you today."

Gavin flipped the napkins over. "It's because of Theo, right?"

He smirked with delight as the twenty-something gently tugged at her blond ponytail, looking astonished. "How did you—"

Before she finished the question, Gavin volunteered, "Never trust a guy named Theo. They're always trouble."

"Do you know him?" Her expression was like that of a six-year-old witnessing an unexplainable magic trick for the first time.

"No, but my first name is Theo. Actually, Theodore, but don't hold it against me." He let the woman off the hook. "The girl who seated me told me that this Theo guy is kind of a pain in the ass."

"He's all right, I guess, just not very punctual sometimes. What can I get you to drink?"

"Coffee—black. And I already know what I want to eat. I'll have the number seven."

"Coming right up."

"Hey, do you know anything about suicides around here?"

She tucked her pen into her shirt pocket. "I know what people say about the bridge, where jilted lovers go to jump in the Hungry Waters. Personally, I think the whole thing is sad, what happened and all, but I don't believe all of what's said around here."

"You don't believe what?"

"Anytime some woman or girl goes missing, there are stories that their heartbreak lures them here to end it all. I know it's good for business and all, but I think it's tacky."

"How is that good for business?"

"You'd be surprised. Did you come in the front door or through the lobby entrance?"

"The lobby door. Why?"

"There's an article in a frame above the coat rack by our front door. I'm told it used to be the only entrance back in the 90s, you know, before the hotel was built. Read all about it if you like." Her smile returned. She was all business again. "I'll be right back with your order."

Gavin waited a moment and then slid out of the booth.

The framed article was just where Katelyn had said, posted above the wooden coatrack pegs. Standing on the wooden T-frame bench allowed Gavin to get a closer look at the dingy newspaper clipping. He gripped the empty pegs for balance. He'd have to be sure to thank Josephine for booking him there. She had to have known about this and probably hoped the local tales and urban legends would inspire him.

The article relayed how a young mother, Victoria "Torri" Barta, suspected to have suffered from depression, threw her infant daughter from the Thanatos Bridge and then committed suicide by leaping in herself. There was something about the picture of her, something about the black-and-white image that was familiar, but he couldn't place it. Even the jewelry around her neck seemed to ignite something far off in his memory, something just out of reach.

That necklace . . . Where have I seen a necklace shaped like a pear before?

"Pretty cool, huh?" a voice behind him asked.

He turned to see a fit man in his early twenties closing the front door. The man resembled a young Tom Cruise, if the actor had sandy-blond hair.

Gavin stepped down from the bench. "Why do you say it's cool?"

"Well, I mean, not that part of the story, but everything else," the man said, tucking a forest-green Hungry Waters Bar & Grill T-shirt into his jeans.

"I don't know the story," Gavin said.

"The part that the paper left out is the 'why' of the story." Before Gavin could challenge this, the grinning man continued, "It says that she was all depressed and that's why she did it—baby depression or whatever."

"Postpartum," Gavin offered.

"Right." He paused, and his smile showed perfectly white teeth. "But what they don't tell you is that her husband was boinking some of the hotel staff. One of the cleaning maids that worked there at the time, some Asian chick. That's why she did it. She walked in on them, and thirty minutes later, splash. Now that bridge is like a Mecca to young girls who want to off themselves. A few dudes too, but mostly chicks. We call them Torries—named after the original one. When we see a girl sittin' alone at the bar or in a booth, we always wonder if she's a Torri trying to get her nerve up to take a plunge and feed the Hungry Waters."

He made a plopping sound and spread his hands in a slow motion splash. "The resort turns a blind eye to all of it because it generates a certain amount of business for them—you know, ghost chasers. Paranormal tourism. There've been claims of strange things happening in the room Torri found them in, people saying it's haunted and whatnot. I kinda doubt it since nobody actually got killed or anything in there, but who knows? Weird, huh?"

He grabbed a menu from a shelf and flipped to the beverage section in the back. "They even allow us to market it. Check it out. We have a drink called 'The Plunge.'"

Gavin took the menu that was thrust at him before realizing it.

"It has an olive in it, for the baby. It's like the baby she threw in, the olive."

"Yeah, I get it," Gavin said, closing the menu. "Pretty gruesome stuff, but that still doesn't explain why this is here." Tapping the small frame of the article with the menu, he asked, "Why would someone want to post this?"

"Guilt, I guess. She was the owner's wife, Mrs. Barta was."

"Torri Barta is married"—Gavin corrected himself—"*was* married to the guy who owns this place?"

"The original owner," the man explained. "But he hasn't been heard from in ten or fifteen years or so. He just up and disappeared when all the suicides and rumors of suicides started. Some even think he might've even jumped in the Hungry Waters himself."

"You knew him?"

"Nah, I've only been here about three years. I give tours. I can take you to the room on the seventh floor where she caught 'em, then go the spot where she jumped. They've got the bridge barricaded off temporarily for that whole Bridge Fest thing for next weekend, but I know a way through. Then we come back here to drink to them. The price of The Plunge drink is included, so the tour works out to only be twenty-two bucks or so."

"You do tours? You must be Theo."

"In the flesh. Hey, if you're staying at the resort, you can charge it all to your room. Are you staying at the resort?"

"Yeah, for a day or so. You said Barta had a room set up for his mistress, like a love nest?"

"I don't think it was much of a romance, just a quickie with one of the maids, an Asian chick named Kawaguchi. I looked it all up from the police report—for the tour, you know."

Gavin suspected that Kawaguchi was not a common name, at least not in Connecticut. There had to be a connection to the murdered dancer.

Theo sped up the tale, enthused to have a listener. "Anyway, they didn't rent a room or anything, but you know how a maid has access to all the rooms to straighten them and whatnot? They just found an empty one that she was supposed to clean, and wham-o."

"You said it happened on the seventh floor?"

Theo was chomping at the bit. "Yeah, Room 719. It's one of the larger suites. I can take you by it, and if the guests have already checked out, I know this girl that can let us in for a few minutes before housekeeping comes by. It's not really a part of the official tour, but I do it from time to time. We'd have to give Tammy, the girl I know, twenty bucks or so, but she'll do it. Hey, what floor are you on?"

Gavin's heart had skipped a beat when he heard the boy say room 719—his room. Surely, Jo hadn't booked him in there intentionally. No, that would have been in bad taste. He played it cool and lied. "Uh, I'm in Room 412—you know, on the fourth floor. Listen, I think I'll pass on the tour and your little macabre drink." He handed the menu back.

For the first time, Theo's face relaxed the used-car salesman's hyena smile. "Sorry, mister. I saw you readin' the article up there and thought—"

"Nope. I am curious, though. The girl who seated me said something about the grill being here before the hotel was built?"

Now that there wasn't a sale to be made, Theo answered more slowly. "Yeah, they built the hotel around the restaurant. Story is that Mr. Barta wouldn't sell the land to the resort people, so they made a deal with him. He'd run the grill like his immigrant father before him, and the company got the novelty of having some local color. The deal made Barta a ton of money, and all he had to do was allow them to remodel the side of his building for an entrance straight from the lobby. I guess all that money that he got made him irresistible to the ladies, and well, you know what happened next."

"Irresistible to the ladies? You said he was sleeping with the hotel staff. It sounds like an act of availability more than anything."

Theo shrugged. "Who can figure out love?"

A slender woman in her late thirties dressed in a black shirt and slacks approached them. She carried a large box labeled "Produce." Her voice was pleasant but firm. "Theo, I need you to tend to station six." She turned her focus to Gavin and offered a well-rehearsed smile. "I'm the manager, Christy Parr. Are you Mr. Gavin Curtis?"

When he nodded, she said, "Then this must be for you." She removed the lid. "Is this a big enough box for what you need?"

Theo butted in. "Oh, man, Gavin Curtis? The writer?" He ran his palm across his sandy-blond hair, laughing. "You really had me going with the line about the 'macabre drink' and all."

Christy shot him a dirty look undoubtedly reserved for wayward subordinates. Unfazed, Theo's smirk returned to full power. "Hey, are you here doing research or something? I could waive the tour fee, be like a consultant to you or something."

The woman clamped a firm hand on the worker's shoulder. "Theo—"

He was wound up and didn't seem to notice her. "You know, people come from all around for the ghost-story angle on this thing. Like I said, I could take you by the room where they say—"

"Theo!" she scolded. Christy put the box at Gavin's feet and then whispered in Theo's ear.

The smile melted from his face, and his body slumped slightly. "I know, but—"

A few heated seconds later, the woman stepped back to face Gavin. Her countenance transformed back into the pleasant, soft smile that she'd first offered him.

Theo looked like a dog thwacked by a rolled-up magazine. "Mr. Curtis, I'm sorry, but I have to get to some things. If you want a tour, just let Ms. Parr know a time and she can arrange it for us."

Theo looked at Christy, who gave him a slow nod, before he added, "Sorry if I was too pushy and all."

"It's fine." Gavin addressed Christy. "I *was* looking at the article."

Theo excused himself before his boss saw the smirk forming on his face, but Gavin saw it.

"Sorry about that," she said, bending to pick up the box. "We don't get many celebrities, and, given the nature of your writing—"

"Don't sweat it," he said, lowering to a crouch to take it from her. "Occupational hazard." Then he inspected the box. "Yes, this will do fine."

The two stood again as he asked, "What was this placed called before the . . . suicide stuff?"

"Before 'Hungry Waters'? I think it was called something like the Riverbed or Riverside Tavern. I'm not sure. That was way before my time here, but I could find out if it's important to your research."

"No, that's okay. Thanks for the box."

Gavin hurried back to his table and tossed the box into the seat across the booth. When his meal arrived a few minutes later, he wolfed it down so quickly, he'd likely have indigestion later. He didn't care. He'd already spent too much time away from his room.

As he finished the last of his onion rings, Theo appeared in his corner booth.

"Hey, man, I'm glad you're still here." The shark-toothed smile was back. "I didn't know if Christy gave you my info yet, so here it is."

Gavin received the scrap of receipt paper from him with no comment.

"It's my email address and cell for your story research about Hungry Waters."

Gavin's server Katelyn approached them with her blond ponytail bouncing in rhythm and swaying with every step. "Here's your check, Mr. Curtis."

When he accepted it, she turned her attention to his unwelcome sidekick. "Hey, Theo, better not let Parr catch you over here. I thought you called in sick again."

"Nah, car just ran out of gas on the way here."

Gavin could tell the two had a thing for each other by the shift in body language.

"Well, at least if you run out of gas, you can't get into any more wrecks."

Theo countered, obviously trying to make her blush, "The car don't need to be rollin' for me to drive in the backseat."

The words caused an idea to flash into Gavin's mind, and he slammed the money for his meal on the table, startling both workers and getting a few heads turned in their direction. He sprang up from the booth, laughing, and grabbed Theo by the shoulders. "That's it! It has to have the gas to run. It won't work without it. Take away what it uses, and it stops and can't go on!"

Gavin released his grip, and the young man staggered backward in shock. The disruption had every eye in the area of the restaurant focused on him, but Gavin didn't care.

A frightened Katelyn leapt to the side as he reached around her for the empty box. He'd taken a few steps toward the exit when he turned back to face where she remained frozen in place. "You two may have just saved somebody from something awful happening to them!"

EIGHT

GAVIN STOPPED IN HIS TRACKS halfway to the elevators. The busy crowd parted around him like a stream flowing around the sides of a rock. Though he was completely still, his mind raced. Now he remembered where he'd seen the jewelry in the newspaper article picture.

The necklace? Is that the connection?

With the box tucked under his arm, he turned and faced the entrance of the bar and grill.

How can I find out?

Then it came to him. His sluggish steps forward turned into a trot, carrying him to the resort's business center on the other side of the area. He found an empty terminal, plopped down in a chair, swiped his resort access card, and began to type.

Two minutes later, he was entering his credit card information into a genealogy website. Normally, he would have balked at the thirty-five-dollar fee to establish an account, but this was important. He was finally on the path to figuring some of this out.

When the answer appeared on his screen, Gavin belted out a loud "Yes!" and slapped the computer table. Two of the other users in the small area responded with a chastising "Shhhhhhh!"

He ignored them as he shot from his seat and raced to the valet station outside.

Nine miles and fifteen minutes later, he pulled up to the curb. Half-expecting Madame Kovács to be in her chair on the porch, he was relieved when she wasn't. It gave him a moment to prepare what to say.

He rapped gently on the screen door and waited.

What if she's not here? Or worse, what if she's next door at the store?

The idea of another confrontation with Puma Jacket made his blood run cold. He knocked harder. "Madame Kovács?"

Muffled yelps rang out from behind the door.

Stupid little dog.

There was the sound of a mild skirmish between pet and master, and the high-pitched barking faded into a back room. Finally, the main porch door came alive. Two locks twisted and clicked into place, followed by the squeak of old hinges.

The fortuneteller cracked the door a few inches and looked through the screen.

Man, she's ugly. Maybe I was wrong about Torri and her.

"Madame Kovács, I need to ask—"

Upon recognizing Gavin, she immediately cut him off. "No, go . . . go from here! The police come for my nephew. You make police come and take him."

"I know, I know. I'm sorry about that. Look, I don't want any trouble, but I need your help."

"No help! Go!"

"But Madame Kovács, the woman in yellow, I know who she is."

"Nothing here for you. Be leaving."

The opening in the door grew smaller.

"Wait, I'm here about Torri! I need to talk to you. I need to speak to you about—"

The door slammed.

Gavin went "all in" and shouted, "It's about your daughter! I need to talk to you about your daughter, Torri."

There was a silence. He knew that she was still on the other side of the door, since the locks hadn't twisted.

"Madame Kovács? I know you can hear me. Look, I'm sorry. I know we got off to a bad start the other day, but . . . "

He looked at his feet, listening for a response from inside.

"Madame Kovács, I . . . I need to know how to stop her. How do I stop Torri?"

To his surprise, the door reopened wider than before.

"Stop? *Szellem* . . . there is no stop, only waiting for her ninetieth year."

She gripped the emerald pear necklace like a first-time skydiver pulling the parachute cord. "Machine not for you. Bad . . . no selling."

She doesn't know I have it.

"Are you saying—her ninetieth birthday—this keeps going until then? All right, okay, but help me understand. How does the machine work? Is it like a horcrux, or a—a whatchamacallit—a Koschei-egg-type-thing that Torri is fused with? The typewriter, it keeps her spirit somehow?"

She shifted her eyes from him, but not before Gavin caught a glimpse of her shame. He asked, "What is it? What happened to her?"

Kovács stared at the ground. "I try . . . you say protect . . . yes, protect her."

"Like with an incantation or something?"

"I not know this word, but I protect her, but . . . she's jumping." She looked up with a hateful grimace that made Gavin shiver. "She jumping because of him." The old woman pantomimed spitting in disgust. "He put his bad blood in her, make crazy, baby bad blood and Victoria crazy. My chant for her long life . . . good, happy life. That is spell, but now she gone."

Gavin couldn't believe it—tears were actually streaming down Kovács's cheeks.

"Protect her. I protect Torri, but when she jumps, it make *szellem*, make ghost. Now she's *korlátozott* . . . you say is 'trapped.' She is trapped, and no to stop for many years."

"Can you undo it—reverse the protection spell or whatever it is?"

She was shaking. "*Korlátozott*! No! She become undone! Gone forever."

"Okay, just calm down a minute. It's okay." Gavin spoke slowly, accentuating each word. "I need you to tell me how to stop this. What happens if I—or someone else—gets rid of the antique?"

She was on the verge of hysterics. "There is not stop—she is *szellem*!"

I'm losing her.

"Madame Kovács, I want to help Victoria—Torri. How can I help?"

"No help. She is *szellem* and is to try to return."

Return? Now we're onto something.

"Return how, Madame Kovács? How can Torri try to return if she died from the suicide? How does it work?"

Her eyes widened. "Back from other side into this world." She gestured making an arc with one hand landing in the other with a clap. "Return. Must not happen this thing bad. She try to recon-sti . . . sti-tu . . . Torri try re-consti-tu . . . "

Gavin butted in. "Reconstitute? Are you trying to say reconstitute, as in re-form into flesh?"

Kovács nodded as she stroked the pear-shaped necklace. "Powerful chant, very powerful magic at work."

"How do you stop it from happening?"

Kovács pointed at him. "No stop. This why she must not do this. She die with much hate on heart. Come back in evil."

She wiped tears from her eyes, saying flatly, "Machine not for you to buy. You must leave alone."

"Or what? What if I get the machine? What happens if Béla sells it to me?" Remembering he'd been taken away, Gavin corrected himself. "What if your other nephew gives it to me or someone else? Then what?"

"Not for sale, too dangerous."

"But what would happen? Please, Madame, I have to know."

She wiped her eyes and stared at him for what felt like an eternity.

"Please. What is it?"

"The *doure sint*," she said in a cautious whisper and then spat on the ground as if expelling a mouthful of poison.

"The what?" He felt sweat roll down the back of his neck and licked his lips to wet his parched lips. "I'm sorry, I don't understand."

"It like a . . . like the coin," she said, pointing at her trembling palm, then to the veiny back of the hand.

Gavin fumbled in his pocket and presented a quarter. To his astonishment, she opened the door and came forward, taking it from him. This was a breakthrough.

She held the coin up, slowly turning it from side to side. "Yes, this way." She pointed to the heads side. "We here." Twisting it to show the tails side. "Torri side. We not to see that side. But with *doure sint*, Torri change to our side."

He knew they were making progress. The very fact that Kovács was speaking to him at all and had even come outside was huge. But what did it all mean? "*Doure sint* is what?"

She handed the coin back heads-up in his palm. "It make person on here," she tapped it, "energy for *szellem* to come back to form."

"But how?" Gavin asked, studying the coin before pocketing it. "How does someone dead—a *szellem* or ghost or whatever—use someone on the living side to rebuild their body? I mean wouldn't they already have a body buried in the ground?"

"Spirit not connected to body, so it use *doure sint* to re-build flesh."

"So, whoever has the machine controls the ghost?"

Kovács shook her head, indicating a frustrated "no." It wasn't just the language barrier between the two of them. These concepts were completely foreign to Gavin, but still he pressed for answers. "So does the . . . *szellem* get the energy from someone when they die?"

Her eyes widened, and though it wasn't a smile on her harelip face, Gavin saw she was pleased. "Yes, like battery."

"The dying energy is like a battery?"

"Not dying, what energy remain."

He pictured taking double-As from a radio to put them into a TV remote with dead batteries. "Let me get this straight. If someone is killed before their time, they have leftover energy in their spirit or whatever?"

He paused as she nodded.

"And that's what Torri would use to make a new form of herself, to make a new body? That energy would be with the dying person to take over into another realm unless something like Torri intercepted it and took it from them."

Kovács nodded again, but he was thinking of the twenty-something-year-old dancer. How many years would she have had left if she had not drowned before her time? What about the boy on the bike? He was at least ten years younger than that. But he'd only had a seizure, right? The grim thought of him dying in the back of the ambulance on the way to the hospital flooded Gavin's thoughts. Had he died?

Gavin forced himself back into the moment. He had to know more. What was going to happen to him? "Madame Kovács, I still don't understand how using the machine works. How does that fit in to all of this?"

"Fit in?" she asked with a puzzled expression.

"The person who types . . . " he felt in his pocket for the coin and then decided against pulling it out again. "How does the machine, the item she's fused with, turn the user in the *doure sint*?"

"It become part of them, too, like it part of *szellem*."

Shit!

This was not what he wanted to hear, that he and Torri were somehow cosmically joined now.

Before he could ask if he were a candidate for possession by the ghost, she added, "Brain is like waterwheel." She placed her hands atop her head and then removed them as she pantomimed the circular motion of the turning of a wheel in front of her chest. "When person awake, thinking, thinking, thinking." She pointed back at her wrinkled forehead. "Always thinking when awake 'Should I do this, should I do that.'" She paused, waiting for Gavin to confirm that he understood.

"Right, I get it. The person is awake, thinking about different things." He spoke impatiently, trying to urge her to the point.

"These things, thinking things, many of things in day we think of, each little energy that make wheel turn." She returned to the hand gestures of a waterwheel spinning being pushed by a stream. "That energy makes . . ." She struggled for a word for a few seconds, finally settling for, "tunnel tube for *szellem* to come from one side of coin to other side. This why no one can have machine."

Gavin scratched the back of his neck. It was moist with sweat. "So, what can be done to stop the connection, to stop *szellem* from coming through?"

Kovács looked confused. Gavin attributed the bewildered look on the language barrier between them. Before he could rephrase the question using different terminology, the old woman blurted out, "How you know these words?"

Now he was confused. "What words? What are you talking about?"

She looked terrified. "'Coming through'? How do you know this?"

"I just asked how someone would keep the *szellem* from coming through."

She backed away, but not to retreat into the house. Her trembling steps were headed in the direction of Béla's shop. "How do you know this 'coming through'?" Her eyes were extremely wide. She accused him, "You have it, don't you?"

"Have what?" Gavin bluffed, but he could tell she was on to him.

"You took it?" she screamed. Her tone was incredulous as she repeated the words, this time in the form of a statement. "You . . . you took it."

Gavin moved toward her as her backward steps carried her to the steps of the deck. The moment was surreal. He realized he'd offered a dumb shrug in his defense.

She was on the ground level now. "You don't push keys?" The question's hopeful tone evaporated as quickly as she uttered it. "No typing, right?"

"Madame Kovács, I need your help, and I can pay you any amount to have—"

Still moving away from him in fear, she shook her head from side to side, but her dark eyes never broke with his. In remarkably clear English, she proclaimed, "Then it has already begun, and we are all in danger."

The words stunned him as he watched her make her way into the shop.

He knew that if he stuck around, he'd likely see Puma Jacket brandishing the shotgun from earlier. Gavin fled to his car and sped away before that could happen.

Gavin returned to the resort, involuntarily replaying Kovács' words of doom. "It has already begun, and we are all in danger." He'd gladly take the antique back there if he could, but he'd never get the chance with Puma Jacket wanting to settle the score. There was one thing left to try, the idea that had come to him while talking to Theo and his would-be girl-friend, Katelyn, in the grill. The hallway of the seventh floor was empty as he exited the elevator. He rushed into his suite, tossed the empty produce box on the bed, and headed for the balcony door.

He stopped short, hearing a series of rapid-fire strikes from outside. At first, it sounded like gunfire, but then he quickly placed it—more typing. Moving as quietly as possible, Gavin peered at the machine from behind the curtain of the sliding door.

Whether she was finished or knew he was watching, the typing stopped.

His heart pounded wildly, and he felt nauseated. The prospect of leaving text on the paper, if only even for a minute, tortured his mind, but he struggled to pull back the curtain.

Gotta do it, Gav. You have to.

He thought of the bicycle boy, who might be dead now, and the murdered dancer. Who knew what new malevolent sentences Torri had typed? He had to stop it, to burn the message. He must go through the door. If he truly was the *doure sint,* he was the only one who could stop this. What if she possessed the power to blow up the hotel and typed something about a bomb? Or somehow set fire to the seventh floor? The lives she'd get from something like that—the power—it was more than he could comprehend. It was up to him to stop this.

He tried to swallow, but his mouth was dry. The door lock clicked more loudly than he expected. With the curtain still drawn, he couldn't see the machine. Gavin listened a moment for more typing, but there was only the labored sound of his breathing.

He had to see what she had typed. He had to know.

Gavin took a deep breath, slid the curtain back, opened the door, and charged through it.

Half expecting it to burn him, he lifted the typewriter from the table and ran back into the suite. He hurled the machine onto the bed. It landed upside-down with its keys clamoring together, jangling as they extended into the center opening of it.

With his body pressed against the nearby wall, he waited for something to happen, for the machine—for Torri—to retaliate.

It didn't move.

What had she typed? He had to know. He had to stop it.

Gavin took a step toward the corner of the bed where it landed, and then he stepped back against the wall. Exhaling another deep breath, he mopped the sweat from his brow. He placed another square of Nicorette gum in his mouth and chewed it frantically.

Finally, he advanced to the machine and flipped it to the upright position. The hammers returned to their ready positions, revealing greasy, black text. A different confusion and fear descended upon him as he read.

```
YOU DISOBEYED ME, GAVIN. I TOLD
YOU NOT TO LEAVE.


THERE WILL BE A RECKONING FOR
ALL THAT YOU'VE DONE, AND IT'S
ALREADY STARTED. IT'S ONLY A
MATTER OF TIME NOW.


OVER HALFWAY THERE ALREADY. CAN
YOU FEEL ME COMING THROUGH?


ARE YOU READY FOR IT?


WANNA KNOW WHAT HAPPENS NEXT,
GAVIN?
```

She knew him.

Remembering what Madame Kovács had said about the meaning of *doure sint*, he accidentally swallowed the gum. A second later, he snapped to. He'd carry out his plan. Gavin lunged for the top of the scroll like a maniac, shouting, "Let's see what you can do without paper!"

He pulled with all his might, unrolling a length of the beige parchment as tall as himself. Throwing the curling ribbon of paper behind him, he reached for where it connected within the machine's undercarriage and heaved again and again.

"If a car can't crash without gas, a story can't be typed without something to print on!"

He heaved at the roll a fifth and a sixth time. The coarse roll of stock curled into a pile around his feet and showed no end in sight. After a few more strenuous tugs at the sheet of stock, Gavin realized there had to be an impossible amount of volume inside in relation to the size of the machine. He stepped back, slipping on the paper that filled the area. Stumbling across the suite, he steadied himself by grabbing the edge of the desk chair.

He sat down to collect himself and looked at the room. The paper scroll covered the floor around the bed like a giant anaconda. Resembling stacks of paper figure eights, the amount of paper from the machine was unsettling in the way it defied physics. As he attempted to process the impossibility of it all, there were a dozen or so sharp cracks from the typewriter.

He sprang from the chair to read the message.

STRONGER

The air was thick with the pungent aroma of lavender, making it hard to breathe. The page advanced upward, and the hammers of the device typed in rapid succession, advancing the page upward with each rendering.

STRONGER

I'M GETTING STRONGER

IT WON'T BE LONG

NOT LONG NOW WITH YOUR HELP

He thought about Madame Kovács' waterwheel analogy. If what she said were true, the very energy from his conscious thoughts was building a bridge for Torri to enter the physical realm. Fear gripped his heart, but he was too hypnotized by the alternating movements of the keys and hammers to look away.

I'M GETTING STRONGER

CAN YOU FEEL IT TOO?

A RECKONING FOR YOUR
SELFISHNESS

UNFAITHFUL GAVIN'S RECKONING

UNFAITHFUL

When it stopped, a dizzying nausea overtook Gavin, causing him to grip his throbbing temples. He collapsed to his knees upon the paper pile.

Through his constricted throat, he uttered, "What reckoning? Why? Because of cheating on Jo? That's nothing to do with you."

Gavin ripped the scroll of paper from the top of the carriage and then grabbed the machine, stormed across the suite to the front door, and slammed it to the ground in the hallway outside.

"Let it be someone else's problem now!" he shouted with his back against the closed door.

Half a minute later, he was looking through the peephole. The device was too close to the door to be seen through the tiny opening, but he felt it there, waiting for him.

A porter or maid would come by and pick it up soon enough. Whether they threw it in the dumpster or kept it for themselves didn't make a difference to him. He'd be free from her, and that was all that mattered.

He contemplated moving it further down the hallway near the elevator so no one would connect it with him.

"Connect it with him." That was the problem now, wasn't it? It would've been a good plan except that he was connected to the device and to Torri. He was the *doure sint*, bound to her and the machine beyond the natural realm, a bond that wasn't as easily discarded as a porter emptying the used dishes from Gavin's room service trays. Besides that, everyone at the hotel knew that the loud typing had been coming from Gavin's room.

Dammit!

Opening the door a crack, he saw the infernal thing just as he'd left it. Of course it was exactly the same. He released the door handle, allowing it to click closed.

He thought about how Torri could type anything and attribute it to him, how she could type a confession for the police about the murdered girl.

Gavin yanked the door open and dragged the machine back into the room. Seething, he made his way to the bathroom and lowered the device into the tub.

Once outside, he slammed the bathroom door.

He had to think.

Come on, Gav. Get control of yourself.

He paced directly outside of the bathroom and lit a cigarette.

The cigarette was halfway to the filter when an idea came to him. He chided himself for missing something so obvious.

Bursting into the area, he knelt, reaching over the edge of the tub, and began to type.

The keys resisted and didn't budge. He tried again, harder this time, striking the keys with the index fingers of his right and left hands—no response.

Had he broken it when he threw it down in the hallway?

Frustrated, he struck the keys with his fist. The impact delivered a sharp pain. Gavin pulled back and examined the cuts on his knuckles.

To his surprise, the typewriter made a metal clank sound. The temperature of the room dropped a chilling fifteen to twenty degrees in an instant. He detected the scent of lavender.

Determined to finish it off, he tried typing a sentence to destroy the device. When the keyboard gave way to his touch, he typed as quickly as he could.

I may only have one chance.

As he typed, he shouted the words. "The writer destroys the typewriter!"

But the result on the page was different. Displayed were the same number of characters that he'd typed, but the message read:


```
IT WON'T BE THAT EASY, GAVIN MY
DEAR.
```


In part panic and part fury, he reached over and turned the faucet knobs on high and exited the bathroom. He retreated into the suite and gathered the rolls of paper that covered the floor. It took a bit of time to compress all of it down into small wads. By then, the tub was close to overflowing onto the floor.

Gavin shoved the paper into the bathroom, turned off the water, and slammed the door again. A couple of seconds later, he opened it, grabbed some towels, clicked the light off, and shut it again.

Stuffing the towels securely under the door of the bathroom, he asked, "What the hell have I gotten myself into?"

He dragged the desk chair across the room, positioning it directly in front of the bathroom. He collapsed into the chair, wondering how to defeat this thing, wondering how much time he had to do so before the *doure sint* bridge was complete enough for Torri Barta to come through.

Nine

MANY HOURS HAD PASSED since Gavin had finished off the pack of cigarettes in his pocket. There were more in the carton on the other side of the suite, but he didn't dare leave his post outside the bathroom door.

As wired as he was, he found himself battling drowsiness after a while. Staring at the blank, white door, he strained to hear any sound from the presence on the other side.

Eventually, his weariness gave way to sleep, and then to dreams. Gavin massaged the cuts on his knuckles and looked up to realize he was at a signing. The bright stage lights of the auditorium made it impossible for him to judge how many people waited in line, lusting for his autograph. The queue weaved through the rows of empty seats. Everyone advanced mechanically in eerie silence. The only sound that filled the vast space was his pen scratching away at the title pages of the books presented to him.

The patrons' attire was a mix of drab greys and muted browns. The one standout was an elderly woman in a neon-blue jogging outfit—Ms. Hodges. She approached the signing table full of life and winked at him.

She dropped a ridiculously oversized book on the table as if it were a stone. The impact caused Gavin's pen to roll off to the floor. Bending to grab it, he saw that his right ankle was shackled to the table leg, which was bolted to the floor. He pulled at the chain with his full strength, but it didn't give.

Eunice peeked under the table and offered a small wave. "Uh . . . Mr. Curtis . . . Yoo-hoo, Mr. Curtis?"

Gavin straightened up and dutifully began writing an inscription in her book. The warmth of her smile comforted him. He looked into her soft, blue eyes as he said, "Miss Hodges, I'm so glad that you—"

Her face contorted and transformed into sheer terror. "Mr. Curtis!" she screamed.

The shriek echoed through the cavernous area. It was like a bolt of lightning shooting through him. She let out another scream, leaving him panicked and confused.

Then he knew why she screamed. He was no longer signing her book, but rather puncturing the remains of a gutted bullfrog with his pen. "Miss Hodges, I didn't—"

"You promised me that you'd be careful, Mr. Curtis. You told me you would, but you're helping her to come through. Helping her to come through to where we are." She recoiled and pulled back from the table. Gavin stood to go after her, but the sharp pain around his ankle reminded him of his restraint. As if it were alive, the chain jerked his leg out from under him, forcing him to fall back into his seat. He frantically struggled with the chain and cried, "Help me, Miss Hodges! Please help me!" But she was already gone.

Though the boys were nowhere in sight, the laughing voices of Gavin's childhood acquaintances, Des and Troy Bridges, echoed through the auditorium. "Look, he's trying to swim away."

Again, Gavin pulled with all his might at the chain. There was an odd sound of bubbling.

Troy's voice boomed overhead. "I got bad news for you. You're not going anywhere like this."

From the open cavity of the frog leaked a stream of gore—much more than could have naturally been contained in it. He slid it off the table with a violent sweep of his arm. To his amazement, the creature landed with a wet plopping sound and proceeded to hop across the floor. With its entrails in tow, the creature left a dark streak of blood across the platform.

Figures amassed at the edge of the stage before him, their books carelessly falling to the floor. They transformed into slimy frog-people, the process ripping their clothing. A low murmuring built to a crescendo. Their torn clothing loosened and slid off their bodies to the floor as they closed in around him.

Gavin desperately struggled again with the shackle. He splashed in a warm puddle of blood left by the frog. His heart beat violently, and his forehead was drenched with sweat. The horde of creatures crowded in on him. Their slick, green abdomens vibrated as they chanted and moved closer.

Then, at once, there was complete silence, and the creatures' shaking ceased. The sudden hush startled Gavin enough to cause him to drop the chain, which splashed at his feet.

One of the creatures croaked so loud that it shook the stage. "Swim, boy!"

A second later, their chests cracked open in unison with the noise of a thousand giant walnuts. Dark blood oozed like viscous lava from their midsections. The oozing became a stream that rapidly covered the floor.

The blood rose, and Gavin's hands shook as he slid the chain up to the top of the table leg. When it met with the underside of the table, he heaved himself atop the surface. As the gore rose around him, he lay flat on the table, gasping for air. The unwelcome image of the dissected frog from his boyhood apartments flashed across his mind, the suffocating creature dreaming of swimming to safety.

The front row of frog-people collapsed like deflated, gelatinous husks falling into the puddles of their own blood and viscera. Another row of the battalion advanced from directly behind them and, stomping on the discarded carcasses of the creatures before, repeated the process.

Gavin squeezed his eyes closed and called out for help, though no one was there to hear his plea. A putrid stench assaulted his nostrils. The table wobbled, and he tightened his grip on the edges. Seconds later, he heard—or more accurately, felt—a crack beneath him as the table legs broke away from the structure. The floating tabletop gave way to the current and swirled around a few dizzying times before leveling off.

He opened his eyes to discover that the auditorium and the throng of amphibian creatures were gone. He was outside, and the deluge of blood had transformed into an acrid stream. The foul-smelling water moved the tabletop so quickly that it created a dank breeze against his hair and face. A violent rain pummeled him. He would have welcomed the rainwater cleaning the slime from his face if not for it pelting his eyes.

He was floating toward a bridge. As he passed under it, the woman in the yellow dress peered over the edge at him. He assumed it was Torri. She held the old typewriter above her head. The brass and copper of the device gleamed like fire in the hard rain.

"Wake up, Gavin. Time for me to come through."

He knew what was about to happen, and he tried to make his way to safety back under the bridge. Despite all his splashing and flailing about, he barely moved any closer to the cover. He couldn't escape by diving under the surface, either. He was trapped like a cork bobbing on the water.

Gavin looked back at Torri as she released the antique. It fell at an impossibly slow rate of speed and blocked out the sky as it descended upon him.

He opened his mouth to scream, only to discover that he was mute.

A blinding light accompanied the pain as the typewriter struck him. The weight of it dragged him under the water like a boulder. The daylight above the surface faded into darkness.

Something beckoned Gavin from the real world, something that shook at his chest. Still in a stupor, he shifted in the chair and struggled to regain consciousness. There was a brief pause, and then he felt it again. As he rubbed the crust from his eyes, it took a moment for him to realize that the vibration in his pocket was his cell phone.

He fumbled for it, grateful to be awoken from the nightmare. Expecting to see Jo's icon on the display, he was annoyed that it was an unrecognized number. Gavin tapped "decline" and slid the phone back into his shirt pocket.

He stretched his arms wide and yawned. He felt a painful crick in his neck as he wiped a strand of drool from the side of his mouth. He supposed it was okay that he had fallen asleep. If Kovács was right, his sleeping would actually slow Torri's transition process. He had to be awake for the path to be finished. And it had been her spell that had fused her unstable daughter to the thing in the first place, so she must know how it worked.

As the room came into focus, he noticed the unexpected appearance of sunlight. Instead of the pale dusk of evening, the warm light of a new morning poured in through the sliding door of the balcony. The realization startled him, and he sat up in the chair, reaching for his cell again. It was 9:53 a.m. He'd been asleep for over fourteen hours. How was that possible?

Still in a daze, he wobbled from the chair to the clock on the nightstand, his reluctant legs as stiff as his back.

The muted cell phone vibrated again, and he declined the call again.

The alarm clock next to the bed displayed 9:52 a.m. in red characters. Hunger pains and a full bladder confirmed that he'd been out for a while, but half a day?

The pain of needing to relieve himself demanded attention. He'd overlooked this part of his plan when securing the machine in the bathroom. Did he dare to go in there? Was this all over? Could it be that he'd drowned it somehow?

He moved to the produce box on the bed. Was it safe to smuggle the machine out to a dumpster now? It was unlikely that anyone would discover it there.

The cell buzzed again, and this time he answered. "Stop calling!" He hung up and debated opening the bathroom door or going down to the hotel lobby to relieve himself. He paced the length of the suite. Was it safe to leave it now if he was only gone for a few minutes?

The phone buzzed again. It was the same person again. He could block the number, but it would take him some time to figure out how. Why didn't they just take the hint? If it was for an interview, they needed to go through Jo anyway. If it was a fan, they shouldn't have his number in the first place.

"Look, I don't know who you are or how you got my private number, but if you call me again, I'm going to sic my attorney on you!"

"Mr. Curtis?"

"Goodbye!"

Seconds later, it buzzed again.

"Listen, I told you not to—"

"Mr. Curtis, please don't hang up. It's about Monica."

"Monica who?" he shouted into the receiver.

"Garcia. My name is Anna. Monica Garcia is my sister. You dated."

"Yeah, so what?" Gavin gruffly added. "We broke up a long time ago."

"She . . . she's . . . something happened last night." The woman's words were punctuated with staccato breaths. Finally, she broke, giving way to sobbing. "She's dead, Mr. Curtis."

"What did you say?" His heart sank, hoping he'd misunderstood.

"I said Monica is dead. Last night. She died last night."

Gavin settled on the edge of the bed. He switched the phone to his other ear and cradled his forehead in his open palm. "How . . . what happened?" was all that he could get out before he was forced to bite his lip.

"She choked." Anna's voice deteriorated into another bout of sobs as she gasped between apologies. "I'm sorry. I'm sorry . . . I'm . . . "

Tears instantly flooded his eyes. Gavin pictured Anna hyperventilating on the other end of the line. Though he'd never met her, he knew of her through stories that Monica had told him about her kid sister. She was very pretty, but a tomboy and a former high-school volleyball champ. He did his best to comfort her. "Anna . . ." He managed to get another phrase out before his own voice cracked. "I'm sorry for yelling. Take your time."

After a few sniffles, she regained her composure. "We were out at a restaurant for an early dinner before going out clubbing. A girl we were friends with during school was getting married today—nothing fancy, just a justice-of-the-peace-type thing at the courthouse. So some of us decided to take her out for a night of bachelorette drinking, the five of us."

Gavin felt a lump form in his throat the size of a golf ball as he waited.

After a pause, Anna said, "I'm sorry. I still can't get used to it." She sniffed again. "We were having fun, getting a little rowdy, but it was okay, and then Susan told a dirty joke. It wasn't even really that funny, but Monica started laughing really hard."

Anna's voice broke again. "She choked on a piece of chicken from her salad. Rosa is a nurse. She feels bad she couldn't save her. She tried to do the Heimlich, but it was lodged too far down. She couldn't . . . " The sentence was left incomplete as she broke into another round of sobs.

"She laughed?" Gavin asked, though he doubted Anna heard him over her wailing. His voice quivered as he repeated. "She laughed? 'The woman laughed.'"

The phone shook in his hand as he fought the urge to vomit. The suite was a blur through his tear-filled eyes.

"Newport. She was at dinner in Newport Beach?"

"Yes, close to where she lives." Anna's voice cracked. "Lived."

Gavin wiped away the hot tears streaming down his cheeks. "But that's three thousand miles away. What time did it happen?" Had he been awake?

"I don't understand what you mean, Mr. Curtis."

It was his turn to weep as Anna relayed in a matter-of-fact tone. "I've been going through her cell phone, calling people who would need to know."

There was a pause.

"You were always kind to her." Anna's voice hinted at being happy for the first time during the conversation, which made it worse for Gavin. He tilted the mouthpiece away from his face so she wouldn't hear him blubbering.

She added fondly, "You may not know this, but you really helped her. You came into Monica's life at a very important time. You meant a lot to her. I think she thought that the two of you would reconnect down the line, but anyway . . ."

Gavin managed to squeak out of his constricted throat, "I'm sorry, Anna, so sorry. I didn't know that it would do that. I didn't mean for anything like . . . "

He sniffed and wiped his nose with the back of his fist. "How could I have known? I never would've—I'm so sorry. I'm . . . I'm sorry."

Her voice was nearly a whisper. "My mother is making arrangements. Is it all right if I call you later with funeral home details?"

He coughed and let out a deep sigh. "Yes, please. I want to know."

"I've got other calls. Goodbye, Mr. Curtis."

"Call me Gavin."

"Goodbye, Gavin."

"I'm sorry."

The phone fell to the floor as he buried his face in the bed, screaming. Gavin wailed until his throat felt as raw as if he'd gargled thumbtacks and acid. Moments later, a realization set in, and he shot to his feet.

"Oh, no! Jo! If she could get to Monica in California, Torri could get to Jo there!"

He scrambled for the phone. Scrolling to her number, he tried to arrange in his mind what he was going to tell her.

"Be careful?" What good would that do? Monica had been safe inside a restaurant, eating a salad, when Torri got to her.

It was dialing. He canceled the call before it connected.

He'd have to handle this himself.

There hadn't been a sound from the device since he'd submerged it in the tub. If a little water quieted it down, what would happen beneath a lot of water?

His heart swelled with hatred and the pain of guilt.

"I'll throw that bitch of a machine from the bridge and let it sink to where it'll never hurt anyone again."

He burst through the bathroom door and clicked on the light. To his astonishment, the rolls of paper crammed in from the night before were gone. Unlike the rest of the suite, the air was as thick and humid as a greenhouse. The strong scent of lavender filled the small space, causing him to cough.

Glancing into the filled tub, his heart skipped a beat. The surface of the water was now a deep burgundy sludge the consistency of coagulated blood. Gavin instinctively pressed his body against the opposite wall as he gasped to reclaim his breath. Whatever the fluid was, it was too opaque to tell if the typewriter remained in it. On the wall behind the tub, a full-sized, distorted silhouette of a human body oozed down the tile, leaving dark red streaks.

Has she come through? Was the typewriter gone? Somehow, he didn't think so.

Small bubbles on the surface of the goo splattered and popped as other bubbles formed to take their place.

Mustering the courage to move closer to the foul-smelling liquid, he pulled at the shower curtain. Some of the rings snapped apart, falling into the tub. Gavin hesitated, watching the goo absorb the plastic hoops slowly sinking into it.

He stood on the toilet seat and reached for the shower curtain rod. When it detached, he quickly slid the remaining rings off the end, allowing the plastic curtain to gather on the floor.

He stabbed at the murky liquid with the metal rod until it connected with something solid. He wasn't certain if he should be relieved or troubled that the device was still there.

"So gross," he said, attempting to shove the object to the back of the tub. It didn't budge an inch. To apply more force, Gavin stepped down, turned to the side of the tub, and then pushed behind him like a Venetian gondolier. This time, the machine slowly scraped across the acrylic bottom of the tub until it came to a rest at the back.

Gavin was going to need as much room as he could get, so he removed the rod from the bathroom. He did his best to ignore the dark red droplets falling from the end of the pole and leaving a trail on the floor. He didn't want to know what that stuff was. If he thought about it too much, he'd lose his nerve for what he was about to do.

He knelt, his knees sliding on the bunched-up polyurethane curtain. Turning his head to the side, Gavin took a deep breath and plunged his hand into the tub. The unsettling warmth of the liquid was unexpected, and he fought down the urge to retch. Fingers sliding on the bottom of the muck, he managed to grasp the stopper and twist it loose. Tossing the cap on the floor, Gavin shook the runny mess from his forearm. From the elbow to wrist, it tingled as if he'd fallen asleep on it.

Seconds later, a large air bubble the size of a fist erupted from above the drain of the tub, followed by a steady gurgling sound.

Gavin returned to his feet.

The thinner part of the substance below the gelatinous crust began to empty out. As it drained, a residue that looked like a mixture of tomato paste and dark red ink lined the sides of the tub. Clumps of a sinewy membrane floated atop the soupy contents. Though a third of it had drained through the plumbing, the putrid smell hadn't dissipated.

Was she reconstituting herself in the bathtub—rebuilding herself from the life energy she'd stolen from Misa Kawaguchi, the bike boy, and Monica? How long did he have?

Gavin covered his nose with his clean arm as the slop lowered to reveal the top of the machine. Rubbery strands crisscrossed the exposed part of the typewriter like thick spider webs, and the parchment looked like stained polyester.

Chewing his lip, he pictured Monica and thought of her family's grief. He returned to the bed and yanked the comforter away from the headboard, and the pillows flew across the mattress, followed by the produce box.

Back in the bathroom, he draped the comforter over the machine and scooped it up, transforming the bedspread into a makeshift cloth sack. He hoisted it out, careful to not drip the gunk onto his feet as he hurried to the center of the room.

Gavin returned to the bathroom, washed the slime from his arm, and then urinated. Halfway through, he heard the unmistakable clacking of the typewriter. He zipped up and rushed back into the suite in time to see twitching movements under the comforter. When he pulled back the covering, the typed question shocked him.

WHO IS THE FROG, AND WHO IS
DISSECTING?

Gavin jumped back from the machine. He'd never told anyone about that scene with the frog. Even as his mother had applied ice to his swollen face and busted lip, he hadn't told her what he'd done to provoke the older boys into beating him.

Knowing that she could access his dreams, his thoughts, and his memories terrified him. How could he expect to outsmart someone who knew his thoughts?

He unfolded the towel that was twisted into an origami swan shape.

"No more typing!" he yelled while wedging it into the opening between the typewriter's hammers and the platen against the paper.

The high-pitched chirping of the hotel phone on the nightstand startled him.

"Who could that be?"

He eyed the bundle of the typewriter and comforter on the floor as he stepped around it. He allowed the phone to ring once more before removing it from the base.

"Hello, who is this?"

"Uh, Mr. Curtis, this is the front desk. You have a visitor—a reporter by the name of Horace Whetstone."

Oh God, she's here!

His heart raced with panic. "Tell her that she has to leave here right now. She has to go right now! It's not safe for her to be here!"

The character of Horace Whetstone had pursued Damien Marksman for the entirety of his fictional detective career. Whetstone, an obnoxious reporter who was always on the heels of the vampire warlock, threatened to find the evidence that would reveal Damien for who and what he really was. Josephine was in the lobby and was using Horace's name for grins.

"Sir, I said Horace, a man—an older gentleman."

"A man?" Gavin asked, completely confused. "Who could—"

"Yes, sir. A man in biker clothing."

"A biker?" Gavin tried to rearrange the pieces of the puzzle in his mind to make them fit. Then he recognized the man's voice in the background of the call. "Billy?" He closed his eyes and pressed the receiver to his ear. The man on the other end demanded that the desk clerk give him the phone. Billy Cavanaugh's rough baritone was unmistakable.

What's he doing here?

He turned to look at the machine on the floor and felt clammy.

"Sir, he's very insistent about seeing you, but I can have security—"

"What? No. Wait, he doesn't know which room I'm in, right?"

"No, sir, of course not."

"Good, then tell him to . . . " Gavin pounded his forehead with his fist. "Just tell him I'll be right down to see him."

He slammed the phone down as the clerk said, "Very good, sir."

He ran to the elevator and rushed inside as soon as it opened. He had to get Billy and whoever was with him to leave—to escape to safety.

When the doors opened on the fifth floor, Gavin repeatedly tapped at the button to close them again while blocking the other guests' access inside. "Sorry, but it's an emergency."

Two young children dressed in bathing suits jumped back to hide behind their mother, and she lifted oversized sunglasses as she shouted, "You're a jerk, mister!"

Gavin pressed the button again, and the door slid shut.

As he rode down the final floors, he realized that his logic about getting his visitors to safety was flawed. Torri had been able to get to Monica thousands of miles away. She'd certainly be able to harm Billy and whoever was with him if she wanted to, wherever they went.

But he still felt a sense of urgency. He thought about how every minute wasted was a minute that Torri grew stronger. Every second that slipped away moved them closer to her so-called "arrival" from whatever realm of existence she presently occupied. He could feel it happening. Like an undertow in his psyche, the device pulled at him. No longer could he ignore the unsettling sensation of something rifling through his mind as if thumbing through a Rolodex. That some*thing* was a some*one*—Torri Barta.

Madame Kovács had warned him that her miscalculated incantation upon the device would somehow commandeer its user. He thought of how she'd told him that it was establishing a pathway for Torri to cross between her world and this one. He couldn't deny that the process had already begun within him, but what could be done to stop its progress? How could he sever this vile connection—or at least stop the waterwheel of his mind from turning and supplying the energy for her to transform?

He needed time to think, and Billy and company were an obstacle at the moment—an obstacle he had to get rid of urgently.

The elevator opened, and he hurried to the front desk at a speed that turned heads. Leaning over the counter, just as the clerk had told him, was a man in his mid-seventies dressed in leather chaps, a denim jacket, and harness boots. He turned and presented a model's stance as Gavin approached. "Like my duds?"

"Billy, where's Jo?" he asked in a huff.

The older man extended a veiny but strong and steady hand to Gavin, saying, "That Horace Whetstone bit was pretty good, huh?"

Gavin ignored the gesture, scanning the area for Josephine. "Where's Jo? Is Beverly with you?"

Billy lowered his hand and tugged at his fingerless gloves. "Josephine's not here, Sport. You made her promise not to come check on you, so she sent me instead." He pointed the wadded gloves in the younger man's direction. "I've gotta say, though, you don't look so hot. You're as pale as a sheet, like you've seen a ghost or something."

"I sorta have. Look, I can't explain, but it's really not a good idea for you to be here right now."

Noticing the clerk at the counter leaning in to listen, he put a hand on Billy's back and guided him away from the desk. "I know this is kind of rude, and I'll explain when I have the chance, but let me get you a cab back to the airport."

As they passed an alcove of lobby couches, Billy made a break for it and slumped down into a posh couch. "I'm not going to the airport."

Gavin reluctantly sat on the couch facing his. He tried to keep his voice low. "I can't go into it, but it really is not a good idea for me to have you here now."

The laugh lines and crow's feet around Billy's eyes tripled. "It's not a good idea for me, either. Wait till Beverly finds out that I rode my hog here."

"You drove your Harley all the way here?"

"Yep, got the bugs in my teeth to prove it." Billy comically mimed picking his teeth.

This is gonna be harder than I thought.

The man's hairline had receded since the last time Gavin had seen him. More hair formed his grey speckled beard than remained atop his head.

"Anyway, Josephine said you were acting a little off and might need some help working out some story arc or something, so she called in the cavalry. So here I am." He slid the denim sleeve back on his left arm, exposing an expensive-looking watch. "I'm all yours for the next hour and a half. Fire at will." He put a hand to the side of his mouth and whispered, with a devilish grin, "Beverly thinks I'm at the golf course."

Gavin was in a hurry to get him on his way, but the statement dumbfounded him. "Since when do you play golf?"

He tugged his beard and let out a mischievous laugh. "I don't, not a single hole, but I got a country club membership at a place that's a few miles down the road from a Store-All unit. That's where I keep my scooter." Billy's blue eyes twinkled when he said it.

"Billy, I mean it. I'm right in the middle of something important, and I really can't be down here right now. I know that you've ridden a long way to get here." Gavin stood. "I appreciate that, I really do. But you've gotta go."

How can I explain to you that dead Torri Barta is trying to regenerate her physical form in my suite?

He reached to help the old man up.

Billy batted the hand away and stopped smiling. "The day I let you tell me what I can do and where I can and cannot go is the day that I—"

"Billy, I'm sorry. There's just something going on."

"Like what?" The old man's expression soured. "Well?"

Gavin didn't blame him for being perturbed. Billy had come a long way to be shut down and sent packing. This was the inversion of their relationship. Though he frequently disagreed with his mentor, he never told him no. It was unheard of.

Billy stood up and put his hand on Gavin's shoulder. The firm weight of it caused him to yield and sit back down.

Billy's harsh Marine face softened to a concerned expression. "Seriously, what's rolling around in that head of yours? What's going on?"

"Something otherworldly, something evil."

This seemed to cheer him up. "So you *are* working on a story."

Gavin looked straight ahead at the floor. "Not a story."

Billy's countenance was contemplative and serious for a moment, and then he erupted into unrestrained laughter.

"Billy, I'm serious. Something's going on, something unnatural. I know it sounds crazy."

The seriousness returned to Billy's tone, and he shrugged. "Well, Beverly tends to be the more spiritual one of the two of us. I think . . . " He paused and rubbed at his beard for a few seconds. "I think she'd say that there are things we don't understand, things that are beyond us—beyond our comprehension. I'd have to agree. To quote Hamlet, 'There are more things in heaven and earth, Horatio, than are dreamt of in your philosophy.'" He leaned in and spoke softly. "We humans think we've got the universe all figured out—everything quantified so that we can slide it in a little drawer, say 'That's that,' and move on. But in truth, we know and understand about as much as a cat chasing a laser pointer on the ground."

He tugged at the beard again. "So whatever it is, Gavin, let me help you. Whatever this is, the two of us can handle it together."

Gavin's eyes were misty. He stood up before Billy could see them. He said in as firm of a voice as he could muster, "Sorry, I have to do this myself. And I need you to go. You need to go. Go now. If you don't leave, I'll have to make you."

Billy bumped Gavin as he stood up. He was half a foot shorter than the writer was, but he had a presence that was nine feet tall. "And just how would you make me?"

"Billy, please . . . just—"

"Show me. I want to see how you'll make me leave."

Gavin's heart was breaking. He didn't want to hurt this man. He loved him.

"Come on, Gavin. Show me."

He never calls me by name.

He leaned in and tightened up. His words were curt. "If I go over to the desk over there," Gavin pointed over his shoulder, "and tell them that you're a reporter or paparazzi hounding me—or better yet, a crazed stalker—the security in this place will throw you to the curb in a heartbeat."

Billy's eyes narrowed to thin slits as he scratched the back of his leathery neck.

Gavin bit his lip, bracing himself for Billy's rebuttal.

Finally, the man simply shook his head in disgust and let out a "Pfffft!" He exaggerated his movements as he put his gloves on. "What's gotten into you? You should be ashamed, threatening to have me tossed out. I oughta crack your jaw, talking to me like that." Billy stared, waiting for Gavin to answer, but a response never came. Exasperated, Billy added, "I'll be eating at the Burger Boy a mile north of here if you should come to your senses within the next few minutes."

Without a word, Billy stormed off in the direction of the automatic doors.

Gavin called out, "I'm sorry! We'll talk at your party next week."

Billy raised his hand without turning around or slowing his pace. Gavin thought he heard him answer "Whatever," but he couldn't be certain.

Gavin let out a sigh of relief mixed with a fair amount of shame as he turned to the bank of elevators. The metal clicks and jangles of the man's biker boots made Gavin look back at him. He was nearly to the exit.

He couldn't shake the feeling that he'd never see Billy Cavanaugh again.

Ten

GAVIN SHIVERED WHEN HE TOUCHED THE DOOR HANDLE of the suite. The brass was frosty cold, and the condensation wet his hand. Wiping the droplets on his pants, he closed the door behind him as gently as possible. His breath was a vapor before him, and his heart drummed madly in his chest.

It's cold enough to hang meat in here. It must be getting close to happening.

He tucked his key card into his wallet and puffed into his rapidly numbing hands. Across the room, the machine looked exactly as he'd left it, bundled in the comforter on the floor.

Without warning, a round of ear-splitting raps erupted from the machine.

Gavin's heart was in his throat. He forced himself to take a step forward to see what was typed and destroy the words. Even as cold as the room was, Gavin felt feverish and clammy as he crept forward.

He expected something horrific about Billy, but the message was even more dire.

LEAVE AGAIN AND THEY DIE.

He shuddered and felt his knees go weak.

As he bent to reach the keyboard, the rollers automatically advanced the sheet upward as if to provoke him into a rebuttal. He knew what the typed line meant and whom it referred to, but he was compelled to ask. Kneeling on the floor, he cautiously pecked out three simple characters.

WHO

The response came quickly as the device backspaced and added two words in front of Gavin's letters.

YOU KNOW WHO

He had no doubt that Torri had the ability to get to Josephine and the others, to make good on the threat just like she'd gotten to Monica. He massaged his temples. There must be a way to get control over the situation—over Torri and the device. Over himself.

"Everybody wants something. Everybody does what they do for a reason."

He used the wall to steady himself as he rose to his feet. "So what is it? What is it that *you* want, Torri? Your baby's dead. Your mother doesn't want anything to do with you, not like this. She's afraid of you—of what you've become. So what does coming over get you? You wanna kill Barta? Or is he already dead? The boy at the restaurant said Barta hasn't been seen for years. He's already gone, isn't he?"

Gavin waited for a response and then shouted, "Isn't he?"

He paced the floor. "Hasn't there been enough death? There's nothing for you on this side. I refuse to help you!"

The machine was silent.

A mix of fear and anger raged through him as he shouted, "I know you're in here, whatever you are!"

The pressure was building in his throbbing head, feeling like it would explode at any second. "Torri, why are you doing this? Tell me. Why?"

The room went dark, and Gavin let out a gasp. He waited a few seconds for his eyes to acclimate to the change, but it didn't help. It was impossibly dark, given that it was morning. Reaching into his pocket, Gavin fumbled for his cell phone. He could use its glow to maneuver around the suite.

After a few desperate attempts to activate it, he realized that it was in vain. But how could it be dead? He had just talked to Monica's sister a little while ago.

Using the wall as a guide, he carefully inched toward the balcony. Though he took slow, measured steps so as not to lose his balance, he still hit the edge of the desk hard enough to make him curse.

The sickly smell of lavender invaded the darkness. He felt like he was suffocating, drowning in a room full of air.

Amber light flickered from under the bathroom door, and there was the sound of running water. He thought of the gelatinous mass he'd drained earlier from the tub. Was she in there?

His legs propelled him toward it one staggering step at a time, moving him awkwardly like an extra in a bad zombie movie.

He knew that he'd demanded an explanation from her, but now he wasn't sure he wanted the answer. What would he find in there?

Cautiously moving past the typewriter on the floor, he didn't dare to touch or acknowledge it. He took small steps, timed with the slow flickers of amber light from beneath the closed door.

Warmth emanated from the bathroom door as he moved closer to it. When he was less than five feet away, the knob turned clockwise on its own.

Gavin froze in place, trying to control his breathing to keep from hyperventilating.

The door burst open, startling him. A blast of steam escaped, making him cough. Inside, the faucet that was running the hot water shut off with a sharp squeak.

Flickering light reflected off the crumpled shower curtain on the floor. The splattered sides of the basin and tiles would not have looked worse if a large pig had exploded in the tub. The smeared silhouette on the wall was gone.

Gavin took an apprehensive step forward, crossing the threshold of the doorway. The steam settled enough for Gavin to see something written in the moisture of the fogged-up mirror. He moved closer, inhaling sharply when he read it: "Adulterer."

The bathroom door slammed shut.

Trembling, Gavin reopened it. There was the pained moaning of a woman. He sensed that someone was in the other part of the suite.

Is that her? Has Torri come through?

He moved slowly, but his heart beat double-time. Cautiously exiting the bathroom, his eyes adjusted to the deep crimson glimmer that bathed the area. He was reminded of the red vision of the kitchen when he'd first held the typewriter in Béla's warehouse. Was he about to see the younger version of Torri? Torri Kovács typing on her favorite plaything?

He took another step toward the sound. He couldn't determine the source of the light. It wasn't from the overhead light or lamps. It was if everything in the room glowed in a phosphorescent red, growing brighter as the moans grew louder and then fading until the next rise.

The temperature of the room went back to normal again. Then, behind him, the flickering amber bulb above the sink made a pop as it exploded into a showering burst of sparks.

When he turned back toward the sounds of pain, a cleaning cart was before him—except that it wasn't. The image of the cart glowed red and wobbled as if he were looking at it from underwater. He reached out to touch the blurred object but only felt cool wisps of air. On the bed, glowing figures moved. It was as if a scene was being projected in red light on top of his suite.

He focused on the glowing figures on the bed and realized the woman wasn't in pain. The female form lifted and fell in time to sounds of ecstasy. The glowing ghost figure of a man lay beneath her, also fading in and out of view. His muscular hands gripped the woman's hips with every upward thrust.

"Torri?" Gavin whispered, moving closer, then gulping. "Mr. Barta?"

He moved to the opposite side of the bed.

Why is she forcing me to watch this?

That the bundled antique typewriter didn't exist in either plane terrified Gavin more than the ghostly couple before him.

The face of the woman looked different from the image in the newspaper clipping. The features were more slender, the eyes narrower, the nose more petite—she was Asian.

Gavin remembered Theo's account of what had happened in this room many years before and realized what he was watching—what Torri Barta was showing him.

He took a step in the direction of the front door, but it wasn't there. In its place was a door-sized rectangle outlined in a pulsating red trim.

It opened.

Bright, amber light in the shape of a woman's dress poured into the entry—the yellow dress from his dream. She was here.

The figure threw down an access key as the faux door behind her closed. The image shoved the ghostly cleaning cart into the bureau, causing it to topple with a crash. She produced a small-caliber pistol from her handbag and took slow, determined steps.

Attempting to remove himself from the line of fire, Gavin stumbled toward the corner of the room.

The events from the past took center stage, shining through with unmistakable clarity.

The image of Torri approached the couple.

That the two lovers hadn't noticed her and failed to notice the noise of the cleaning cart infuriating her even more. Only when the gun was placed against the maid's head did they stop.

The man shouted at her, "Torri, don't be a fool! Put that away!"

Without a word, she mechanically aimed the gun at Barta's naked chest.

The hammer clicked as she readied the pistol to end him.

He pleaded. "Okay, baby, I made a mistake. I'm . . . I'm sorry. Please put that away."

The trembling, naked woman straddling Barta didn't move.

Barta shouted in a voice that reeked of desperation. "Think about what you're doing. This isn't the way."

Torri wiped her eyes with her free hand.

To Gavin's astonishment, she turned the gun to her own temple. "You're making me do this. You!"

The maid took the opportunity to slide off Barta, taking the sheet with her as she fled the room.

After the ghostly door slammed, Torri turned back to her husband. "You did this to me! You said you wanted a baby, and then—"

Barta sat up with his back against the headboard, attempting to conceal the evidence of his arousal with a pillow. "Please put the gun away. You don't need to do this. I'll give you a divorce if you want. Whatever you want, just tell me."

"Whatever I want?" she screamed. "What I want is gone! What I wanted was *you*, but not now. Not after this."

Gavin's eyes grew wide as Torri's yellow dress burned the bright orange and red colors of flame. She pointed the gun at Barta again.

"Torri, no, don't!" Barta shouted. "The baby! Think of the baby!"

After a few seconds of intense contemplation, she slowly clicked the hammer down with her thumb. "Yes." She sniffed. "Think of the baby. How could I leave the baby with some-one"—she corrected herself—"*something* like you?"

Gavin saw the rigidity drain from her muscles and her arm go limp by her side.

Barta's shadowy figure must have seen it, too, as he made a move to get closer to her. Gavin wasn't sure if the gesture was to comfort her or to simply take the gun from her. Either way, it wasn't received well.

Torri pointed the gun at him for a third time, shouting, "Stay away! You stay away from me!"

Barta retreated to his original position against the head-board.

"Just stay away from me!" Torri threw the pistol at his head. The throw was awkward and missed her target by a foot or more, but her message was received loud and clear.

She bounded over the debris of the spilled cart and rushed from the room. Hoping to escape, Gavin followed her, hurrying through the phantom cleaning products scattered on the floor.

He reached the door—the real door—only to discover that the handle didn't work.

"Noooooo!" he shouted as he beat against it.

He looked back across the suite toward the memory image of Barta, but it was gone. In his place lay the typewriter, glowing with a fiery red-orange that lit the room.

Gavin returned to alternately working the handle and slapping at the door with sweaty palms. "Someone help! I'm trapped in here! Help me! Please help!" He broke into sobs, shouting, "Help me! I'm Gavin Curtis! There's a . . ."

How could he describe what was happening? The glow from the device was as bright as a spewing volcano. He opted for a lie that would suit what someone passing by might see under the door. "There's a fire in here! There's a fire, and I'm trapped! Help me!"

From out of nowhere, the image of the bookstore clerk popped into his mind.

Fire!

Gavin raced across the suite to the desk chair. He positioned it beneath the sprinkler on the ceiling and stood on the seat. Setting off the fire alarm would force guests into the hall. They'd hear him and get security to open his door from the outside.

It was a long shot, but it was all he had.

As he tried to ignite his lighter, the overlay image of the room from the past started spinning. His room remained stationary, but the room of Torri's memory started to rotate, accelerating like a children's merry-go-round.

Determined to set off the sprinkler, Gavin closed his eyes to block out the dizzying images around him. He flicked his lighter, but as the room spun faster, it produced a wind that snuffed out the flame every time.

He opened his eyes to see why it wasn't working, a miscalculation he paid for by dropping the lighter, and it was caught in the increasingly fast whirlwind and spun around the room.

The items, furniture, and structure of the room from Torri's memory revolved around him at an incredible rate of speed. This resulted in a vortex of cool air, capturing the smaller objects of the suite, including the lighter, and hurling them in a wide circle around the room.

Gavin was frozen in fear and amazement as the phantom tornado knocked over the metal bed lamp, slung a pen and notepad against the wall, and even unplugged the clock radio. Everything small and lightweight in the suite spun clockwise.

The only stationary object other than the furniture was the brightly glowing typewriter on the bed. It was the hub—the eye of the storm—and all the loose items orbited it.

Gavin held on to the back of the chair. It felt as if the machine was trying to suck him into itself or to draw him to it.

He fixed his vision on the chair and lowered himself to the ground. "Torri, make it stop! I'm not typing anything for you—or whatever it is that you want. Make this stop, all of it!"

The image of Torri reappeared next to the machine on the bed, her hair lifting slightly as if by a spring breeze. The sharp crack of typewriter hammers cut through the noise of the room.

"No more typing! I command you to speak! I know you can. I just heard you. Now make it stop!"

"You command me?" an incredulous feminine voice asked, coming from everywhere at once as the machine typed her words. "You are nothing, simply a means to an end."

The whirlwind abruptly snatched the chair from Gavin's side. It spun around the room a few times before shattering with a loud crack against the wall.

Gavin felt faint and nauseated.

Shouting above the noise of items striking the walls, he asked, "What . . . what do you want?" His fists were knotted and tight, but he knew there was nothing tangible to strike. "I told you, there's nothing here for you!"

Torri lowered her hands to her ghostly hips. The typewriter hammered out her words into the page as if taking dictation. "You still haven't figured it out? Taking my mother's machine, bringing it into Room 719, what you did with your little slut? You set all of this into motion. And there's no going back now!"

The carriage return of the antique made a loud ding, accompanied by a bright flash of red. Gavin barely dodged the remains of the wooden desk chair hurled in his direction. The shards punctured the wall behind him like wooden daggers before the furious cyclone swept them away again.

"Monica was a long time ago!" Gavin shouted. "That's between me and Josephine. It's none of your business."

"Wrong!" The wind within the suite grew. Gavin had to lean into the direction he tried to walk, like an unfortunate weatherman assigned to give a live report from a hurricane.

Slowly and methodically, he placed one foot in front of the other until he reached the sliding door. It was opaque, as if the sheet of glass had been coated with tar.

He played the hunch that what he was seeing was false, just as fake as the exchange that he'd witnessed between Barta and his lover. Gavin reached for the handle to slide it open and pulled back when he felt an electrical shock.

She doesn't want me over here, which can only mean one thing— the way out!

He rammed the door with his shoulder a few times, but the glass didn't break. Each attempt delivered a punishing jolt of electricity through his body.

The fury that Torri displayed showed that he was on to something. She voiced an unearthly scream. "If you leave me here before the transformation is complete, everyone you've ever known will die before their time, and you'll be the last to go so that you'll see it's true! I'll search your memories like a catalog, calling up everyone you've ever met. What a lucky girl I am to pair up with someone who's as well known as you, Gavin Curtis—someone who knows so many people to choose from."

The sound of her sarcastically uttering his name gave him chills as he returned to the desk and lined it up with the sliding door. He batted away the small objects that rained on him from the whirlwind—a pencil, the empty carton of cigarettes, the clock radio, and his own dirty socks.

Sensing that her power was growing, he knew that he had to make this count.

Tossing the laser printer to the ground, Gavin pressed his shoulder against the edge of the ornate desk and rammed it into the glass. After a loud impact, he desperately checked for damage, but there wasn't a single crack in the slate-black surface.

Torri protested. "I'll extract every memory out of your brain. You've become a conduit, and I'll destroy everyone you've ever thought about, everyone you've met, everyone you love."

The typing reached an inhuman speed. "I'll feast on their energy as they leave. Do you hear me? All of them—everyone—and send your unfaithful, cheating heart into cardiac arrest!"

Ignoring her, he tried again, this time with the desk already pressed against his target. He lunged forward, resisting the pull of the vortex. A thin line of white light no wider than a pinprick peeked through the glass. The fracture in the glass looked like a black-and-white photograph of a lightning storm, but it was undeniably there. He was breaking through. Encouraged, he returned to the task, finding an extra reserve of strength. He felt the white-hot glow on his back from the machine on the bed.

Torri sounded desperate. "I'll destroy them!"

Gavin shoved at the desk. More random cracks of light splinters shone through the glass.

"I'll kill them all, and it'll be your fault!"

The fractures grew, looking like a drunken spider's web stemming from the collision point.

"Do you hear me? I'll kill them all just like I did with your choking little Mexican whore!"

He heaved at the desk as he enunciated, "Monica didn't do anything wrong!"

Large shards of glass snapped and struck the surface of the desk as it broke through a quarter of the way.

It worked!

The specter shrieked and wailed, but Gavin didn't turn around. He shoved at the desk through what remained of the shattered glass. The smell of soft summer rain filled his nostrils. The swollen grey sky was the most beautiful thing that he'd ever seen. He laughed and cried simultaneously.

As the desk made it two-thirds of the way onto the balcony, the front legs skidded on the concrete and snapped with a loud crunch. The abrupt lack of support from the front sent

Gavin's end upward. He slid forward uncontrollably and struck his chin on the edge, slamming his teeth together, then hit the edge with his forehead, leaving a deep gash.

Determined to break free from the horrors of the room, he crawled under the desk, lifting the fallen end when he was outside.

The typing ceased.

When he made it to the balcony's railing, he looked back inside the room. Though the room was a wreck, the whirlwind had stopped. More importantly, the glow from the machine was gone, and so was Torri Barta. Or at least she wasn't visible.

What's she up to? Is she coming through? Is it starting?

The rain picked up, but he didn't mind the drops hitting his head and soaking his clothes.

He felt reborn.

Gavin surveyed the area for help, but the parking lot was empty. He felt his shirt pocket for his cell to call the front desk until he remembered that it was dead. Behind him, the rain tapped a steady pattern on the metal railing, striking the same discordant note over and over again. The other raindrops bounced off the smaller fragments of broken glass, making them dance in the tiny puddles that collected on the concrete.

Gavin felt something heavier than the rain bump his shoe, and he looked down. He instinctively jumped back when a small, dark-green creature leaped from his foot to join another one near him.

He turned to the destruction the desk had made of the glass door. Thousands of frogs were in the suite. He remembered the story of the plague of frogs he was taught at Catholic school in St. Anne's Elementary. The sudden, unnatural manifestation of frogs was shocking, yet he found it strange that Torri was using the memory of the frog dissection against him. It wasn't as if he had a phobia of frogs. She'd misinterpreted the memory.

Whatever her capabilities of reading his thoughts and dreams were, they were fallible. She still had to interpret their meaning. This revelation inspired him to believe that there might be a way out of this after all.

For the moment, the horde of frogs in the suite moved toward him in random, uncoordinated leaps and bounces. With a wide, sweeping motion of his foot, he slid the four small ones that had already gathered near him to the lip of the patio balcony. They fell from the ledge, too small for him to see their impact on the lot below, not that he was able to see much of anything through the downpour.

The frogs felt real enough, not like the phantom cleaning cart. More of them emerged from around the sides of the broken desk.

How much weight can the balcony hold before collapsing?

He ushered a second wave of frogs, mixed with bits of broken glass, over the edge. His drenched clothing made each move clumsy, and thick strands of his wet hair continually fell into view, blocking his sightline. Frantically brushing it out of his eyes, he looked at the bed.

While frogs of all sizes covered the bedspread, they gave the machine a wide berth. Next to it, they outlined a perfectly proportioned human form free of frogs—as if an invisible person were lying on the bed with her arm around the typewriter.

He studied the spot, expecting to see Torri materialize in it at any second.

I have to throw it over the edge before it kills me.

The frogs came around the sides of the slanted desk more quickly. The writing table vibrated from the bombardment of hundreds of them making their way onto the balcony.

He grabbed the edge of the desk that angled upward and rocked it back and forth. Finally, there was enough momentum for him to heave it toward himself. He jumped clear as the top of the desk landed flat on the balcony with a sickening squishing sound. He closed his eyes.

I'm sorry.

The noise from the frogs was considerably louder now that he was in the suite, but at least he was out of the rain. Everywhere he stepped, he crushed and crunched the creatures beneath his feet. He tried not to think about all of these poor frogs he was killing, only concentrating on throwing the typewriter over the balcony—but he couldn't ignore it. The soles of his shoes slid on their guts and blood-slickened bodies, making each step both awful and uncertain.

He felt like he'd have a heart attack.

As he made it to the bed, he witnessed the impossible again: half a dozen frogs of various sizes emerged from the center opening of the device and hopped to the edge of the bed.

So that's where they're coming from.

He glanced at the paper roll from the machine. For the most part, it was a word-for-word transcript of all that Torri had threatened. He ripped the sheet from the device. He was fed up with all of this.

Gavin grabbed the device. Expecting it to shock or burn his hands, he was surprised to feel the cool sides of its metal casing. More frogs exited from the center opening of the device. Gavin batted them away before the next batch materialized.

The machine was heavy—too heavy. Despite straining with all his might, he couldn't lift it from the bed. He'd have a better chance of lifting a cement truck. He slid his hands between the bottom of the device and the bed sheets. A tremendous weight pressed down on his hands as if to crush them. Gavin cried out in agony but managed to wrangle them free before they were crushed.

Another wave of frogs appeared from within the machine as the box spring of the bed bent inward and collapsed. The silhouette of Torri's form on the bed filled in with frogs as they toppled downward.

Where was she?

Gavin lost his footing on a cluster of frogs. His soaked and weary body fell hard, but never actually made contact with the suite's carpet. The decorative pattern was hidden beneath quivering mounds of green.

Frogs from around the room made their way to where he lay. He struggled to sit up, but the weight of them held him down. They jumped onto his head and into the openings of his clothing. A tiny one found its way into his mouth, which was more than he could bear. He spat it out and kept spitting as he rolled to one side and then to a pushup position. Pushing himself up along with countless frogs, Gavin clumsily returned to his feet. Frogs flung off in every direction as he shook his head and limbs violently. Gavin hobbled on the backs of crushed frogs on his retreat to the balcony, feeling nauseated by the sensation of the frogs under his feet.

In a panic, he scanned the parking lot for any sign of help, but he only saw spears of rain ricocheting off evenly spaced cars.

The drops were colder than before, and a large mass of dark clouds swelled on the horizon. This wasn't going to be a summer cloud burst.

Gavin moved past the upturned desk to the railing closest to the other balcony and wiped the water from his face. "Hey! Hey, is anyone there?"

The distance was less than six feet from where he was to the railing of the neighboring enclosure. The challenge was that it wasn't a straight shot. To ensure privacy, each balcony followed the contour of the round building, like ends of flower petals pointing away from the center. The only way to see another guest was for both of them to lean forward.

The croaking noise of the frogs grew louder as they exited the room to the outside.

Gavin moved past the upturned desk to the rail closest to the other balcony and shouted again. "Hello, can you hear me? Is anyone there? Help! Help me!"

Gavin's heart pounded like it would explode. There were units positioned diagonally above to the left and right, but he could only see the underside of them. He returned his focus to the neighboring balcony.

He could never make a jump like that, especially in the rain.

He turned back to the broken sliding door. The amphibian exodus had already grown to three or four layers deep, causing the balcony to shudder under the extra weight.

The darkened sky lit up when a dazzling burst of lightning shot across the heavens. Gavin paused as the bolt crackled with energy, thin, veiny tributaries disappearing from view over the bridge.

A bridge! Yes, a bridge!

He moved with purpose, grabbing the two remaining legs of the desk. Hundreds of frogs of different colors hopped across the now-exposed underside of the desk. With as much strength as he could summon, he skidded the desk right and left across the tops of the helpless creatures, wincing and muttering apologies, until he made it to the balcony's edge. He hoisted it upright, propping the side with the broken legs against the rail. Frogs fell over the side as if being poured from a bucket.

Gavin shoved the desk toward the neighboring balcony with such force that a clang sang out when it slammed into the other side.

Heh, still got a little fight in me, Torri, you bitch!

Gavin wiped the rain from his eyes. Only a few inches of the far left corner of the desk actually balanced on the top of the rail, but it couldn't go any farther. It was alarmingly wobbly, and his blood ran cold as he contemplated what he was about to do.

He told himself that at least if this stunt didn't work—if he died—it would be his own doing and not at the hands of Torri Barta.

The wind howled as he hoisted himself onto the edge of the desk. He knew he couldn't hesitate. If he waited even for a minute, he'd convince himself not to go through with it.

Locking a death grip on the sides of the desk, he inched forward on his knees. His heavy, waterlogged clothing clung to him, and the blood dripping from his forehead kept getting into his eyes. He resisted the temptation to look at anything but the surface of the desk. Even though smears of frog guts made him wince, it was a more welcome sight than the ground seven stories away.

Just as he was beginning to master the agonizingly slow and precarious process of moving forward one limb at a time, another startling explosion of lightning and thunder paralyzed him with fear. He was nearly halfway across, but he was now stuck, frozen in place like a statue, too afraid to proceed and unable to blindly retreat backward. His left hand cramped from clutching so tightly, but both hands refused his command to release their grips from their respective edges. He closed his eyes and sobbed uncontrollably for a minute or so until he began to hyperventilate.

Forcing himself to focus again, Gavin lowered his head and concentrated on breathing. Pain pulsated from white knuckles, shooting through his wrists into weary arms.

He had lost all sense of time. Though his rational mind pleaded otherwise, it felt like he'd been trapped in the middle of the desk for hours.

The noise and vibrations of thousands of frogs gathering on the balcony behind him snapped him out of his daze.

He bit his lip and returned to crawling painstakingly across, first his left hand and then his right hand, followed by his left knee, a shift in his weight, and then his right knee. It was the longest five-and-a-half-foot crawl of his life. Each inch gained was an act of sheer will and defiance of the malicious creature in his suite. Each move was a testament to his refusal to forfeit control to her. He was freakin' Gavin Curtis!

Nearing the edge of the desk, he maneuvered his legs around until he was in a sitting position. Dark smears of frog blood and goo stained the knees of his trousers. He then cautiously scooted on his butt until his feet could touch the concrete. On solid footing, he turned and looked back at the other balcony and exhaled a sigh of relief.

The frogs tried to follow him, but only fell to their deaths in droves off the side of the balcony where the desk bridge was.

Safely away from the hellish scene of Room 719, a question formed in his mind.

Why didn't she kill me just now? A gust of wind would've easily knocked me off. Why did she hold back? Why now?

The answer would have to wait. Gavin took a mental inventory of all that he'd abandoned in the room and decided that everything was replaceable and not even worthy of trying to get the resort to send to him later. He'd made it to safety away from Torri Barta, and it was time to flee this mess as quickly as possible.

Eleven

GAVIN WAS GRATEFUL THAT THE SLIDING DOOR of the neighboring suite was unlocked. He rushed into the room, gasping, "Hello, is anyone in here?"

Wiping the gunk from the desk onto the perfectly made bed, he noted that the suite wasn't as nice and roomy as his was.

"Hello? I'm just walking through. Don't shoot me or anything." The announcement trailed off once he realized there were no personal items anywhere, just a room prepped to receive resort guests.

He picked up speed as he rushed for the front door. He flung it open. A shocked bellhop wheeled a brass-plated luggage valet up to the entrance. They exchanged dumb looks for a second.

A preppy man in his mid-thirties forcibly emerged from behind the bellhop, complaining, "Room 717 is supposed to be empty."

The bellhop's shrug was interrupted when a blonde trophy wife shrieked, "Look at him! He's been shot!"

Gavin realized that he must've been a sight, out of breath and dripping wet, but the kicker was the frog blood on his trousers from the knees down and the blood oozing from his forehead.

He decided to go with it.

"Yeah, that's right. You've gotta get out of here. It isn't safe!"

When the men didn't respond, Gavin pushed his way through the door. He shoved the towering luggage cart, causing some of the smaller bags to fall. "I said go!"

Preppy Man protested, "Hey, what are—"

Gavin cut him off. "We gotta go *now*! There's no time to explain!"

The blonde was already jiggling down the hallway to the elevator.

"Marcia, wait!" the man yelled, starting to trot.

Meanwhile, the bellhop was returning the fallen luggage pieces to their original places on the valet. He pointed to something on the floor.

"You dropped something there."

"Huh?" Gavin looked at the ground at a faded sticky note, a note that had lost its adhesiveness many years ago. He slowly crouched to pick it up.

The bellhop start heading down the hallway, leaving the valet next to 717. He still eyed the wet, bloody man suspiciously.

Gavin turned the note over and saw the small printed image of a unicorn, its horn impaling the stick man that he'd drawn what seemed like a lifetime ago.

"Aren't you comin', mister?" the bellhop asked from the open elevator compartment.

Gavin turned the note over and saw the small printed image of a unicorn, its horn impaling the stickman that he'd drawn for what seemed like a lifetime ago.

He didn't look up. "You go on, kid. I'll take the next one down."

Gently rubbing his fingers over the handwritten note, which read, "This one is you, Gavin. Love, Jo," he muttered, "I love ya too, baby."

He'd gazed at it a thousand times before, but he couldn't peel his eyes off it now.

From nowhere, he remembered Torri's words—that she would use him as a pathway to get to others. He'd witnessed firsthand how her power had amplified from taking the life of exotic dancer Misa Kawaguchi, the kid on the bike, and finally, Monica. He suspected she'd be unstoppable if she had the chance to feast on the dying energy of a few more lives.

Staring at the note in his palm, he sluggishly moved to the elevator.

He extended a finger but hesitated to push the elevator call button.

He couldn't do it. He had to finish this.

He pictured Ms. Hodges, Thad, that annoying Theo guy from the bar and grill, Billy C., and even that Puma-jacket-wearing jerk—every one of them at risk, everybody an unknowing target of the vindictive spirit whom he was fused to and who would be manifesting soon. Though he didn't see or hear her, now that things had settled down a bit, he could feel the time of the transformation drawing closer. It wouldn't be long now—of that he was sure.

And there was Josephine. Why should she be punished for his mistakes? Hadn't she paid enough already?

A tear wet the sticky note, and Gavin sniffed.

How many people had he met over the years at movie premiers and book events? Were those people in danger, too? The toll would be in the thousands. Could he just walk away and allow this spiteful being to destroy all of them?

Clenching his fingers into a ball, he lowered his fist to his side and turned to look down the hallway.

"Aw, Jo," he said, returning his eyes to the unicorn and stick man. "I really need your help here. You always help me, always know just what to do and how to fix what I screw up." He laughed as he sniffed and leaned against the metal threshold of the elevator. "So how do we go about fixing this one?"

Though Gavin imagined himself having a dialogue with his ex-wife, Billy Cavanaugh's voice butted into his head. The imaginary response from the old man was two chilling words: "Reichenbach Falls."

"Hell's bells, Billy. Who invited you into my head?"

Then, all at once, he knew the reason why Torri hadn't pushed him off the balcony with a gust of wind—why she hadn't killed him.

He knew her weakness. More importantly, he knew how to exploit that weakness.

Gavin slowly shook his head from side to side. It was an awful solution.

Addressing the imaginary editor, he pleaded, "You said it didn't even work when Doyle did it in *The Final Problem*."

He studied Josephine's note in his hand, staring at the last two words: "Love, Jo."

The bad idea grew stronger and took root. In his mind's eye, Gavin pictured the scene as if it were straight out of a Damien Marksman story.

It was the worst idea he'd ever had, but he couldn't argue with the logic of it, and what else was there to try? Imaginary Billy, just like the actual Billy, was annoyingly right. And who knows? Maybe Gavin could keep all those people from being harmed.

Maybe he could protect Jo.

Twelve

ADRENALINE COURSED THROUGH HIS VEINS as Gavin slid his key card into the door mechanism one last time. He'd wheeled the cart with the preppy couple's bags up to his room. When the lock clicked open, he stacked their suitcases against the open door. He definitely wasn't going to be trapped in his suite a second time.

The air in the room was moist as the storm raged outside. Most of the frogs had pursued Gavin and fallen off the balcony, but a few stragglers hopped toward him. Ignoring their advances, he wheeled the luggage cart around them, stopping at the bed.

He paused, wondering if Torri knew his plan from reading his thoughts. She'd been wrong about the frogs, assuming that he was afraid of them rather than sympathetic to them. Maybe he could misdirect her now. By force of will, he'd think about anything but his newly devised plan, just to be safe and throw her off the scent.

He took in a slow, deep breath. This was the final round. This was for all the marbles. He exhaled even more slowly.

The room was a mess. It was the kind of destruction that would have made legendary rock stars like Keith Moon envious.

So much for staying at the Droverton Resort ever again. Not that it matters.

He clutched the sticky note with the unicorn and stick man in his hand.

Other than the remaining frogs jumping at his feet and the violent weather outside, the room had an eerie calm to it.

He'd expected Torri to have typed something when he entered, some kind of snarky welcome back message or something, but the typewriter was motionless, still displaying its last message—threats of how she'd kill everyone Gavin knew.

Was she lying in wait? Was this a chess game and his was the next move, or was it something else?

Suspicious of the antique in the middle of the collapsed bed, he slowly bent and positioned his hands to the sides of it. He didn't touch it yet.

He took in another deep breath.

"I love you, Jo." As he said the words, Gavin grabbed the device and heaved, expecting it to still be impossibly heavy. It was its normal weight again, and he stumbled, spinning, and the device landed on its side with a loud crash.

It hadn't shocked or burned him.

Keeping a wary eye on it, Gavin picked up the sticky note that he'd dropped. This was too easy. Something was wrong. Where was she?

He took a pillowcase from one of the pillows on the floor and rammed it between the platens to keep it from typing.

Seconds later, he wheeled the cart to the front of the suite, bulldozing the luggage that propped the door open.

"Sir, I'm going to need you to come with me," a uniformed man said, approaching from the bank of elevators at the other end.

Gavin didn't respond. He just pushed the cart faster.

The olive-skinned man was short but stocky. Since his outfit was dark green, Gavin knew he wasn't a cop, so he was likely unarmed.

The man mumbled something into a radio on his shoulder and then addressed Gavin. "Sir, leave the cart."

Even at a closing distance of fifty feet, it was clear that the man was all muscle. Gavin was at a full run now, and the cart swerved to the left and right. He didn't want to ram this guy, but he'd do whatever he had to do.

The security guard broke into a run toward him. "Sir, I said leave the cart!"

Despite the momentum that Gavin had built up, when the guard grabbed the ornamental brass posts of the cart and dug his heels in, the carrier stopped abruptly.

The typewriter slid forward to the edge, stopped by the brass railing. A clang like a small gong reverberated through the posts.

Gavin also slammed into the cart with his nose and then his forehead. There was a white flash of pain. He feared he'd lose consciousness and wake up in a holding area.

Gotta keep going. Can't stop.

The guard came around the side of the cart. "Are you okay, sir? I'm sor—"

Before Gavin knew what was going on, there was a loud smack, and he felt a sharp pain in his hand and wrist. To his amazement, he'd decked the guy. The pint-sized Atlas was down on the floor, and Gavin had put him there.

"You broke my frickin' nose, you crazy son of a bitch!"

Fights in real life are never like movies or TV, but the blow he'd delivered was straight out of a Damien Marksman fight scene. He'd never hit anyone in his life.

His bewilderment was shaken loose when the bloody man on the ground called for backup.

"Look, man, I'm sorry. I didn't mean to . . . I can't explain why."

The words were lost on the guard as he gave a rambling description of Gavin, finishing by calling him a "perp."

Gavin returned to pushing the cart, accidentally running over the boot of the security officer as he went. "Sorry. Really sorry!"

The elevator came quickly, and Gavin was grateful to see that it was empty.

A few seconds into the elevator's decent, the cabin lights flickered. Then the lights exploded in the same way the bathroom light had blown.

Gavin was in complete darkness for the second time that day.

The compartment stopped moving. He groped until he located the brass posts of the carrier and braced himself. The all-too-familiar clammy sensation accompanied the strong aroma of lavender.

She's in here. I'm trapped in here with her.

His heart was in his throat, but he wasn't afraid to die anymore. He was only afraid of not ending this.

"Torri?" He felt for the sticky note in his damp pockets. "Mrs. Barta? Mrs. Barta, I'm begging you to—"

The deafening strikes from the machine nearly made him jump out of his skin. He covered his ears from the assault as he slammed himself against the farthest corner of the compartment. What had happened to the pillowcase he had stuffed in there?

"No!" he screamed, drowned out by the Gatling-gun rhythm of the typewriter.

He failed to notice the elevator start up, so he was shocked when the doors slid open, revealing light from the resort lobby. Gavin shoved the cart and quickly pushed it by onlookers who froze in their tracks.

The entire lobby gawked at the spectacle, but who could blame them? It was quite a sight. He was wet and haggard from his balcony escape, a dark, viscous substance dripped from his shins, blood dripped from his face, and occasionally, frogs leapt from the cart, but most noticeable was the loud clacking from the typewriter. It sounded like a sequence of long-fuse firecrackers going off at evenly timed intervals.

Adults pulled their children back by their shirt collars, and hobbling retirees scrambled to safety against the walls.

Everyone cleared a path as Gavin shoved the unwieldy cart through the area.

He didn't care what they thought, nor did it matter that each of them avoided eye contact. He had a job to do, and for all he knew, one of them could very well be the machine's next victim if Torri were allowed to get to them.

The security staff must have abandoned their posts in the lobby to help on the seventh floor. Gavin rolled the cart unhindered through the automatic doors and into the covered valet parking zone.

Looking as dumbfounded as everyone inside, the young men of the area didn't offer any resistance. Gavin hurried past them and pushed the carrier from under the awning into the hard, cold rain.

Following the straightest path to the bridge entrance on the hill, Gavin didn't try to avoid the puddles.

Almost done. Almost done.

The barricades were a little over a thousand yards away.

His arms were sore. He did his best to ignore the anguish and fatigue of his legs, but he cursed himself for being so out of shape. Each cumbersome step he took was punctuated by the strikes of the typewriter.

What is she typing?

He didn't dare to look, not yet—not until he reached his destination.

The dark afternoon sky rumbled and exploded with discharges of lightning. Worse than the pounding rain were the gale-force winds that had picked up. It felt as if the rain was being thrown at him—hurled against his face—and the wind was in a shoving match against the cart.

After making it a quarter of the way up the incline of the hill to the barricade, he abruptly halted when a hot, bright flash of light shot up from the ground only a few yards in front of him. The boom followed instantly, and Gavin fell to his butt, startled and covering his ears. It took a moment for him to realize that he hadn't actually been struck by the lightning but had come close.

The cart rolled down the slope away from him.

As he pushed himself up, he dropped Jo's sticky note. He scurried to catch it, but it disappeared in the fury of the wind.

Doesn't matter now.

In the distance, the rolling cart leveled off on the flattened terrain of the parking lot. It bumped into one of the cars in the last row, setting off an alarm. Gavin wearily headed down to the lot, his heart still pounding. He wiped the rain from his face and looked up to the seventh story. He could barely make out the oversized writing desk connecting the two balconies.

The continual noise of the typewriter grew as he approached. He tore the scroll sheet from the carriage and read it.

It was a list of names. Some he recognized—his twelfth-grade English teacher, the man who had done the yard when he and Josephine had lived together, the guy who owned the motorcycle shop near his home, the female barista at his favorite coffee house, his mechanic. Many were unknown to him.

It was a list of targets.

He scanned the sheet for Josephine, Billy, and Beverly until he remembered Torri's promise that she'd kill those he loved last.

Has she already started? Is it happening?

He was horrified. Not knowing what else to do, he wadded it up and tossed it onto the asphalt.

The machine resumed typing.

"Let's see who has the stomach to end this," he said, snatching up the device and carrying it.

The lightning strike from before caused him to abandon the luggage cart. He wasn't sure if the carrier's brass poles and canopy acted as a conductor of electricity or not. He thought there was something about the rubber tires offering some protection, but he wasn't about to take the chance—not after what he'd just been through.

The strikes of the keys shuddered through the metal of the typewriter as he cradled it. He considered removing his shoe to jam it in the mechanism but decided against it. What she typed wouldn't make a difference in a few minutes anyway. He'd be to the top of the bridge soon enough.

Thirteen

GAVIN REACHED THE BARRICADE of the massive bridge. Several five-foot-high plastic barriers were plastered with signage from radio station WHCN 105.9. The notices celebrated the completion of the restoration project, announcing the 5k Fun Walk for the March of Dimes the coming weekend.

There was a gap between two of the barriers, just like Theo had said. The opening was small, but he could squeeze through it.

Placing the typewriter on the shoulder-high ledge of the plastic, he sucked in his gut and shimmied through the crack. The cold rain bouncing off the slick plastic barrier sounded like a continuous round of applause.

Gavin reached for the device from the other side, tore off and discarded another list of names, and proceeded up the four-lane bridge.

Is that all you got, Torri? Threats?

Curiously, the typing stopped.

He was exhausted, but he forced himself to ascend the steep bridge step by step.

Keep going, Gav. Nearly there.

Even through the downpour of rain, he saw faint traces of graffiti that the city had attempted to cover up. Faded spray-painted slogans like "Hungry Waters Bridge – Come on in, the water's fine," "Take the Plunge," and "TKB-Torri Knows Best" ran along the walls of the middle concrete barrier. It was like a twisted shrine to a woman who went nuts decades ago.

Though the rain was brutally cold, the metal of the machine was growing warm to the touch.

"It won't work," a calm female voice said behind him.

Gavin sped up without looking back. He needed to go further up the bridge. A gust of cold wind at his back made him stumble forward, but he didn't drop the device, and he didn't stop.

Gotta get higher.

"I said, what you're doing won't work. Throwing it over won't matter now. Turn around and look at me." Torri's voice sounded satisfied and proud. "I'm past needing it. I'm no longer fused to it—no longer bound to it. And just a few minutes from now, the transformation will be complete. You'll have a front-row seat."

When he didn't answer, Torri shouted with a voice loud enough to block the noise of the storm for a few seconds, "I said *look at me!*"

Holding the typewriter against his chest, he hurried up the incline. At the rate it was heating up, he wasn't certain he'd be able to carry it with his bare hands for much longer.

He ran beneath a lamppost with a surveillance camera mounted to the top of it. The sound of the light exploding behind him filled his ears, but he kept going without looking back.

Can't stop . . . reach the top.

"Stop running!" Torri ordered. "You're going to give yourself a heart attack."

Another gust of cool wind pressed against Gavin's back as a flash of lightning draped across the sky for a few seconds before disappearing.

The device in his hands had a faint, fiery, red-orange glow. As it heated up, the glow intensified.

Keep going.

"I said *stop!*"

He felt a hand shove him, forcing his knees to buckle. The scent of lavender filled the air. He fell forward, stopping his fall with the palms of his hands as they scraped against the pavement. The typewriter tumbled ahead of him, bouncing once and then skidding to a stop a few yards from him.

Gavin pushed himself up on his knees and brushed the gravel from his cut hands. The top of the curved bridge was in view, but farther away than he'd hoped. He'd only made it halfway to his destination.

A red-hot glow emanated from the device, illuminating the area like an overexposed photograph. After a few seconds, the light began to fade as raindrops sizzled and turned to steam on the surface of the device.

The shimmering image of Torri walked into his view with a casual and confident strut. Her ghostly form was unaffected by the storm—a perfect image of her in the yellow dress with her hair softly blowing in a breeze from another time and place. Her appearance was more defined than before, sharper and more detailed than she'd been in the hotel room. She was hardly transparent at all. The emerald necklace around her neck gleamed bright green.

Gavin wiped the rain from his eyes as Torri's form grew brighter and the glow from the typewriter on the pavement behind her began to dim.

Then, like a high-priced CGI effect in one of the Damien Marksman movies, the ghostly image of Torri Barta started to fill in with thousands of tiny, swirling, multi-colored lights that zipped through the area she occupied—a spinning kaleidoscope of colors in a frenzy of energy.

The sight stunned him.

After a few seconds, the dazzle of the lights faded, replaced with flesh tones. The moving specks made it appear as if her skin were boiling, bubbling at varying degrees of temperature.

This was it. She was coming through.

None of the areas were entirely formed yet, allowing Gavin to see rain through the larger openings. It was like looking through an incomplete jigsaw puzzle.

He regained his composure and made a break for the machine while she was distracted. It was now or never. Once she was completely formed, there'd be no stopping her.

As he ran past Torri, he felt a cold blast of air and the concentrated smell of lavender. He reached the typewriter—it was still warm to the touch, but he could handle it. He made his way back to the side of the bridge, ignoring her spiteful laughter.

The woman waved a bubbling finger at him like a grade-school teacher and made a "tsk tsk tsk" sound. "You haven't been paying attention, Gavin."

She moved closer, her visage still shifting to take on solid form. "That was my favorite thing to play with as a little girl, even more than dolls or tea sets, but I told you, I don't need it anymore."

A tremendous gust of wind responded to her uplifted arms. She lowered them and laughed again. "Now we're partners, you and I."

With the machine tightly cradled in his arm, he wiped away more rain from his face with the other hand.

She offered a mocking curtsy. "As much as I appreciate you looking after my toy, you're all I need now. You became the pathway once I had claimed enough energy from the deaths of the boy and your little tramp, Monica, and that bastard child, Misa Kawaguchi—who was a little whore just like her mother."

Gavin closed his eyes and lifted his face to the rain. He let it strike his cheeks for a few seconds.

He was ready.

Continuing to face her, he took small steps backward to the side of the bridge. "Torri, I think I figured something out, but I want to hear it from you. Back at the hotel, why didn't you kill me on the balcony? Just a little push, a little gust of that wind you like so much?"

It was obvious that the question irritated her. Her unfinished form glared brighter for a moment, and her steps toward him took on a defiant stride. "Do you think I'm bluffing? Already, I am becoming more powerful, and after I take a few more of your people, I'll be unstoppable."

"I don't doubt it in the least." He stopped moving backward when he heard the rain ricocheting off the metal railing behind him. He'd made it to where he wanted to be, against the side of the bridge. "Just answer me. Why didn't you do it there, or why didn't you just kill me in my sleep? You could've had some aneurysm pop in my head or something." Shifting the typewriter to the other arm as she approached, he said, "If you can lodge a piece of chicken in someone's throat thousands of miles away, surely you're capable of something simple like that, right?"

Her eyes blazed. Gavin recognized the hateful stare from the way she had looked at him as a child in the vision in Béla's warehouse.

"Don't you believe that I am becoming more powerful?"

"Oh, I think you are. I think that's obvious. But you made a mistake."

The statement noticeably caught her by surprise. "I don't make mistakes."

"Of course you do. You made a mistake by marrying Barta, by having his kid . . . by killing your baby."

A frustrated scream accompanied a chilling blast of air that slammed him against the safety rail of the bridge.

It took a few seconds for him to regain his balance. Straightening himself, he continued, "I think you do make mistakes, even now, even as you are in this form, Mrs. Barta."

"Stop calling me that! My name is Kovács, Victoria Kovács! I despise and reject everything about that man, especially his name."

"Fine then, *Victoria*. What I mean to say is that you need me, at least for a few more minutes, and while I don't understand all of the mechanics of this *doure-sint*-metaphysical-conduit-passageway thing, for this to work—whatever this is—for it to work you need to be connected through me, and that's why you won't kill me. You can't—not yet, at least. Not until the transformation's complete. So that's what I mean, you made a mistake in connecting through me. It's a dead end, and now that I'm on to you, I won't let you take any more lives, not a one."

The ground trembled, electricity filling the sky above their heads. "A dead end? I don't think so. Shall I show you another death? Who shall it be? The old man? Or would you prefer his wife has a heart attack at his birthday party? How's that for a present? But no, I'd prefer not to wait that long. How about I just go to the top of your list to the lovely Josephine?" Her tone reeked of sarcasm. "Crossing a busy intersection can be oh so tricky."

"Listen to me, you crazy bitch! You're not going to touch any of them! I'm not going to let you."

"Hmph, and how can *you* begin to stop *me*?"

"Control. I take the control from you." Gavin leaned in as he said this.

"What do you mean?"

He turned and placed the typewriter on the edge of the guardrail. Positioning himself directly in front of it, he turned to face her.

Her countenance changed. She looked confused. "I said, what do you mean?"

He laughed and took the time to run his fingers through the wet mop of his hair. "So you can't read every thought, can you?" It was his turn for sarcasm. Judging by her unfinished form, he had another few minutes. Speaking in the kind of saccharine-sweet voice that one reserves for talking to a four-year-old, he said, "Now, listen up here, sweetie. I'm gonna think about it really, really hard." Gavin touched his temples with both index fingers and squinted comically as if straining to make a thought bubble appear. "Let's see if you can guess."

After a few seconds, he opened his eyes. The change in the spirit's body language was unmistakable. Her anger had turned to fear.

"Wait, you can't. I haven't finished. There's not enough energy yet. I'm not ready. You can't—"

"Wrong!" His shout seemed to reverberate off the heavens.

She was pleading now. "No, please, I can't—"

He nodded with a sly smirk and returned his hands to his side. "Till death do us part, baby. You see, Mrs. *Barta*, I'm Gavin Curtis, and anyone who reads my books knows that Gavin Curtis is the king of the plot-twist ending. I'm the master of surprise. So, me and your little toy behind me, the two of us are going for a little swim to the bottom of the river. When I'm gone, you'll be cut off, the path—the *doure sint*—will be sealed shut, and you will go back to wherever nasty little things like you come from and stay there until the ninetieth year of your birth. At that point, according to my favorite harelipped soothsayer, you'll slip away from existence for good."

The appearance of her dress flickered a brilliant yellow, then turned into a jaundiced hue and then back. "No, wait. Wait. I don't have to take your friends. We can work together and only take bad people—or people you barely know, fans that you've only met once, a long time ago, even."

Gavin turned and hiked his leg onto the slick railing next to the machine. "Only kill my fans? That's your best offer?"

He placed his other foot on it and carefully balanced as he turned to face her. "You gotta do better than that. You'll only kill my fans?" He laughed. "Wrong, my dear. I love my fans."

"What's wrong with you?" she screamed.

"What's wrong with me?" With a determined nudge of his foot, he sent the typewriter over the edge of the guardrail. He listened patiently.

It seemed to take forever, but he guessed that it was three full seconds.

Then, finally, even through the clamor of the storm, he heard the plop and splash of the device in the water below. It'd sink like a stone to the bottom of the river.

"What's wrong with me? I'll tell you what's wrong with me." He made a royal bow and then spread his arms wide as he leaned backward. "What's wrong with me is—I'm Gavin Curtis!"

Torri ran to him, but he was already falling and out of reach.

Three seconds until impact . . .

There was no fear. The sound of the wind rushed past his ears. Raindrops appeared to fall in slow motion, reflecting the lightning like a million stars. Those tiny globes of light above and beside him glided downward at the same pace he did, everything following the same route to the same destination—to become one with the mighty river below.

Two seconds . . .

The peculiar sensation that he'd encountered when he'd first touched the machine in Béla's shop enveloped him. He had a keen awareness that Torri's connection was fading, being unraveled like so many strands of string twisted together to make a rope. Her image peering over the bridge began to disintegrate.

He'd won.

She'd never come through now. Her form had fallen apart like a house of cards collapsing in on itself. It was over. She'd revert back to being confined within the typewriter, and buried in the silty bottom of the river, there was no chance it'd be discovered before the incantation expired. Soon, she would return to simply being a memory, a faded article posted above a coat rack in a bar.

The people he loved were safe again. Jo was safe.

For the first time in his life, Gavin felt satisfied and at peace.

One second . . .

A hint of sunlight peeked behind the swirl of clouds.

He closed his eyes and smiled.

He could smell the salt in the water now. It'd probably be cold, not that it mattered.

He breathed in.

Goodbye, Jo. I love you.

Then he was gone.

Epilogue

ONLY THE OLDER COUPLE REMAINED in the intensive care waiting area. Except for the small section of wall with a flatscreen TV mounted on it, the entire area was a glass enclosure.

"Seriously, another *Judge Judy* episode?" the woman scoffed, wearing a droopy pink sweatshirt that read "Grandma is Awesome!" "This is torture. Why don't they have a remote in here?"

Without lowering his large book, her companion answered in a barely audible mumble. "Beats *People's Court.* Judy's got spunk."

The woman nudged him. "Here she comes. William, put your book away. Here she is."

The old man complied, folding his reading glasses into his breast pocket as he stood.

A smartly dressed, middle-aged woman immediately raced to hug the elderly one in the Grandma sweatshirt. They embraced without reservation.

After a few sniffles, the younger woman kissed her cheek and then hugged her even more tightly. "Oh, Beverly, thank you so much for being here." She buried her face in Beverly's plump shoulder. "I didn't know what else to do when they told me. When I heard the news, I just . . . I just thought—"

Beverly gave her a comforting pat on the back. "Being here is the right thing, Josephine. This is important . . . for all of us."

Josephine took a tissue offered by the older man. "Thank you, William." She blew her nose softly.

He nodded. "You should've seen this place an hour ago. Security had to do crowd control. It was absolutely crazy."

She sniffed and forced a smile. "Yeah, I had to pass through a group of supporters outside and show my ID to a guard to get in here."

He tugged at his grey, speckled beard, a nervous habit that Josephine had come to adore over time. He cleared his throat and said, "I've always said Gavin Curtis fans are bright. Guess it didn't take too much to figure out he'd be in one of three hospitals in the area once the media released the story."

Tears welled up in Josephine's eyes again. "Did he say anything to you yesterday when you saw him? Anything about doing this?"

"No, not exactly. I mean, he was acting a little off, though, but nothing that he said hinted at anything like—" He bit his bottom lip and shook his head.

"I know, I know. We talked on the phone two days ago. He said he was going through something but wouldn't tell me what. I should've come then instead of sending you, but I promised him I wouldn't." Tears ran from Josephine's eyes. "They say he completely trashed his room. I think it's 'cause we kinda got into a fight on the phone . . . about Ray."

Beverly quickly shifted her eyes from Josephine's gaze.

After a few more sobs, Josephine continued, "I should've come. I should've known that he . . . I coulda . . . coulda—"

"Now, both of you stop it," Beverly ordered. "There's no way to know what's going on in somebody's head. If somebody is contemplating something like this, there's no way to know unless they come out and tell you—no way at all. Whatever he did, for whatever reason he did it, is nobody's fault but his. Josephine, my dear, none of this is your fault, not one bit. Am I clear?"

She answered with a nod and a sniff. Wiping tears from her cheeks and eyes, she regained her composure. "What are the doctors saying about the chances of recovery?"

Beverly looked to her husband, who'd found something remarkably interesting to stare at on the ground. A few awkward seconds passed before Beverly answered. "Well, they say it's too soon to tell. They did two surgeries before we arrived here this afternoon. That helped get the blood off the brain. According to the second surgeon, he seemed to come through that pretty well, but the trauma Gavin took to the head was pretty severe. So they're in a 'wait-and-see' mode for the next few days."

"You've seen him, right? How . . . how does he look?"

"Yeah, I've seen him," Beverly said. "I just came out about fifteen minutes ago. They had to do some routine checks, and policy is that no one can hang around while they're doing that kinda stuff. He looks . . . well, you know . . . considering everything . . ." She put her arm around her husband. "William isn't ready to see him just yet."

He looked up. "I've got better things to do than watch Gavin Curtis take a nap." The wink he offered Josephine made her smile.

Always one to get the final word, Beverly added, "I think he's afraid he'll lose it if he sees all the tubes and things, but it's not that bad. It's really not."

"I told you, I'll see him before we go." His response was curt, but his eyes never left Josephine.

She jumped in before Beverly could retaliate. "Thank you both so much for being here. I can't believe you came all this way."

Beverly left her man's side to rub Josephine's shoulders. "Nonsense, sweetie. The drive only took a couple of hours, and we didn't want you to face this by yourself."

A black woman in dark blue scrubs approached the trio, addressing Beverly with a trace of a Haitian accent. "We're done for a bit if any of you want to go in there."

"Brigitte, this is Josephine Garner, Gavin's former wife. She just flew in from California."

"Hello and welcome. I'm Mr. Curtis's nurse until seven tonight. Would you like me to take you to his room?"

Josephine extended a handshake and exhaled. "Yes, that'd be good."

She turned, offering her designer purse to Beverly. "Can you keep this for me?"

"Of course I will. William, hand her some more tissues."

He offered three and held up his thick book in his other hand. "I'm only a third of the way through, so take as much time as you need."

Josephine gave him a peck on the cheek. "Thanks again for coming."

The nurse led her through a set of double doors into the unit.

Half an hour later, the door clicked open again, and Billy wedged a bookmark in the middle of his book.

Josephine emerged alone. Beverly was quick to hand the purse back to her, along with more Kleenex.

"Thank you," Josephine said, dabbing the mascara at the corner of her eyes. "The nurse told me that coma patients can hear people talk to them."

William said, "I seriously doubt that with all the drugs that they have him—"

A hard nudge and a dirty look from Beverly silenced him.

He defensively asked, "What?"

A nervous laugh escaped from Josephine. "I don't know if it's true or not, but I told him that we were here, that we loved him. That I . . . I loved him."

Beverly clasped Josephine's free hand. "I think that's good, dear, and really brave of you. That could be just what he needs to wake up, and they do sometimes. A lot of times, they do."

She signaled to William like a stage actor who had forgotten his line.

"Uh, yeah, right. All the time. If I know Gavin, he's just faking it to get out of the last few stops on the book tour."

The rebuke from Beverly was instantaneous. "William Randolph Cavanaugh! That's an awful thing to say! How could you even think of—"

"No, it's okay, Beverly. It's funny. He's right. Gavin hates doing tours." Josephine's expression turned curious. "I want to ask you something, though. When you were in there, did you notice anything odd?"

"Like what exactly?" Beverly asked.

"Did you see his hands—his fingers?"

"Are you talking about how they were moving?"

This got William's attention.

"Yes." The answer snapped out of Josephine. "His fingers were moving the entire time I was in there. The nurse said that she'd seen something like it once before and not to worry. But what did you think of that?"

"I dunno. I just figured it was a reaction to the medicine or something."

"No, the nurse said it wasn't."

"What are you saying, dear?"

"I know it sounds crazy, but did it . . . do you think he was typing?"

"Well, now that you mention it, I can see how it would look like he was typing. Yes, I could say that, possibly." Beverly turned to her husband with a questioning look.

"Don't ask me," William said. "I haven't even been in there yet, but there have been cases of coma patients dreaming. They told us he's not brain dead—in fact, far from it. So I guess it's possible that he could be—"

"Sleep-typing?" Beverly said before he could finish.

Josephine nodded as she formed a half-smile.

William scratched the back of his neck. "I know one thing. If he is writing, or sleep-typing, as you say, I guarantee you that he's not writing a Damien Marksman story."

Josephine smiled. "That's true."

Beverly looked confused, not getting the joke.

He stroked his beard. "However, I do wonder—sincerely wonder. What story do you think Gavin Curtis is writing now?"

It was Beverly who saw her first and quickly moved to place herself between the woman and Josephine.

"Jeez Louise!" William exclaimed, nearly dropping his book. "How long have you been standing there?"

The old woman with the harelip ignored the question and took a step closer to the trio. Pointing to an old publicity photo of Gavin in the newspaper she was holding, she asked, "Are you this? The writer?"

Josephine, ever the publicist, moved from behind Beverly's human shield and extended a hand. "Are you a fan? Do you read Damien Marksman books?"

The old woman asked again, "You are this? For him?"

Josephine shot a glance behind her to William, who seemed to be scanning the area for security. When their eyes met, he shrugged.

Josephine turned back to the woman, who looked like she was wearing a homemade dress. Before she could answer, Beverly said, "Yes, we are Mr. Curtis's . . . family. Are you a Gavin Curtis fan?"

Satisfied, the woman folded the paper away and addressed Josephine. "No, I'm not reading the stories, but I come telling you something, something important for your ears." Though she was not an attractive woman, the three could not take their eyes off her as she said, "He did good thing when he jumped. He stopped—"

A gasp from Beverly called William into action. Pointing an index finger at the woman, he rebuked her. "I don't know who you think you are, but you'd better turn around and head back out that door before I put my boot up your—"

Josephine lifted a hand, stopping him short. Her voice wavered, but she managed to ask, "What do you mean—what good thing? He stopped what?"

"My daughter. He keep her from doing bad thing, very bad. It over now."

Beverly moved to steady Josephine.

William demanded, "What are you talking about? Is this some kinda prank or something?"

The old woman shook her head from side to side. "He not jump because of sad. He jump to keep bad away—to protect."

Josephine was crying again.

"No sad, no sad," the old woman said in a comforting tone. "Wait, I have something for happy." As she pulled the green, pear-shaped necklace from around her neck and over her head, she asked, "You the wife? The writer wife, no?"

Josephine sniffed and nodded repeatedly.

"This for you, for happy. It's gift."

Josephine waved her hands before her in refusal. "I can't . . . you don't need to do that."

"The writer stop my daughter from doing bad thing. It's gift."

After a few seconds of looking into the persistent stare of the woman, Josephine gave in. She stooped to allow the woman to place the necklace over her head. "Thank you. What's your name?"

The woman ignored the question. "It make you happy to wear it, you see. It make you happy very soon."

Josephine received another tissue from William as Beverly offered a comforting shoulder squeeze.

"I will go now, but remember I said the writer not jump because of sad."

Acknowledgments

A big thanks to friends and family who gave their support to this project (even though it had no robots this time). Of special note is the input from Team Armageddon members Jason Aydelotte, Shannon Winton, Carrie Patel, Dominick D'Aunno, Erik Hailey, and Christian Roule. A special thanks goes out to Vicki Estes who tirelessly served once again as my first reader and to the talents and unfailing guidance of my editor, Hilary Comfort.

No frogs were harmed in the making of this book, except for that one (and that was a long time ago).

Thanks for reading,

GWP

About the Author

George Wright Padgett has always had a passion for storytelling.

Born in Houston, Texas, he grew up consuming a steady diet of science fiction and comic books. His time is divided between being a husband and father of two, a jazz piano player, a graphic artist, and a playwright. With what time is left over, he writes science fiction, horror, and the occasional mystery while sitting on the sofa next to his mini dachshund, Jenny.

Connect With George

Email:	georgewpadgett@gmail.com
Facebook:	facebook.com/Author.GWP
Web:	george-p.com/author.htm george-p.com/cruel.htm
Mail:	P.O. Box #844 Humble, TX 77347

GREY GECKO PRESS

Thank you for purchasing this book from Grey Gecko Press, an independent publishing company that focuses on new and emerging authors, bringing readers great books at reasonable prices in all formats.

With books in nearly every genre of fiction and non-fiction, there's something for everyone, and you can be sure that buying books from us leads directly to the support of independent authors.

You can help by reviewing our books on your favorite website! Reviews are the word-of-mouth of the digital age, and help us find new readers just like you.

Visit our website to purchase our titles, preorder upcoming books at a discount, sign up for our free email newsletter, and find out about two great ways to get free books, the Slushpile Reader Program and the Advance Reader Program.

Don't forget: all our print editions come with the ebook free!

Your Favorite New Indie Authors

www.greygeckopress.com

store.greygeckopress.com

www.ingramcontent.com/pod-product-compliance
Lightning Source LLC
Chambersburg PA
CBHW061435210726
48287CB00007B/2218